Old Enough

C. L. Kraemer

Published by Rogue Phoenix Press
Copyright © 2015

ISBN: 978-1-62420-226-1

Credits
Cover Artist: Designs by Ms G
Editor: Christine Young

Dedication

To Larry, whose love and enthusiasm helped our marriage survive the artistic process.

One
Oakdale, Virginia
Circa 1999

Diane sat stirring her strawberry margarita. She hated the thin, delicate glasses most bars used to serve the blended drink so she and Mark, the bartender, made a pact when he first started working at The Bar. He served her margaritas in a sixteen-ounce beer glass, and she paid him an extra dollar. It worked for both of them. Diane's beverage arrived in a decent sized glass and Mark put an extra dollar in his tip jar.

In Oakdale, The Bar, located in the same building for as long as anyone could remember, was where respectable people in this small community of 17,500 went after work for a tall, cool one. There was one other bar at the edge of town by the Wal-Mart shopping center, but no decent person admitted going there. Club Nouveaux offered exotic dancers and seemed to do well in spite of the empty front parking lot. Everyone knew who visited the Club and who didn't since, with the exception of a few people like Diane, everyone had been born, raised and would probably die in Oakdale.

"So, why do I get the pleasure of your company tonight?" Mark leaned over the bar to gaze into Diane's eyes.

She returned his look. "I'm tired of sitting in my house watching TV with only my dog for company, and I'm not inspired to surf the net tonight. So," she waved a hand at the semi-empty room, "I thought I'd come in here and watch the circus."

Mark pushed away from the bar. A customer at the other end was signaling for another drink. Diane occupied herself by surveying the room in the wall length mirror that ran behind the bottles on the bar counter.

She could view the action without turning and looking interested. This hidden local bar was a smorgasbord of young bodies, male and female. Stopping into The Bar tonight reminded her how little the dating game had changed since she had been a willing participant. Two unsuccessful marriages and one very painful love affair convinced her falling in love again was not a doable option as far as she was concerned. She and Mark had dated at one point. They concluded during the middle of their first, and only, date the best thing they could do for each other was to become friends, so a great friendship had blossomed.

"This is for you," Mark placed another strawberry margarita in front of Diane.

"I didn't order a second one yet. What's this for?" Diane asked.

"I mixed up an order Tami gave me," Mark replied.

"Mark, you have the ears of a spy microphone and memory of a computer. You don't make mistakes. What's up?" Diane's eyes narrowed as she peered warily at Mark.

"A nice guy at the end of the bar said you look like you could use this: no strings attached," Mark stepped backward.

"Mark, you've known me for what, three and a half years? When was the last time you saw me accepting a drink from someone I really don't know?"

"Oh, come on, Diane. Lighten up! It wouldn't kill you to accept one drink from a guy I'll swear is a bona fide gentleman."

Diane glared, her mouth set in a thin line as she silently slid the drink toward him. "You can take the drink to the gentleman and give him his money back or not. I don't care. I thought you knew me enough to know I prefer to buy my own drinks; eliminates any obligations. I'm here to relax, not cruise for company, so to avoid any further problems, I'll take off," Diane picked her purse off the bar and grabbed her jacket.

"Whoa! I've never seen you so touchy. What's wrong?" Mark leaned against the back counter and crossed his arms.

Sitting down, Diane draped her jacket on the back of the barstool and dropped her purse onto the bar. She sighed heavily. "You're right. It's been more than one of those days. It seems like it's been a week of *those days* wrapped up in one obnoxious package."

"It's Timmy, isn't it?" Mark scowled.

"Timothy."

"Whatever."

Diane smiled at the obvious disdain in Mark's voice as he talked about her ex-husband.

"He's decided since I did not immediately jump into another marriage, like he did, I must *have it real bad* for him. He has no clue our divorce was the best part of our marriage. He sends flowers weekly, and calls once a day, every day of the week. I've threatened to call his new wife, but he's got her convinced I'm unstable because it was *such* an emotional shock for me when he ended our marriage. So, she calls to see how I'm doing. My mom didn't keep track of me this much when I lived in Hawaii! It's really beginning to wear on me. The man has an ego the size of T-Rex."

"And the brain to match. Why haven't you sworn out a restraining order for stalking on the guy?" Mark asked.

Diane chuckled, "I tried. I called the Police station here in town and asked to speak with one of the deputies about my ex-husband. After several minutes of hemming and hawing, they switched me to a female officer. I explained how Timothy was calling and sending unwanted flowers and generally making life uncomfortable. She said 'Whatcha complaining about? Most women would be happy to have a guy send 'em flowers.' I tried explaining what he was doing was stalking me. She snorted and replied, 'Stalking! Honey, you been watchin' too much TV. Around here the only thing that gets stalked is deer. Now, if you want a license to hunt deer, I can switch you to the license office, but a restraining order 'cause your ex-husband is sending you flowers? Not gonna happen anytime soon.' I hung up. I've just sort of dealt with him since then."

"Well, as I have often heard you say, don't take it out on the rest of us. The guy who bought you this drink doesn't cause trouble and tips well. If you want to give the drink back—do it yourself," Mark said.

He walked away leaving Diane sputtering for a response. He

began carrying on a conversation with a younger man who had captured Diane's attention the moment he'd walked through the door. Alternately peering sideways at him through lowered eyes or quickly glancing in the mirror behind the bar, she guessed he must be a construction worker. His shirt did little to hide well-developed chest and arm muscles. *Although he might be a gym rat, I doubt it. Those muscles undulate too easily and that tan, mmmm, doesn't have the color of a lotion or tanning booth. Dark hair, light eyes—my kind of eye candy.*

~ * ~

Justin glanced anxiously at Mark.

"Don't worry," Mark leaned his lanky frame against the counter, "she's just having a bad day. Got a genuine flake of an ex-husband who's convinced she still loves him. Hell, he thinks every female he talks with falls in love with him. Guess he's bordering on the edge of stalking lately. Their divorce has been final for two years, but he won't accept she's moved on because she didn't jump into another marriage. If you're interested, really interested, have patience. Diane's worth the wait."

"Then why haven't you two..." Justin blushed letting the thought die. "Listen, I'm sorry. It's really none of my business."

"You're right. It is none of your business. But there's no secret about it. We dated once and realized we didn't want to ruin a good friendship. Diane's like the sister I never had. She's level headed, has no problem telling me when I'm being an ass and I do the same for her. I really think you two would get along. Let me try to talk to her again. You in a big hurry?" Mark nodded to the cocktail waitress waving to get his attention. "Gotta actually earn my pay. Be right back." He headed toward the waitress station at the end of the bar.

Justin turned his glass of beer around with his fingertips. He'd been coming into this club for about seven years and hadn't been attracted to most of the ladies who frequented the place. Diane's confidence first grabbed his attention. Her poise and overall demeanor spoke to the fact she was probably older than most of the bar's regular clientele. Justin

4

smiled. *I think confidence is as sexy as a great figure.* He peered into his beer as though it were a crystal ball. The amber liquid was slightly cloudy and he couldn't tell anything except he was getting close to needing another beer.

~ * ~

Diane slipped off her barstool and marched toward him. *This is ridiculous.* She shook her head slightly. *He's no different than any other man.* The dive-bombing butterflies in her stomach threatened to destroy her bravado.

As she drew closer, she realized he was younger than she'd assumed. *Make that young man. He puts his jeans on one muscular tan leg at a time. The closer I get, though, the more I can see I was right about his incredible physique.* His plain cotton shirt strained over well-formed chest and arm muscles developed by hard physical work, not hours in the gym with weights. The spicy scent he wore sent Diane's hormones stampeding. *God, this isn't fair. He smells yummy!* She took a deep breath. *I'd better do this before I lose my nerve.*

Justin jumped when the five-dollar bill slapped down on the bar beside him. He snapped his head around to face flashing, fiery brown eyes.

"I believe this is yours. I pay for my own drinks. You'll need this later when the young ladies begin to arrive. I understand they require lots of these," she picked the five off the bar and waved it in the air, "to keep them interested."

Justin opened his mouth to reply, but Diane had turned on her heel and marched away, leaving him with his mouth gaping. He snapped his jaws closed and watched the rhythmic sway of her hips as she moved away from him. *Whew. What a spitfire!* Justin leaned back in his chair. *She's going to be a challenge and I love challenges.* He turned to face a smirking Mark.

Mark swept his arm in the direction of Diane's disappearing back, "I see you've met my friend, Diane Wallace. What do you think? Worth waiting for?"

Justin turned his glass. Looking at Mark, his eyes twinkled as he answered, "In every man's life there's one challenge he feels destined to take. She's mine. She's confident, takes nonsense from no one, including you, and she's a woman, not a girl, unlike most of the others who sit on the barstools in this place. I like older women. They don't *need* a man in their life."

Mark took a bar towel and absently wiped at invisible dirt. "Well, you're right on all counts. But be careful what you wish for because she has the ability to sting like a scorpion."

Moving away, he continued to wipe the bar as he gravitated toward Diane.

"You're a real piece of work, Diane. Personally, I like Justin. He's a helluva guy who'd treat you with respect. You know, that stuff Timmy hasn't got a clue about? Got to go. As you can see, the place is beginning to get busy and I have customers who need me."

Mark picked up his pace as the crowd started gravitating through the doors. The cocktail waitresses were congregating near the register, placing drink orders while the bar filled with townies and kids from the nearby college. The volume on the jukebox had amplified in relation to the volume of increasing chatter in the room. A blue haze of cigarette smoke curled toward the ceiling coloring the room in a muted glow. The happy buzzing of voices swelled as time drew closer for the band to play.

Diane picked up her glass and swirled the contents in the bottom. The frenetic atmosphere crackled, raising the hair on her arms. A stream of cigarette smoke blown her direction triggered a coughing fit.

A stocky man reeking of Jade East cologne and wearing multiple gold chains accenting a three-piece white suit suddenly occupied the barstool next to her. His dark dyed hair was heavily sprayed to hold a style he should have quit wearing in the seventies. Chain-smoking, he kept blowing smoke in Diane's direction.

"Hey, gorgeous, how about letting me buy you a drink?" An ugly sneer covered his puffy face.

"I buy my own drinks," Diane half turned toward the stranger just as he blew another stream of smoke in her face. She closed her eyes against the acrid stream and wrinkled her nose at the stale smell invading her senses. He reached out a nicotine-stained finger and touched her nose.

"You have a cute little nose," he said.

Grabbing his finger and bending it toward his arm, Diane glared at him. "I will break every bone in your body if you touch me again. Do I make myself clear?"

Wrenching his finger free, he smiled widely, revealing yellow tinted teeth. "You're quite a little pistol, aren't you?"

He turned to the bar and waved his hand at Mark. "Hey, bartender, bring the little lady a drink!"

This idiot isn't listening. She snatched her purse and jacket and slid off the stool. Her nose tingled in identification of the spicy aftershave she noted Justin was wearing.

"Gosh, honey, I'm so sorry, but you know Dave when he starts talking about fishing. A man could lose an ear. Want to dance to this song?" Justin stood wearing an apologetic smile and lightly touching Diane's elbow.

"Look, bud, I don't know what your game is but I'm buying the lady a drink. Take a hike." The Retro Man moved to get up.

Diane slipped her arm through Justin's, "I'd love to dance. Hey, Mark! Will you put my things behind the bar?"

Mark snatched Diane's purse and jacket set them on a shelf under the counter.

"Bartender, give me a gin martini, very dry. Oh, yeah, *shaken not stirred*." Retro Man swiveled his barstool to face the quickly filling dance floor.

Mark prepared his drink and set it on the napkin.

"Bitch," Retro Man muttered as he turned and grabbed his drink.

"What did you say?" Mark's eyes flashed.

"How does a young punk like him rate with an older broad like her?" Retro Man scoffed.

"I suspect he treats her like a lady."

"Hell, any broad who comes into a bar is looking for one thing and one thing alone, you know what I mean?" he sneered in Diane's direction.

"Yeah, I do. And I think you'll be a lot happier heading down to Club Nouveaux," Mark picked up the drink he'd just placed on the napkin and motioned to the door.

"You can't kick me out," Retro Man started to protest. "I haven't done anything."

Pointing to a sign taped at the center of the bar mirror, Mark read out loud. "We reserve the right to refuse service to anyone." Turning to the man he added, "I have just exercised my right. There's the door. Don't bother coming back." He nodded to a video camera in the corner, "we have your picture. I'm letting you know you've been permanently barred. Now take your money and go!"

Grabbing his bills from Mark's hand, Retro Man turned toward the dance floor. He glared at Diane and Justin smoothly flowing together to the slow music.

"This isn't over yet," he muttered. "We will meet again, little lady."

"Is that jerk looking this way?" Diane asked.

Justin glanced toward the bar. He could see Mark's firmly set jaw as he removed the drink from in front of the man and handed back his money.

"He's still leering at you. We'd better follow through until he gets the message," Justin suggested.

"I guess so," Diane said.

"Don't sound so excited. I'll go back to my beer and you can wrestle Mr. Seventies if you like. I thought I'd offer some assistance, no strings attached. But, for the record, I am a fairly decent dancer."

Justin, Diane's hand in his, pulled her close to him. He felt her warm, quick breath through the material of his shirt. Her stiffened body began relaxing as they fell in step with the song playing on the jukebox. The fresh clean fragrance of her hair drifted to his nostrils. He inhaled slowly, deeply to imprint her essence in his memory.

"Normally, I don't slow dance, but under the present circumstances, I'm making an exception. I do agree that you are a good dancer," Diane admitted.

"Thank you, I think," Justin gazed into her beautiful face.

Too soon the song ended and Justin felt Diane pull from his embrace. He watched her lovely hips sway back to the bar. *If there was just some way I could convince her I'm not some womanizing monster. Well, that isn't going to happen tonight.* He was beginning to doubt his own sanity. *Mark's right.* He had no problem getting dates with younger women. It was just, they drove him crazy.

They were constantly concerned with how they looked, if their friends were watching, how much money was being spent on them, and on and on. Justin had concluded younger women felt the only way a man could prove how much he cared was to go broke.

He had one ex-wife who lived in his ancestral home. The court ordered him to sell stocks bequeathed to him by his grandfather and awarded half the money to her. She was, currently, fighting to acquire fifty percent of the construction company he'd started and built right after the divorce had become final. By the grace of God and his best friend, a lawyer blessed with the ethics of a shark, he still retained his company.

Justin strolled back to his seat and surveyed the scene beginning to unfold in front of him. *I can have just as much fun if I pick up a six pack at the convenience store and go home. There, I won't have to put up with the cigarette smoke and loud music.* Dancing with Diane had fed the fire of his passion to be near her. *I hate wanting something this much!*

But, as his father used to say, "You're old enough for your wants not to hurt you." Justin smiled sadly. He'd hated when his dad spewed platitudes at him. No matter how Justin would plead the answer would still be no. He hadn't thought about his parents for a while. He really missed them. The old pain began to creep up on him, and he signaled Mark for another beer. Maybe he'd stay a little bit longer.

~ * ~

Diane leaned against the back of her chair and placed her right hand on her left pulse point. Was it racing as much as she thought? *Yep.*

It's doing the flamenco. She couldn't believe she was reacting like a schoolgirl to the touch of this--this kid. The warmth of his hand holding hers made her heart pound. And his scent...*Oh, man, I'm in trouble.* He smelled the way a man should smell, outdoorsy and masculine. She'd fought the urge through the entire dance to bury her face in his neck. The closeness had verified, beyond any question, his muscularity. His chest was taut, solid and his legs rippled as they moved. She could picture herself wrapped around him in front of a roaring fire. *I have got to stop thinking about him or I'm going to hyperventilate myself into the emergency room.*

Diane headed to the bathroom. What she needed was a shot of cold water and she needed it now. She tore several paper towels from the dispenser and wet them with water from the spigot, mopping her forehead then placing the cool towels on the back of her neck. A blonde cocktail waitress emerged from the toilet stall. Washing her hands and running the damp towel across the back of her neck, she asked Diane if everything was all right.

"Yeah, just freshening up. You know how mucky it gets in here."

"Yeah," the blonde smiled, "I do the same to keep from going to sleep when it's slow. See you later."

The waitress pushed out into the noisy bar.

Diane decided to follow. *I'll finish my drink and head home.* A lot had happened in the last hour, and she wasn't in a mood to tempt fate. She kept reminding herself this guy was young. When she'd gotten moved closer to him, he appeared to be in his early thirties. *There are millions of reasons not to get involved with someone so young. I don't like having to explain my taste in music, for one thing. Besides, who says he isn't here on a bet from his buddies? Which brings up another point—buddies. They can be great fun or a huge pain in the butt. Most young guys drink too much; chase girls—even though they are attached to someone nice—and require great amounts of time bonding while watching sports.* She'd been shredding her napkin while making the case to herself for not becoming involved.

Mark, arms crossed and frowning, stood in front of her.

"What?"

"Look at this mess. You know who has to clean it up? Me, thanks," Mark started sweeping the little bits of paper into his hand. He placed another napkin under her drink.

"If you shred this into little tiny pieces like you did the last one, I'll indenture your body for clean up when we close this place down. Do I make myself clear?" he warned.

Diane had no intention of staying any longer than it took to finish her drink. Sucking up the foam at the bottom of the glass through her straw, she carefully set the empty glass in the middle of the complete napkin. She waved Mark over.

"What do you need now?"

"You stowed my things behind the bar, remember? May I have them?"

"Sure," Mark turned and retrieved Diane's items bringing them to where she stood.

"Here. I don't think they match my outfit. What do you think?"

"I think you've lost your mind, but what's new? Thanks. I'm going home. I've had more fun than I can handle. See you later."

"Whoa! Whoa! Hold up there! If you think I'm letting you walk out to your car alone, you're out of your mind," Mark caught the attention of the blonde waitress. "Tami, take over while I escort Diane to her vehicle."

"No problem," Tami moved behind the bar.

"Now, shall we take a short stroll to your chariot?" Mark motioned to the door.

"What? You think I might be drunk? After one drink?" Diane raised her eyebrows.

Mark shook his head.

"Then what?"

"I don't want to take any chances your psycho ex-husband will try anything. Okay?"

"Fair enough; to my chariot!"

~ * ~

Justin watched Mark and Diane walked through the front door arm in arm.

If only that could be me. I'm going to convince her to go out with me at least once. Justin smacked a fist into his open palm. *I guess it's time I went home too.*

Even with the influx of young faces and bodies, he didn't feel interested. Diane had captured his attention, and she'd just walked out the door. He glimpsed "Mooch Mary", a nickname given her by the guys in town, heading his way. He quickly downed his beer and headed for the front door.

"Justin! Justin!"

He moved quickly, using the loud music to feign deafness. The last thing he wanted to deal with tonight was someone expecting him to buy all her drinks because she graced him with her presence. He dashed out the door before she caught up with him. Pausing in the shadows to retrieve keys from his pocket, Justin spied Mark and Diane standing next to a newer dark Corvette.

Mark held out his hand. The jingle of keys hitting Mark's palm echoed against the building. He opened the car door and held Diane's hand as she lowered herself into the vehicle. Returning the keys, Mark closed the door and waved as Diane started the car and drove away. Justin found himself staring down the darkened road after the red taillights. *I'm impressed.* He passed Mark on his way to his pickup truck.

"Goodnight, Mark."

"Justin. You're finally taking off?"

"Yeah, I spotted Mary and I'm really not in the mood to pretend interest tonight."

Mark chuckled, "I know what you mean. Looks like I'm going to be earning my tips tonight. If Mary's in her usual form, I'll be making every oddball concoction in the bartender's book, and a lot of guys will be going home frustrated."

Both guys laughed.

"Diane has a nice looking Corvette."

"The car was a gift to herself for putting up with her ex-husband. He nearly had a stroke the first time he saw her driving it. She'd driven from the car lot over here to show off her new toy. He'd spotted her getting out and followed her into the bar. That's when the interrogation began."

"You're kidding," Justin said.

"No, he asked who she was doing to get that kind of gift. She leaned against the back of the barstool looking him directly in the eye and coolly answered, 'Your father'."

"No way!"

"Yeah, his face started turning this funny shade of purple, and I really thought he was going to explode. He sputtered and lurched toward her, clenching and unclenching his fists. I stepped between them then escorted him outside and threatened to call the police if I saw him in here again. When I walked inside, Diane was laughing so hard tears were rolling down her cheeks. Only then did she take me out and show me the car. Her ex was irritated because she'd acquired something he'd wanted for years. Listen, got to go. Tami can't handle the bar when it gets busy. See you later."

The irritating ring of a cell phone split the air. Both men reached toward their belt. Realizing it wasn't his, Mark ambled into the bar.

Justin flipped open the phone, stopping his forward motion to answer.

"Justin Anderson. Anderson Construction."

"You'd better watch your back," a muffled voice whispered. "Someone wants you dead."

The phone clicked then silence. Justin squinted his eyes to read the number on the display. He couldn't see anything. A move to the edge of the sidewalk to use the light from the street lamp to read his display, and he was still having difficulty. Across the street an engine roared to life and a set of headlights blazed. Justin snapped his head up in time to see the same headlights bearing down on him. He dove for The Bar door feeling the rush of wind ruffle his hair. The car passed within inches of his body and sped away.

Scrambling to his feet, he leaned against the building shaking from head to toe. *What is going on? First the phone call, then the car?*

"It's time to go home," Justin announced to the darkness. He picked up his phone and keys from the ground. He needed a shower and a warm bed.

Tomorrow he'd try to see if he could retrieve the number of the anonymous caller from the cell phone's memory.

Two

Smoke rolled out the open window. A red glow from the cigarette the only visible light inside the plain white four-door sedan. Retro Man pulled the flask from the inside pocket of his suit and drew a long swig from the silver container. Screwing the cap on tightly, he watched the door to The Bar open and Diane step out. He set the flask on the seat and reached for the car door until he saw Mark step out behind her.

"Damn." He really wanted to talk with this broad. He was sure he could convince her to have a drink with him.

He watched Mark open her door and secure her inside the dark Corvette. Lighting another cigarette, he dropped the lit match between his legs onto the seat of the car. "Shit!" Raising his butt off the seat, he frantically slapped at the lit match until the flame extinguished, looking up in time to see the disappearing taillights of her car round the corner. He cranked the engine over on the rental car and started pulling out to follow her. He glanced down feeling a desperate need to grab his flask. As he looked up, he realized he was moving directly toward the young buck she called her boyfriend.

"Holy..." He bumped over the curb and accelerated down the side street.

Hope I got the kid. His eyes slowly adjusted to the road. *Serves him right for getting me kicked out of this backwater dive.*

He spotted the distinctive taillights of the Corvette. Obeying the speed limit and driving twenty-five miles per hour through the residential streets, she slowed and turned into the driveway of a ranch style home.

The garage door opened automatically, and she drove straight in. When the door closed, the driveway light went out.

He parked the rental car a block away from her house, grabbing the flask and turning it upside down.

"I've gotta get to a bar. I'm ou-outta booze. Maybe she'll have a bottle inside her house," he said to the empty seat next to him. He watched as lights came on inside and tried to focus on his watch. Holding it at arms' length, he narrowed his eyes. "Eid-thirdy. I'll wait ten minutes and knock on her door. Yeah, that'll work."

~ * ~

Diane parked the car in the garage and entered the kitchen. As she locked the garage door, she caught a whiff of herself. *God, I reek.* Now a two-decade reformed smoker, she was more sensitive than a nonsmoker when it came to the stench of cigarettes.

Since she'd quit, the lingering aroma of smoke on her clothes and especially in her hair, made her nauseous until she'd cleaned everything. Diane headed for the bathroom to wash away the smell. As the water sluiced down her body, her mind kept wandering back to the feel of Justin's taut shoulder muscles against her hand and a pair of jeans designed with his body in mind. She could fool Mark a little; however, the truth was she was very interested in Justin.

"You can fool everyone except yourself, Diane." The truth echoed against the tiled bathroom walls. Diane realized she'd spoken the thought out loud. He was deliciously good looking but seemed unaffected by the fact. He exuded a musky, masculine scent, danced well, and was chivalrous—a vanishing trait. *In short, everything I'm looking for in a guy—if he was older and had appeared many years earlier... Oh, well, that's the way things go for me. Woulda, shoulda, coulda. Enough wishful thinking and excuses.* Stepping out of the shower and drying, she put on comfortable, warm sweats and padded down the hallway to attack the work she'd brought home.

She was carefully grooming an advertising campaign where the money involved could reach six figures. According to the investment broker, Diane's contact, his client was a finicky perfectionist. If this campaign met with his approval, she'd be rewarded with the financial freedom to put her house on the market and move to a smaller one. Bought to provide room for children who never came, the house had been the most reasonably priced on the new home market when she and Timothy, her second husband, were searching. When they divorced, he felt he deserved the house because he'd immediately remarried and started a new family.

Thankfully, she had a lawyer who proved, during their tempestuous coupling, Timothy had contributed little to the marriage or the household. Diane emerged from the divorce with her old pickup, her business and the house.

She opened her briefcase and spread work papers over her dining room table. Her present project had been somewhat of a surprise. A phone call from a friend had started the ball rolling.

"Diane!" the female voice had chimed.

"Kate?"

Both women squealed.

"What have you been up to?" Diane asked.

"Well, I've been trying to get my business off the ground and haven't had much luck. Everyone keeps telling me I'm going to fail, but I can *feel* I'm on the right track. I've opened a specialty coffee shop with computers available to use by anyone who pays the hourly rate. I think it's right for the times. I just can't seem to find my customer base," Kate said.

"Who are you targeting?"

"Boomers. You know, the forty-somethings with money," Kate answered.

"That's where you're making your mistake," Diane said.

"What do you mean?"

"Let me work up an ad campaign for you. I think you'll do much better if you target the college and twenty-something generations. Older consumers can afford their own computers and specialty coffee at home. They don't feel the urge to congregate like they did when they were in college. I'll have the campaign ready for you by the end of the week. Let's run it for a month and see if we get any noticeable results. If not, I won't charge you. Fair enough?" Diane said.

"Fair enough. I hate taking your money, Diane, but somebody's got to do it," Kate giggled and hung up.

Three weeks later, Diane received a large check in the mail from Kate with a short note attached.

"Business is booming. The first two days I was sure I wouldn't have to pay you; day three and all others after that have proven to be pure gold. I'm gladly paying this bill. After all, I can afford it! I've recommended you to a friend. I hope you don't mind. Yours, Kate."

One phone call later and Diane had landed the biggest contract she'd ever imagined—signed, sealed, and delivered by special messenger. She needed one hook for the radio commercial. If this worked, they'd talk TV ads. She sat twirling her pen between her fingers and staring at the partially finished work, hoping for an epiphany. She pushed her purse to the edge of the table and caught a whiff of Retro Man's aftershave. *How could he have handled my purse when Mark had it behind the bar?* She quickly inventoried its contents and confirmed nothing was missing. Setting the bag on the floor, she leapt from her chair to rummage through her old cassettes. Finding the one she wanted, she popped it into the cassette player, dancing around her living room to disco music for ten minutes.

~ * ~

He laid back against the headrest, his eyes drooping as his head nodded forward. The sound of a slamming door jolted him awake. Swearing, Retro Man realized he'd fallen asleep. Focusing on her front door, he staggered up the sidewalk to the house he'd seen Diane enter. He leaned against the door frame and knocked softly on the dark wood door, but the pretty brunette didn't answer. Squinting hard at the door frame, he leaned his bulk against it, accidentally pushing the doorbell, and jumped at the sound but no one answered. *I know I saw her go into this house.*

The only reason she din't talk to me wuz that punk kid.

He could hear the pulsating beat of loud music.

"Hey! Let me in!" he pounded on the door.

He stumbled off the front porch. Weaving along the sidewalk to the back yard, he spotted a sliding glass door which opened onto a covered patio. He hovered outside the ring of light cast from the porch light watching as Diane danced in front of the door. His heart began to pound against his ribs in rhythm with the thumping of the music and his breathing quickened with the thought of the little brunette close to his body. He watched her hips wiggle back and forth and breasts jiggle with the beat. Wiping his sweaty hands on his pants, he licked his lips in anticipation.

"Perfec. Shez in the mood."

He stepped into the ring of light and maneuvered his way toward the glass door.

~ * ~

Breathless and feeling out of shape, Diane slumped down at the table and started drawing. Retro Man had given her the best marketing idea she'd thought of in the last ten years. She glanced up at the reflection in the sliding glass door. It took a full fifteen seconds for her to realize she was staring into the lust filled, glazed eyes of Retro Man on her patio lunging toward her house. She heard a scream and realized the sound was coming from her own lips.

Retro Man wiped his mouth with the back of his hand. The luscious brunette dancing in front of the door in sweat pants and a sweatshirt made him hard. This would be his lucky night; he could just feel it. He wobbled up one more step toward the door. Suddenly, the brunette's eyes widened and she opened her mouth to let escape an ear-shattering scream that overrode all other sounds. He watched her disappear into the other room.

"Damn." He slammed a fist into the sliding glass door and ran unsteadily down the steps and across the next-door neighbor's front lawn.

He couldn't afford to tangle with the local cops. His heart pounded against his chest to the rhythm of his ragged breaths. Sides aching and head throbbing with the beginning of a massive headache, he pulled open the car door and fell inside. He tried to turn the ignition switch. *Keys, where are the keys?* His mind raced as he reached under the front seat, finding them where he'd shoved them before he'd crawled out. Fumbling the key into the ignition, he turned it one more time. The sound of the engine rumbling alive was sweet music to his ears. Blowing out breath he hadn't realized he was holding, he accelerated out of the neighborhood. Luck was with him so far, no police.

"Now whut wuz the name of tha' club the bartender tole me bout? Club NoNo. Thas not it. Club Novo. Yeah, thas it. Club Novo, here I come!"

~ * ~

She bolted from her chair into the kitchen and snatched the phone off the wall.

"911. What is your emergency?" the operator sounded bored.

"There's somebody in my backyard. Please send the police, right away!"

"What's your address?"

"715 Elm Street. Hurry!"

"We're sending someone out. It shouldn't be more than two minutes."

Two minutes? I could be dead by then! Where's Princess? Diane hung up the phone and cautiously crept toward the dining room and sliding glass doors. Her heart pounded, the sound drowning out the disco music coming from the living room. Steeling herself against what she might see, she peeked out to the patio. It was empty; no one was looking through the glass. She was sure she'd seen Retro Man out there, but the only way to verify it was to go outside. Right this moment, the last place Diane wanted to be was in her backyard.

She trudged back to the kitchen and picked up the phone and

called 911.

"911. What is your emergency?" the operator still sounded bored.

"Yes. I just called about an intruder? Please cancel sending out the police. He's gone."

"Are you sure, ma'am?"

"Yes. I'm sorry I wasted your time."

"If you're sure ma'am, it's not a waste of our time to make sure you're safe."

"I'm sure."

"All right. Have a nice evening, ma'am."

"Thank you. Goodnight."

Diane felt like a total idiot. Her imagination had gone completely over the edge this time. *Where is Princess? Oh, yeah. Locked in the laundry room. Just like I do every day.* Diane was feeling even more foolish. She had protection in the form of her rescued Greyhound dog, but it didn't do any good if the dog was locked up. Which reminded Diane the dog needed to be let out.

Diane walked to the laundry room, carefully opening the door and pressing herself against the wall. A silver streak shot out of the room, making a beeline to the sliding glass doors while woofing furiously with each step. Diane unlocked the mechanism and slid the door to one side. She opened the screen door and stepped out. Princess pushed out and dashed to the grass beyond the concrete patio. She quickly did her duty and began intently sniffing the entire yard.

Diane shivered. The scent of Jade East hung heavy in the air; he had been here. Maybe he was still here? She called Princess and the two retreated into the house. Diane locked the screen door and turned out the back porch light. If he were out there, he'd hurt himself trying to find his way out. She headed directly to the entry door to set the alarm. She should have done this when she first came in but had been so lost in thoughts of Justin she'd forgotten.

Alarm set, Diane picked up the phone and called Mark. She needed to hear a comforting voice and, who knows, maybe he'd come and stay in the extra room tonight. She was sure Jennifer knew they were friends and nothing more. That would ease her mind considerably.

"Hello, Mark?"

Three

Justin lurched to his truck. It had been a long day, made longer by the dive to the concrete he'd just performed. Ten hours on the construction site, two hours at his lawyer's office to sign papers, and now diving to the ground like he was playing college football again. "I'm getting too damn old for this stuff," he muttered as he climbed into the cab of his truck. Leaning against the seat, he recalled his visit to the office of his friend and lawyer, Tom Manning.

Ashlee, his ex-wife, wanted more money. He willingly paid $400 a month child support for his daughter, Briana. However, Ashlee was determined to get the judge to double his child support since she'd heard about the new contract his company had secured to build a major hotel. Justin was juggling to make ends meet because the agreement to let Ashlee and Briana live in the family home had forced him to buy a home for himself. Those bills, along with his company's costs, kept him teetering on the brink of solvency. The money from this completed contract would help put his bank account in the plus column. Tom advised him not to be concerned about the situation.

"How can I not be concerned, Tom, when every time she's petitioned the judge, he's handed her everything she wanted?" Justin was exasperated.

He hated the ping-pong ritual of court.

"I'm conducting an investigation. If my information is correct, you'll come out on the winning side."

Tom Manning and Justin had been best friends since grade school, playing on high school and college football teams together, and joining the same fraternity at Old Dominion. Tom continued to Harvard to study law where he decided after graduation to come back to his hometown and practice in his father's law firm.

"What are you talking about? Don't lawyer babble me, you know how I hate it," Justin replied.

"I don't want to jeopardize what I have, so, if my information is substantiated with hard evidence, things might ease up on you. I won't know for certain until tomorrow afternoon. I'll let you know, good or bad," Tom said.

Justin left his friend's office feeling uneasy. Tom liked his dramatics, they served him well in the courtroom, but he'd always been careful with Justin and their lifelong friendship. Justin's ex-wife had been so controlling after the divorce she'd only made his daughter, Briana, available for visits twice in the last year. Justin shook his head. *I miss the dimpled smile and bounce of my little girl. Good Lord, she's going to be twelve this year, nearly a teenager.*

Tonight, he'd decided to stop at The Bar and have a beer instead of his usual routine of going home. He smiled as he remembered the clean smell of Diane's hair when she'd moved next to him to slap the five-dollar bill on the bar. He'd actually been able to hold her in his arms. He could still feel her body molded against his, moving perfectly with his every step on the dance floor. Snapping himself out of his reverie, Justin inserted his key into the ignition. He drove the three miles to his home thinking of the small brunette. Her musky fragrance still tickled his nose. Parking in the driveway, Justin walked to the front door which he unlocked and opened. He stepped over the pile of mail that had been pushed through the door slot, recognizing most of it as junk mail. There was one bill, which he opened and placed on top of the ever-growing pile of flyers and discount coupons on the entry table.

He was getting a queasy feeling in the pit of his stomach, and his head was beginning to spin. *I've only had two beers. I shouldn't be drunk enough to be dizzy.* Justin wobbled down the hallway to the kitchen where he plunked his lunchbox on the counter.

The smell nearly knocked him to his knees. He wrinkled his nose and staggered to the garbage disposal. Grabbing a flashlight sitting on the counter, he lifted the rubber lip of the disposal and, with a flick of his finger, shed light into the metal grinding machine. He was rewarded with a shining bright, empty unit.

What the heck is that smell? It's so familiar; kind of like...rotten eggs!

Patting his shirt pocket to be sure he had his phone with him, Justin stumbled out the back door off the kitchen into the yard. He pulled his phone from his pocket before dropping his head down and pulling fresh air into his lungs. Five minutes of breathing clean air cleared his head enough for him to realize he needed to contact the gas company and police. He flipped open his phone and dialed the emergency digits.

"911. Police, fire or ambulance? What is your emergency?" the Operator asked.

"I believe there is a gas leak in my home. Please send whoever is available right now," Justin's voice wavered slightly.

"What is your address, sir?"

"I live at twenty-one ninety-five Meadowcreek Lane in Oakdale. When I came home after work tonight, the overwhelming smell of rotten eggs permeated my house. Can you send someone out? Soon?"

"Yes, sir. We'll send someone as soon as we can."

Justin clicked off the phone. He needed to contact the gas company, but the number was on the bill, in the hallway. He swiped his hand across his forehead to push away the sweat beginning to trickle into his eyes. The crazy phone call, a car narrowly missing him, and now this. He'd have to hold his breath and get the bill from the hall table.

Justin sucked air deep into his lungs and moved as fast as his unsteady legs would carry him. He snatched the pile of bills from the side table turning and escaping the hallway. He sat on the wooden plank bench of his picnic table and spread out the envelopes searching for the one with the cutsey flame person. His flashlight started to dim, brightening when he gave it a good shake.

"Here it is." Justin dialed the number listed as the emergency phone number and waited for an answer. When the voice of a real person answered, he gave an explanation and his address to the company representative. Her estimate of getting someone out was approximately thirty minutes.

Justin dropped his head to his hands. What the heck was going on?

The changes made on his will at the lawyer's appointment tonight were confidential. Tom and his law clerk were the only ones aware he had put everything in trust and was having his sister, Irene, act as the trustee. Tom guaranteed no one would have knowledge until the changed will was filed Monday morning.

The whine of a siren interrupted his concentration. *Best meet them out front.*

Justin made his way around the side of the house, noting a familiar form lumbering to the front door.

"You think someone is trying to blow you up? I'm expected to believe this is not some kind of hoax you and Tom cooked up?" Detective Corey Williams had been a year ahead of Justin and Tom in high school and college but had taken the two under his wing when they'd all played football.

"Why did they send out a cop?"

"Gosh, I've got goose bumps all over coming to see you too. It's a small town, Justin. Whenever anything happens, we get a courtesy call. I wouldn't have made the decision to come out if I hadn't recognized the address. You sure this isn't some prank Tom concocted to one-up you?"

Justin slanted a disgusted look Corey's direction. "Tonight as I was leaving The Bar, I received a warning call—it was actually more of a warning whisper—telling me to watch myself. I shrugged it off as somebody's phone prank gone sideways. The stench in my kitchen, however, is no misdirected prank. I think it would be best for you to experience it yourself."

Detective Williams followed Justin around the house to the back entrance. He reached out an arm and pushed aside the homeowner to investigate the problem without interference.

Justin hung back. The gas had been spewing into his house for nearly half an hour by now. Was there a real possibility of an explosion or was that just television theatrics?

"Corey, be careful."

The detective turned around. "I have no intention of becoming a shesh-ke-bob. Stay back, Justin." He opened the door as carefully as he could manage, allowing the inside air to assault his olfactory senses. Once the recognizable rotten egg smell blasted him, the detective slowly pulled the door shut and moved toward the center of the back yard, grabbing Justin and taking him along.

"Could you have forgotten to shut off one of your burners on the stove?" Corey took a small tablet from his shirt pocket to scribe the answers. "Rumor has it you've been putting in a lot of overtime."

Justin shook his head. "No. The only items in the house fueled by gas are the water heater and forced air heat. My stove is electric as is the in-window air conditioner. Besides, I use the microwave to cook most of my meals."

The detective scribbled furiously in his notebook. "So, there is no way you could have done this?"

Justin turned a glare his direction. "Look...I get up at the crack of dawn to go to work. It may take me two cups of coffee before my blood starts moving, but I'm not numb enough to try and blow up my own house. No, there is no way I could have done this myself."

Corey let a smirk cross his lips. "I had to ask. It's part of my job."

Justin lifted his head to the heavens. "I know but I'm exhausted from work and dealing with, well, you know who."

Vehicle lights brightened the side of the house, and the two men made for the front yard. A white van with official lettering on the side pulled next to the patrol car and parked.

"I've got two hours left on shift and this'll take up most of my time with paperwork, real or not." Corey groused.

A harried looking gas worker, replete with jumpsuit and *John* embroidered on the right pocket, shuffled to the front porch where Justin and Corey stood waiting.

"What's the problem?" John, the gas man, looked at the Detective.

"Ask him. He's the homeowner," Corey jerked his thumb Justin's direction.

The worker turned and repeated his query. "What's the problem?"

Justin's jaw twitched as he steadied his voice to answer.

"I believe there's a gas leak in my house, but I won't know until it has been checked out. The aroma of rotten eggs sucked the breath out of me when I came home. Confirmation," he pushed through gritted teeth, "I believe, is where you come in."

Justin watched Corey stifle the urge to snicker.

"Oh. Well, that means I'll have to go back to my van and get my equipment." The gas company rep trudged to his vehicle, creating a ruckus as he searched for his gear.

"Corey, please keep me from choking the life out of this idiot."

"Well, I would have to stop you as choking the life out of someone is against the law. I'm a policeman and it's my duty to stop those kinds of actions." He allowed a smile to cover his face.

"Thank you for the astute observation."

"You're welcome."

The technician returned with face mask in one hand and a rectangular silver box with long black antennae in the other. "Where did you notice the smell first?"

Justin proceeded to lead the worker to the back of the house and indicate the offending area as his kitchen. Once the gas man had donned his mask and turned on his meter, the obnoxious sound of high pitched beeping permeated the air in conjunction with the overwhelming stench.

The gas rep backed out of the house and bent over near the foundation, manipulating his hand held device near the base. The man reached the connection from the house to the meter. There was one long piercing sound cutting through the night air. Hands over his ears, Justin walked around the side of the house to the front porch.

A figure wrapped in a chenille robe sporting flip flops on her feet, trundled across the darkened street to sidle up to Justin.

"Hey, kid. What the hell is going on?"

"Oh, hey, Edna. Gas leak."

"Really? I thought the guy this afternoon would have fixed it," she took a step away from his home.

The speed with which Corey moved from his car to the robed figure caused her to gasp.

"Wha—who are you?" She planted her hands on her ample hips.

"It's okay, Edna. Corey is a detective and a friend." Justin patted the arm of his across the street neighbor.

"Do you remember what the guy looked like and when he showed up?" Corey had flipped open his notepad and held his pencil at the ready.

"You mean you don't know? Why that lying, two-faced..." Edna threw up her arms and started to pace. "He said the company had received a report of a broken main in the area and was checking those houses with gas appliances. I asked him if he would take a look at my stove, and he started to make some excuse when his phone rang.

"Can't tell you exactly what was being said, but the poor guy looked like he was gettin' his ass chewed but good. He closed the sliding door on his white van and took off, screeching the tires on the street as he left."

Corey lifted a brow at the extraneous explanation. "Did you see him go into the house?"

Edna humphed and rolled her eyes in Justin's direction.

"I caught him comin' out the side of the house with one of them wrench things in his hands."

Justin and Corey exchanged looks. Justin picked up the thread. "Did he have on gloves, Edna?"

"No, uh, wait a minute." She stood and tapped her chin. "You know, I think he did. I scared the bejesus out of him, that much I know. When I asked what he was doin', he jumped and hollered." She offered a wicked grin. "Been a long time since I had the pleasure of sneakin' up on somebody."

Corey took her aside and attempted to gather further information about the illusive gas man from the afternoon.

John, the current gas company representative, having deposited his tools in the back of his van, walked up to Justin with a metal pad and paperwork.

"So what's the verdict?" Justin held his impatience in check.

"Well, Mr.," the tech looked at the name he'd written on the paper, "Anderson, you can't stay in the house tonight."

"What!" Justin felt the heat rushing up his spine. "Why not? I've got to work tomorrow and need to--"

The tech held up a hand.

Justin started toward the man only stopping when Corey, appearing suddenly, threw a heavily muscled arm out to waylay his motion.

"I'm sorry, sir, but as unstable as the situation is, I couldn't, in good conscience, allow you to enter your home. There's no telling what might set off the fumes. We won't be able to get out our specialist until the morning. You're going to have to find somewhere to stay the night."

Justin huffed out a breath. "I really don't need this now."

"And I think you should know...this was no accident." Scurrying to his truck, the gas company tech left Justin standing bewildered, a stunned look on his face.

"No accident? Hm," Corey sauntered up to his friend. "You said you received a phone call earlier this evening. Did you happen to get the number?"

Justin pulled the phone from his belt, looking at the display and groaning.

"What's the matter?" Corey asked.

"I guess when the car sped at me and I dropped this thing, the power pack disconnected. I'm not sure I can retrieve the number." He plugged the power pack into the phone. Using light from Corey's flashlight, Justin searched the phone memory for the most recent numbers.

"I can't find anything here I don't recognize," he said.

"Well, let me take it to the boys in the computer lab and have them do their magic," Corey held out his hand to take the phone from Justin. "You got a place to stay tonight?"

"I can find a place between here and Billington."

"I'm glad because we're going to be all over the house for the next few days."

"I figured as much," Justin said.

"Justin, you really pissed off somebody." Corey leaned back against his car and crossed his arms. He conferred with a couple of the patrol officers who had approached him.

Justin felt as if he'd been sucker punched. *Who'd do this?*

Corey watched his friend's shoulders sag and asked, "You going to be okay?"

"Soon as I get my truck, I'm out of here."

"We want to keep your truck and give it a bumper to bumper search, but I might have a solution. Since you're not really going anywhere for a while, I'll drive you to your motel tonight, and when you get up in the morning, you can call me and I'll see you get to the rental agency."

"Why don't you drive me to The Bar and drop me off. I think maybe I can get a ride with Mark, the bartender. I don't think I could go to sleep right now, anyway," Justin said.

"Are you sure? It's really not a problem for me to make sure you make it to a motel," Corey replied.

"Nah. I'd like to be around people for a little while. Okay?" Justin said.

"Sure, no problem." Corey waved Justin to the car and the pair headed down the street. Ten minutes later, in front of The Bar, Justin saluted as the state vehicle pulled away from the curb.

Four

Justin strolled into the bar. He hadn't realized how much he was shaken by the fact someone might want to kill him. Moving to a barstool farthest from the front door, he nodded at Mark who nodded back, almost dropping the bottle he had in his hand.

Recovering, Mark set the bottle on the bar. "What are you doing back here? I thought you called it a night?"

"I did, but something came up and I didn't feel like staying home by myself. There's a bunch of police at my house who chased me away and told me I can't come back for a couple days. So, I decided to stop in before calling a taxi to take me to the Snooze Inn. How about Coke? Since I still have to work tomorrow, I'd better keep a clear head."

"Police? Why?" Mark asked.

"Oh, something about a deadly gas leak in the house," Justin said.

"A gas leak? You need to get more rest and stop walking around in a daze. I'd invite you to stay at my apartment, but I've given it up and moved into Jennifer's house."

Justin smiled for the first time in an hour, "You haven't told Diane, have you?"

Mark shuffled uncomfortably, "No. I don't need to hear the 'if it's real you can wait' speech. Jennifer and I are doing okay. I know we could break up at any moment and I'd be on the street but, right now, things are just fine."

Mark's defensive body stance made Justin laugh out loud. "Boy, Diane sure has you on the run. You'd think she was your ex-wife or something. Why don't you tell her what you told me? I mean, what difference does it make to her?"

"None. Except, I gave the 'if it's real it can wait' speech to her the last time she was thinking of moving in with somebody. I could see the guy had nothing but dollar signs in his eyes and she wasn't thinking clearly. I hate having to eat my words. Wait a minute. Diane called about forty-five minutes ago asking me to come stay tonight. She said she saw the guy who was bothering her earlier peeping in her windows. I told her I wouldn't be able to come over tonight. I think I can solve everyone's problems."

Before Justin could object, Mark disappeared into the office. Emerging ten minutes later, he was smiling.

"When I called Diane, she said the news station just broke the story there is a large suspicious gas leak on Meadowcreek Lane. Were you going to keep all the excitement to yourself? I told her that considering what you just told me, it was probably your house and suggested you staying with her would serve two purposes. She'd have a trustworthy male presence, and you'd have a place to catch a few winks more desirable than the Snooze Inn; she agreed. Here are the directions to her house, but you'd better get moving. She said, under the circumstances, the front door locks at eleven-thirty sharp."

"There's just one problem, Mark."

"What?"

"I don't have any transportation," Justin said.

"Take my car. I'll have Jennifer pick me up after work. Now, you have no excuse."

Justin noted the smug look on Mark's face and realized arguing would be futile. He'd been committed to staying at Diane's as a charity case. Staying at a hotel wasn't all that bad, and he would've preferred to be *invited* to Diane's under more agreeable circumstances. Finishing his Coke, he picked up the keys Mark had set on the bar and trudged out to the large four door Mercury he was borrowing.

Justin turned on the inside light of the car and read the directions Mark had handed him. Driving and trying to remember the directions was a different story. He made all the turns Mark had designated but had problems finding the house numbers. He'd made a third pass down the street, when he noticed a porch light that wasn't lit the other times he'd driven past. Pulling in front of the house and turning off the engine, Justin checked the number. This was the right place. He was impressed with the neat, well-kept lawn, and not too much frilly stuff out front. Hopefully, the inside would show the same taste.

Five

Justin dutifully locked the car and walked to the front door. Hand poised to knock, he blinked in surprise when the door opened. Diane ushered him into the tastefully designed living area. Simple and elegant were the words that sprang to Justin's mind. The decor was neither masculine nor feminine but artfully functional and open. He felt comfortable.

"Welcome to my home. Let me show you where you will bunk tonight."

Diane led him down a wide hallway that served as an art gallery. The taste of the collector reflected an interest in Native American works. He stopped midway to gape at a picture of an Indian maiden peering coyly out from behind a feather fan.

"Wow! This picture looks like you!" Justin marveled.

"It is—sort of. An artist friend borrowed the dancing outfit and asked if I would act as his model. He'd promised a Native American style picture to a client and he was facing a close deadline. He painted two pictures. This one, where I'm peering out with the fan held up and in the other I'm looking off into the distance with the fan at my side. This was my birthday present."

Diane was slowly beginning to blush as she spoke of the picture. Justin decided not to press the issue any further.

"It's very beautiful. He's a talented man." Justin stood for a moment, gazing at the oil painting. The artist had captured a mischievous twinkle in her dark eyes. The buckskin dress clung sensually to her slender body, outlining her full round breasts then, at a slit on the thigh, fell open to reveal her shapely bare leg. He inhaled slowly and deeply. He needed to get hold of his imagination. He'd promised himself he would act like a gentleman.

"Now, where am I staying?" he asked using his best casual voice.

Diane continued to the end of the hallway and turned left. Opening a door at the end of the short T-shaped hallway, she presented a comfortable looking room complete with a queen sized bed, night stand, dresser and TV on a stand. She moved inside the room to another door and opening it, explained he had his own bathroom with shower.

"I start moving around at about five a.m. and usually leave by seven. Let me show you where the kitchen is located. There'll be a pot of coffee, real stuff, no decaf, ready in the morning. You're welcome to have some. Please wash out your cup and put it in the dishwasher before you leave."

Justin heard whining and scratching as they passed a closed door halfway down the hallway. The sounds were the only indication Diane had a pet. He wouldn't have known otherwise. There weren't the usual signs—chewed toys and the smell.

"Princess! Settle down. I have a rescued Greyhound. She shouldn't be any problem, but if she happens to wander into your room, move slowly. She's a bit skittish and not fond of males. Her trainer was not a nice man and, consequently, she's snapped at a couple of people. Mark found out you can't rush over and pet her. He has a little scar on his left hand that taught him to slow down. Well, that's the fifty-cent tour. I'm really bushed so I'm going to bed. Please see if you can be up and out by seven or seven thirty at the latest so I can lock the house."

"I'm usually up and gone by six, so if you want to show me how to make coffee in your coffeemaker, I can make it in the morning."

"No, that's okay. I have a machine with an automatic pre-set. Good night, I'll see you in the morning."

"Diane?"

"Yes?"

"Thank you. I appreciate it."

"You're welcome. Goodnight, Justin." Diane wandered to the kitchen to make coffee. She liked the sound of saying goodnight to him. It was nice to have the sense of security a man's presence gave. After she assembled the ingredients for tomorrow morning's brew, she leaned against the counter, breathing air deep into her lungs. Showing Justin around the house had tested every nerve in her body, and she needed to slow her pounding heart. His aftershave lingered, leaving a faint reminder of his presence. When he had been looking at the painting in the hallway, her eyes had revisited his taut, muscular physique. She was sure he knew she'd been checking him over, and she'd blushed to her toes at being caught.

She walked down the hallway to the laundry room and stepped back as she opened the door. Princess came charging out of the room, busily sniffing all the new smells. Tail wagging, she moved to Diane and nudged her thigh.

"Sit down. Good girl. We have a visitor so you behave yourself and don't bite him. He'll be gone in morning so I won't lock you up tonight. Okay?"

Diane knew the dog didn't understand anything said to her. The only issue was getting undivided attention. Princess's eyes sparkled and she danced a little as she watched Diane.

"Come on, Princess, one last visit outside before bedtime."

Diane gravitated to the patio door, the silver dog close at her heels. She put her hand on the latch and hesitated. Still seeing the face of Retro Man staring at her from the back yard, her hand shook as she opened the door. She watched Princess streak to the back of the fenced yard. The clock in the kitchen ticked loudly, and Diane was about to set out to rescue her wayward pooch when the silver animal trotted to the door. She hustled the sleek canine indoors and locked the screen and patio doors checking, again, to make sure they were impenetrable.

"Let's go to bed."

The two padded to the master bedroom on the right of the short T-shaped hallway. Diane glanced in the direction where Justin was sleeping. The door was open just a little.

Probably just uncomfortable in a new place.

Diane felt the breeze of movement against her legs as Princess nosed her way into the occupied guest room before Diane could grab her collar.

"Princess!" she whispered through gritted teeth. She waited. No response. She didn't know Justin well enough to go barging in the room to retrieve her dog. So far there hadn't been cries of pain, so Princess wasn't eating him alive. Diane would have to let Princess stay where she was.

She entered her room, leaving the door slightly ajar in case her wayward dog opted to sleep in her usual spot at the foot of the bed. Completing her nightly ritual, Diane heeded the beckoning of her warm covers. Sleep overtook any thoughts about Justin or Princess.

Six

Diane stood naked, her arms wrapped tightly about her body, on a glacier in Alaska. Alaska? Emerging slowly from the fog of dreaming, she started to shiver. It was cold! That was the key. She was cold. Where was the body that normally spooned against her back keeping her warm? Where was Princess? When she'd awakened enough to grab for the blanket at her feet, the alarm went off. She slogged into the bathroom. Exiting, a little more awake and ready for the day, her next stop was the kitchen. She searched all of Princess's favorite snooze spots on her way from the bathroom to the kitchen but couldn't locate her. Grabbing a mug and the newspaper on the counter, Diane headed for the table in the dining room.

She stopped. *I grabbed the paper off the counter top—not the front step.*

She peered around the corner into the dining room. What she witnessed was her greyhound, head resting in Justin's lap, gazing at him expectantly.

"Okay, Princess. I'll pet you until Diane gets up BUT we have to keep it our secret you slept with me. You're a very good blanket, big eyes." Justin tenderly ran his hand between Princess's ears and down her body as he talked to her. She scooted her back end closer so he could reach further down her body. She lifted her head from his lap, lowered her ears and began skulking away from Justin.

Diane stepped around the corner, "So this is what happened. I woke up freezing this morning because my extra blanket wasn't there to keep me warm." She sat down at the table.

"I hope she wasn't a bother. She obviously didn't bite you." A smile flickered across her face.

"Listen, I'm sorry. About fifteen minutes after I went into the room and crawled into bed, a long silver nose and two big eyes peeked around the door. You didn't mention she was such a beautiful dog. I sat up, slowly like you told me, and held my hand out to her. She hesitantly moved near, sniffed my hand then hopped up on the bed, circled three times and lay down. I didn't want to make a scene because you said she might bite, so I lay down and went to sleep. We've taken a walk and eaten this morning. That's okay, isn't it?"

Diane shook her head. Princess avoided new people and would disappear when her former dates had shown up. She'd actually nipped a couple of guys who'd tried to pet her. Diane later agreed they needed nipping. But right now, Diane was staring into two pairs of questioning eyes.

She burst out laughing, "Of course it's all right. Gives me more time to read the paper and drink my coffee. As soon as I'm done with the paper, though, I'll leave for work."

"How did you happen to get her?" he asked. "Isn't she a special racing breed?"

"One of the customers who frequented The Bar when I was bartending there some years ago had spent enough money at the track to be on a first name basis with most of the handlers and trainers. He'd been given an opportunity to go inside the kennels with a guest and invited me along. Once inside, I heard the most wretched whining. We rounded a corner into the center of the ready room, and this trainer was jerking one of the racer's dog collar to the floor and forcing it to lie on the ground by placing his foot on the dog's head," Diane's eyes flashed as she recalled the scene. She felt her heart beating heavily against her chest and realized she was clenching her hands into and out of fists.

"What a jerk," Justin frowned.

"That was the most polite thought I had. I reacted by rushing over and shoving his foot from the dog's head as I yanked the leash from him.

The poor dog cowered on the floor, obviously expecting a beating. I spat out that if he were smart, he'd leave before I called the Humane Society and reported him for the abuse I'd witnessed. I added I was sure the Racing Commission would be interested in his methods too. He sputtered something in Spanish and stomped from the room."

"Bravo. That's the *how* you met this beauty, now, *how'd* you get to bring her home?" Justin pulled his coffee cup closer and wrapped his hands around the sides.

"Well, my chaperon was certain I'd ruined his career at the track and grasping my elbow, promptly escorted me out of the kennels and sped me home. Once he'd cooled off and won a couple of races without the insider information he thought was helping him, he started coming back into The Bar. I asked him what had happened to the dog. He made some flippant remark they were going to have her destroyed because she wasn't any good to the owning race kennel due to the abuse she'd suffered. She wouldn't run for any of the trainers. Frantic, I called the track and spoke to someone who put me in touch with a rescue organization for greyhounds that are destined to be destroyed."

"I didn't know they had such a thing," Justin said.

"I didn't either until that day, but I was glad I found out about it when I did. I filled out paperwork, paid a small fee and within two weeks she was mine. It took six months before she quit cowering every time I got near her. Oh, jeez, would you look at the time? I need to get moving. Are you about ready?" Diane asked.

"Take me only about ten minutes," Justin got up and walked toward the bedroom.

"Justin?"

He stopped and turned at the door to face Diane. She had lost the morning glow he'd noticed when she'd first entered the kitchen.

"What?" Justin tried swallowing past the tightening in his throat.

"The paper quotes the police spokesman as saying..." Diane picked up the paper. The headlines screamed, *SABOTAGED GAS MAIN IN BLUE MOUNTAIN COMMUNITY*, "'We found evidence of tampering with the gas main on the outside of the house. It also appears as if the brakes on the pickup truck had been cut just enough that when the driver attempted to use them, they would fail. Why? We're not sure. We'll investigate further before we comment."'

Justin slumped against the wall. Head throbbing and heart hammering, he sucked in short quick breaths, feeling as though the air in the hallway was being pumped out the opposite end.

"Are you okay? You don't look so good," Diane rose. The strong chivalrous man who had held her close to his sinewy body last night was propped against her wall looking very shaky.

"I don't believe it," Justin muttered.

"Justin? Are you all right? Is there someone I can call for you?" Diane's stomach rolled as she clutched the back of her chair.

"I'm all right, I'm all right," Justin straightened. "When you hear about sabotage at airports or post offices the news is disconcerting; when you hear about it in your own house, reality punches you in the gut."

"Is there anything I can do to help?"

"Would you listen for a few moments? I'm not a confiding sort of guy, but I need to talk to somebody. I trust Mark's judgment and he seems to trust you. After all, I did sort of bail you out last night." Justin mustered a weak smile at Diane.

"You do realize this is blackmail?" Diane asked.

"Blackmail? I hadn't thought of that. Okay. This is blackmail," Justin said.

"I've got about," Diane looked at her watch, "ten minutes then I really have to leave for work. Will that help?"

"Thanks. I'll take it," Justin and Diane moved back to the dining room table.

"Would you like another cup of coffee?" she asked.

"Please." Pouring two cups of coffee, Diane placed one in front of Justin and sat with hers across the table from him.

"What's this all about, Justin?" Diane asked.

Justin took a sip of coffee before looking up to talk.

"The only thing that has kept me going, for a long time, is my eleven year old daughter, Briana. Would you like to see her picture?"

Justin pulled his wallet from his back pocket. It automatically fell open to a specific picture which he handed to Diane.

She looked at the school picture of a beautiful dark haired, light-eyed child. The innocent full-lipped smile revealed perfect white teeth and deep perfectly matched dimples. Her heart ached at the thought of what she had been unable to attain.

"She's absolutely gorgeous, Justin. You're going to have problems pretty soon. Hope you have a big shotgun," Diane smiled as she handed back the wallet.

"Yeah, I know what you mean. Unfortunately, my ex-wife, Ashlee, has made my visits with Briana fewer and farther between scheduled times. When we divorced, things started to get vicious quickly. It didn't take me long to realize just how much Briana was affected by our arguing and court shenanigans. So to avoid putting my baby through hell because of her mother's avarice, I agreed they should live in the home I inherited, until my ex-wife remarries. It's the only home Briana's ever known. I was to have as much time with her as I wanted according to the divorce documents, however; her mother uses every visit against me. Even though she somehow managed to be awarded alimony, it doesn't seem to be enough. She still tries to control my life through my visits with Briana similar to when we were married.

"Meanwhile, my poor daughter is becoming withdrawn and distant. The last time we saw each other I left after only half an hour because I could see Briana was uncomfortable. Ashlee has joked about having me *'push up daisies'* if I don't follow her instructions to the letter. She laughs and brushes it off later when people ask if she is serious. After last night, I don't know. I'm just getting paranoid thinking she might have tried something. Right?" Justin put his elbows on the table and leaned toward Diane.

She sat against the back of the chair, unconsciously running her hand through her short hair. She could relate only too well to Justin's current situation. Timothy, her ex, was making life a living purgatory with his demands, but she didn't think he'd resort to attempted murder. He didn't have the initiative to think of it or the courage to follow through.

"You don't think she'd actually do something as stupid as tamper with your car or house, do you?" Diane asked.

"I'm not sure what she'd do," Justin said, "I heard a rumor she has a new boyfriend she has dancing on a string, but if she eliminates me, they both lose. She'll have to go to work at a real job to support him. He's some sort of competition bodybuilder, and his job is to work out in the gym. One thing I know for sure is Ashlee likes her pampered life style too much to work for a living. The only reason I'd suspect her of attempting to follow through on her threats is my daughter inherits everything I have when I die. I'd originally arranged to have Ashlee as the executrix of the money until Briana was twenty-one but I've recently amended my will. If Ashlee found out, she'd personally shoot me just for the thrill of it."

"Oh, come on, Justin, you can't mean that," Diane frowned.

"I don't really know anymore what she would or wouldn't do. I just want to spend time with my daughter before she falls too much under her mother's influence."

His slumped shoulders and the disappointed tone of his voice tugged at Diane. Fighting the urge to gather him up in her arms and soothe away his pain, she got up from the table and put her cup in the dishwasher. She turned to him. "You're going through a rough period right now. I suspect you won't be able to get into your house for a couple of days if this police department works like most. You're welcome to stay here until they clear your home. Princess has taken to you, and I've learned to trust her instincts. She's never wrong. There are ground rules if you decide you want to stay. We can discuss those when you make up your mind." Diane said. *I might regret this later.*

Justin stared at Diane in amazement. Twelve hours earlier, she was pushing him away. Now she was offering the safety of her home.

"Thanks, but until they find out who's been sabotaging my life, anyone near me will be exposed to the same danger. I really like Princess," the silver dog nudged his hand with her wet nose, tail wagging, "and you're not too bad either…"

"Gee, thanks."

"I couldn't ask you to put yourself in danger. I'll be very careful and watch my back at home. They'll probably have extra patrols past the house until they get this figured out. I mean, this is the most exciting thing to happen in town since Miller's Drugstore burned to the ground in 1957."

"Well, I applaud your courage but just in case you come to your senses," Diane handed Justin a business card, "call me on my cell or leave a message. I'll get back to you before five tonight. Are you ready to head out?"

"Let me get my things," Justin retrieved the few articles he'd managed to grab from his home before his exile.

They set off through the kitchen to the garage. Planted in front of the door was Princess.

"Damn. Princess, come on, you need to get out of the way. This is not the first time I've left for work." The dog didn't move a muscle. Justin moved to her side and, squatting down, petted the silver beauty.

"Let us go to work now and I promise I'll come visit if Diane approves. Okay?"

Slowly the greyhound trudged to the laundry room. She turned and gave such a soulful look back that Justin and Diane started laughing.

"I've never had her do that before. What did you do to my dog?" Diane asked in mock anger.

"It's my secret," Justin smiled.

"Should I put her in the laundry room today? I guess I'll let her roam the house. After what happened last night, it won't hurt to have her out. Maybe whoever was here will think twice about breaking in if they hear her bark."

Justin opened the door as Diane used the automatic control to open the garage door from the inside. He walked out to the borrowed sedan parked at the curbside. Diane's Corvette slowly slid down the small incline onto the street parallel to Justin, the passenger window sliding open.

"Now, remember, if you need a place to stay just call. I have plenty of room," Diane flashed Justin a dazzling smile, waved and the black Corvette disappeared down the street.

Seven

Justin drove to the police station determined to get an update from Detective Williams. Maybe he would take up Corey's offer to drive him to the rental car place in Billington. Consciously locking all the doors, he set out for the three-story building that sat on one side of the town square and served as Police Headquarters, the courthouse, and County Jail. Inside, he followed the signs to the Detective Division and approached the Sergeant-on-Duty asking to see Detective Corey Williams. After the Sergeant checked Justin's identification, he motioned him to sit in the designated waiting area while he phoned the office. It wasn't long before Corey lumbered down the hall toward him.

"What can I do for you, Justin?" Corey asked.

Justin stood. "What's going on Corey? Has anything been uncovered yet?" Crossing his arms and planting his feet, he continued, "I really need my truck for work, so I can pay my ex-wife. And *NOT* wind up on the coroner's slab."

Corey placed a hand on his friend's shoulder, "Let's walk back to my office, and I'll update you on what we have so far. Then we'll see what I can do about getting your truck to you," Corey moved toward the door marked Employees Only. He swiped his ID card and motioned for Justin to pass through. Corey took the lead and walked Justin past several desks in various stages of orderliness. Each area had the identical look of Government Issue—one three-drawer desk, battleship gray, a four-drawer filing cabinet, also battleship gray, and one slightly sprung battleship gray chair. He set off to the only glassed-in office. The doorplate read, Corey

Williams, Chief Detective. Entering, they sat on opposite sides of the desk.

"You realize anything I tell you stays in this office. This is an ongoing investigation and everything is considered evidence not to be shared. You clear about that?" Corey emphasized.

"Yes."

"Good. Basically, we have very little right now, except the connection from your gas main to the house had been loosened and your truck brakes were expertly cut. We have two clear prints on the undercarriage of the truck. The gas meter outside the house provided a partial and several smeared prints. My guess is you weren't expected to survive the blast. Whoever set this up got careless. We've sent those prints to the crime lab in Billington to be processed through their computer. *They* are tied to the national data base. Remember all the wonderful equipment the town council budgeted for and loudly promised would be delivered? Well, none of it has shown up, so we have to rely on Billington PD to help us with the technical end of things.

"Most of the evidence we located can be easily explained away as normal wear and tear. However, we do have one ray of hope."

Justin sat forward in his chair. "What's that?"

"Your lady across the street—what's her name again?" Corey shuffled through the paperwork on his desk until he located a small green spiral notebook. "Edna Jones?"

Justin smiled, "Yeah, our neighborhood busybody."

"Well, it's a good thing for us she is," Corey added. "The stranger she noticed yesterday drove a white van. He was dressed in coveralls like the regular meter reader, and she wouldn't have given it a second thought except Buddy Allen, who's been the gas company meter reader in your area for ten years, had just been there the day before.

"Edna remembers because Buddy always stops in for her fresh baked muffins and a cup of hot coffee. She said she was watching the birds near her feeder when this guy parked in front of your house, not on the side like Buddy does. First thing that made her curious was his overall stature; a hundred and eighty pounds and blonde. Buddy's nearly three hundred pounds and has jet-black hair. Next, was the brand new van; Buddy's is falling apart. About that time, Edna decided this needed closer investigation. She crossed the street to see if she could help the young man, stopping to note down the license plate. She said he came running from the back of the house and, *'nearly knocked me down. Didn't say excuse me or anything'*. She did get a good look at his face, though.

"We're running the plate through the National Crime Information Center in Washington to see who the registration on the van comes back to.

"When she was talking with the patrol officers this evening, she said the one thing that really triggered her suspicions about this guy was a pair of Ostrich skin boots he wore underneath the coveralls. She knew they were Ostrich because she'd bought Ned, her husband, a pair two years before he died. She knew how expensive they were fifteen years ago and wondered how someone working for the gas company could afford to work in such an expensive pair of boots."

Justin sat in the chair, dazed and breathless. He'd resented Edna's snooping before—but not this time. It appeared her personal neighborhood watch might help.

"Where do we go from here?" Justin asked.

"*We* go nowhere. The police department will continue to question people in the neighborhood, your employees and anyone who appears as though they might've had a motive to blow you into the next county. Which, of course, includes Ashlee and her latest boyfriend. But you? *You* do nothing. You don't go storming over to Ashlee's and accuse her; you don't go investigating ex-employees; you do nothing. This is a police matter not a vigilante hunt. Go to work. Carry on like nothing happened, and we'll keep you informed of our progress."

"Someone tried to blow me up! I'm supposed to act like nothing happened? Corey, get serious. How would you feel? Why can't I go back to my house? You've found everything by now, and in the last twelve hours no one's tried a repeat performance, so why can't I go back to my house? And when do I get my truck back?" Justin pushed up from his chair, pacing in front of Corey's desk.

"Listen, Justin, we haven't finished investigating the house. We're sending your truck to a specialist from the State Police to examine every inch. You'll need to make arrangements to stay somewhere and get transportation for the next couple of days until we have checked everything thoroughly. If you don't have any place to go, we can probably put you up in a safe house. As for the truck, I don't know what to tell you. Don't you have anything at your construction site you can use?"

Justin leaned against the side of the desk. "Corey? That is my company truck. It just happens to be my personal truck as well. Most of my guys drive their own rigs and my money is tied up in my big equipment. I could drive my big dump truck, but if I drove it down Main Street, you'd probably give me a ticket for disturbing the peace. I was hoping you'd let me call the rental agency from here and maybe give me a ride to pick up a car?"

Corey turned his phone around to face Justin and handed him the phone book.

"Go for it."

Justin flipped through the pages. Finding the number, he marked it with his finger as he dialed.

"Hi. Yeah, I was wondering if you might have a pickup for rent. No? Nothing? You don't have anything until Saturday. How come? Oh, convention in Billington. Can I put my name on a waiting list? Yes. Justin Anderson. Four three four, five five five, two one four nine. It's my cell phone and you can reach me anytime. Thanks."

Corey raised his eyebrows. "Well?"

"Seems there's some kind of convention going on in Billington and every rental car in town has been reserved. She'll call me when something becomes available. Meantime, Corey, I'm stuck. Can you think of anybody who'd rent me their car for a day or two?" Justin began to pace in front of Corey's desk again.

"I'll tell you what, why don't you cool your heels in the lobby for about ten minutes or so, and I'll see what I can scare up," Corey stood and lacing his hands behind his neck stretched backward.

"Keep me posted, Corey," Justin said.

"When I have something, you'll be the second to know, okay?" Corey stepped from behind his desk and opened the door. "Just follow the corridor to the lobby and I'll be out shortly."

The two men shook hands, and Justin trudged to the lobby where he sat in the government-issue chair while he waited.

Corey's phone jangled angrily. Picking it up, he barked, "What? Yeah, this is Detective Williams. What can I do for you? I see. You say the van was stolen two nights ago between nine and ten in the evening. Who's the registered owner? The Manning law firm. Why would a law firm need a van?" he muttered to himself, "They said it's a shuttle van for their three offices? I see. Who reported it stolen? Humph. Okay, thanks, Officer Varvarinski. This'll help. Yeah, you too. Bye."

Corey had no love for the Mannings. His former wife of nine years had taken his four kids, house, and new car with a divorce decree that'd been drawn up by Thomas Manning. Despite the fact Thomas offered to help raise Corey and his sister when their family was killed, it wouldn't have hurt his feelings to lock up one or both of the Mannings. Oh, well, he'd have to pursue other leads more intently.

Corey picked up the phone and called the front desk.

"Sarge? Is there still a dark haired guy sitting out in the lobby area? Yeah, that's the one. Give him the extra set of keys to my truck. Yes, that's what I said, the keys to my new truck. Hell, I know where he lives and works. I'm not worried. I'll just drive the squad car until he gets his truck back. Thanks."

Corey hung up the phone. He needed to track some viable leads. Ashlee Anderson had the most to gain if Justin was out of the picture. He'd give her a call and set up an appointment for her to come in and answer questions. Then he'd call the Mannings for interviews. This might turn out to be a good day after all.

~ * ~

Justin shifted in the institutional chair. *I swear they make these things uncomfortable on purpose.* He wasn't good at waiting and, right this moment, his patience was fraying. The faint scent of Jade East tickled his nose. He glanced at the Sergeant's desk and saw Retro Man retrieving his personal items. The dark growth on his face, rumpled white suit, and black eye required Justin to squint to verify his suspicions. Stuffing his wallet into his coat pocket, Retro Man stumbled past Justin without acknowledgement.

"Excuse me, Sergeant?" Justin leaned forward on the chair and nodded at the figure pushing through the glass exit doors to the parking lot. "That guy looks a lot like one being a real pain to a friend of mine at The Bar last night. He just wouldn't take no for an answer. When I left to go home, I'd swear he tried to run me over."

"It might be the same guy. Some out-of-town businessman here with a convention that got pretty liquored up last night and tried to manhandle the girls over at Club Nouveaux. When Brian, the bouncer, warned him to keep his hands to himself, the guy wouldn't listen. The second time, Brian escorted him outside and told him not to come back. He wasn't welcome. The bozo walked back in and tried to pick a fight with Brian. Not a smart move. Brian punched him once and knocked the guy out. We were called to pick him up and dump him into the drunk tank. When we ran a check on him, we discovered he has a history of this kind of behavior. He's pretty well known in the Washington, D.C. area and not allowed in most of the bars over there. Guess he figured we hicks in the country wouldn't mind if he mauled our female population. He found out different."

Justin sat back in the rigid chair. At least, Retro Man was able to leave and go home. He wanted to sleep in his own bed and drive his own truck. Which reminded him, Corey had told him he might have a temporary solution. He went to the front desk and asked if Detective Williams had left a message for Justin Anderson. The Sergeant tossed a set of keys to Justin.

"It's his personal vehicle. He said since you were a friend you could use his truck for the next couple of days, and he'd drive a police car until you got your wheels back. Better take good care of it. That's his baby." He called one of the police clerks to escort Justin to the vehicle.

The two walked out to the employee parking lot.

"Which one is it?" Justin asked.

"The big red Ford pickup," the clerk pointed.

Justin gaped at the sparkling cherry-red four-wheel drive pickup truck. It stood three feet from the ground to the bottom of the truck door. He couldn't imagine Corey Williams trying to get his bulk into it without a ladder and snickered at the mental picture.

Justin pulled a number from his wallet and dialed his cell.

"Hey, Mark. Yeah, thanks for letting me use your rig last night. No, I've got something for now. You want me to come get you? Okay, well, it's in front of the police station. I'll leave the keys with the desk sergeant inside. Thanks again." Justin walked to the desk sergeant. "May I have an envelope?"

The sergeant handed him a blank envelope from under the desktop. He wrote Mark's name on the outside and handed the envelope, keys inside, to the sergeant.

"There'll be a dark haired guy come in for these."

The clerk looked at the name on the envelope.

"Oh, you mean the bartender from The Bar."

"Yeah, that's the one."

"No problem."

"Thanks."

The police clerk and Justin walked out to the employee parking lot, and he opened the driver door then grabbed the steering wheel to pull himself into the cab of the truck. This was going to be a challenge. He'd driven dump trucks closer to the ground than this rig. He started laughing as he pulled out of the police station and rumbled down the road toward the construction site. No one could miss him now.

Eight

Justin's construction business was doing well in a floundering economy. He'd been thrilled to be approached about building a hotel in Oakdale. The area was scenic—imposing mountains and breathtaking waterfalls—but not a tourist destination. He'd been skeptical until Ed, his foreman and friend, convinced him if some idiot wanted to waste his money building a high rise hotel in Oakdale, who were they to stop him? It would put his construction crew to work and bring money to the local townsfolk. What could go wrong?

Justin accepted the job and, so far, was keeping the project on schedule and below cost. If they continued their present rate of work until grand opening, each member of the crew would receive a large bonus. It was intoxicating motivation.

Justin pulled the big red truck onto the graded dirt lot housing the construction office, a single wide trailer with two offices. The front served as the reception and general office. It housed the usual secretary's desk and file cabinets as well as a drafting table. The back portion of the trailer was Justin's private office. The only difference from the front office was the model of the finished project on a table of its own. There was a door between the two offices for privacy when needed.

Justin drove into the area designated as his parking spot—a painted rock with his initials placed beside the trailer. The mobile vending truck was parked next to the trailer and several of the construction crew stood gathered around arguing the merits of reheated breakfast sandwiches versus donuts. Considering how bad the food was from the vending truck, Justin figured if his guys had time to argue about the merits of junk food, they needed to return to the job at hand.

"Well, it's about time you got a decent truck," Ed nodded his approval in the direction of the large red truck, "and a Ford to boot. It's taken three years but you finally listened to me. Can't go wrong with a Ford." Ed took a large bite out of a donut his waist didn't need. He held a steaming cup of coffee in his other hand.

"I hate to disappoint you, Ed, but the truck is not mine. The police confiscated my truck and sent it to their lab. Seems they want to go over every inch. I'm borrowing this rig from a friend." Justin realized Ed probably hadn't heard about the tampered gas main he'd discovered the night before. He really didn't want Ed or his wife Belinda, Justin's secretary, worrying any more than normal.

They'd signed on with the construction company Justin's father had built two years before he'd been killed. Ed learned so much from Martin "Andy" Anderson, he'd quickly moved into the position of Andy's right hand man. When a drunk driver killed all of the family except Justin, Thomas Manning, Andy's silent partner, asked Ed to run the company for him. Justin hired on right after college. When his divorce from Ashlee had become final, Justin made the decision to start his own business. Ed and Belinda moved over to Justin's construction crew and appointed themselves his guardian angels. They quizzed him about the girls he was dating and made sure he didn't spend holidays alone. He trusted them as he trusted no one else.

"Why does the police department need your truck? Did you find yourself somebody's wife? How many times I gotta tell ya, Justin, stay away from them married women," Ed was grinning.

Justin was about to shoot back a scathing reply when Belinda opened the trailer door and hollered for him to get his butt in the office. The phones were ringing off the hook, and she needed him to help out. Justin trotted to the trailer as Ed and the crew filed into the huge hole being excavated for the underground parking garage beneath the hotel. Today, the second crew was to secure the huge stanchions in the ground that would support the fifteen-story building. They were running four days ahead of schedule and, so far, the weather had been clear and sunny.

Belinda stood behind the desk, her hands parked on her rounded hips. The lights on all the phone lines were blinking.

"I thought you said the phones were ringing off their hooks? They look busy to me and it's quiet in here," Justin's wide-eyed expression didn't fly with Belinda.

"Don't even go down that road, Justin Anderson," she shot back at him. Belinda sounding harried this early in the day was not a good sign for Justin. She ran his office and mothered him whether he needed mothering or not. Her strength had gotten him through many a crisis with his ex-wife. Belinda always took the lead in screening his calls-personal and business. But today, he'd placed her in the dark and she wasn't happy.

"You'd better tell me what's happening or—I'm walking out of this office and not coming back," she threatened.

Justin closed and locked the trailer door. Belinda's eyebrows shot up in surprise. Justin seldom resorted to cloak and dagger antics. He sat her down in the chair across from his. Sitting on the edge of his desk, looking at his friend, he began his story.

"I stopped at The Bar last night for a drink. The older woman I told you about was there, and I stepped in and helped her out of a jam. When I went home, I nearly choked to death from the rotten smelling fumes overwhelming the house. After the police arrived, they discovered a break in the gas line in the back of the house. That's why every reporter within twenty-five miles will probably call today. Sorry."

Belinda's silence pervaded the small space.

"You're welcome to leave," Justin said.

"Have you lost your mind? You need me now more than ever. I don't know who you've pissed off, although I can probably guess, but, honey, if they take you down, I go too. Now, open the door and let's get this hotel built. I'll think of something to tell these vipers."

He'd often envied Ed. Belinda was a little plump but had the face of an angel, could handle a trailer full of construction workers, and stop a full-grown man in his tracks with one look. When Justin opened his construction company, Belinda had walked into his office the first day and, sitting at the desk across from him, managed his business into success. Justin knew if anyone could handle the press, it was Belinda.

"I'm going to try to get some of this paperwork done. The investor is pushing to see some sort of a progress report before the weekend. If I draft the report, will you type it for me? Please?" Justin begged.

"Maybe, but it'll cost you a trip to the beauty salon tomorrow afternoon. Deal?" Belinda crossed her arms over her ample bosom and grinned at Justin.

"Why do I feel like I've been had?"

"Because, you have," Belinda shut Justin's door. He could hear the phones ringing continuously in the other room. The small town reporters in every surrounding county must've gotten wind of the story. He was happy to give Belinda tomorrow afternoon off. After today's insanity, she'd deserve it. Belinda's voice crackled over the intercom.

"Justin? Corey Williams at the police station, line four. You'd better take it."

"Thanks, Belinda," Justin punched the blinking button of line four.

"Hey, Justin," Corey said, "I've received the report from the lab about your truck. Someone knew exactly how to cut the brake lines so you'd have driven a couple more days before they wore through and you crashed. No one would've questioned it."

Corey's report sent chills up Justin's spine. Someone was serious about stopping his breathing. His organized, simple world had become complicated overnight. Justin buzzed Belinda on the intercom.

"Belinda?"

"Yes, boss?"

"You got any aspirin?"

"Sure. How many you need?"

"A handful."

"Done."

He went into the outer office and washed three of the little white pills down with a fresh cup of coffee. *Aspirin and coffee; recipe for an ulcer.* Justin fled to his office and retrieved the business card Diane had handed him that morning. He left his name and office phone number on the answering machine when prompted.

If her offer were still open, he'd take it. If not, there was always the Snooze Inn on Route 15 outside of town. Glancing at his watch, Justin realized he was late for a scheduled meeting with the subcontractor to discuss the timetable for installing the stanchions. They had agreed to meet near the site. The ground had been prepared to be almost as hard as the concrete itself. The walls would be poured for the basement parking structure and set up. The floor would be molded and allowed to dry. Soon after, the building would quickly rise to the sky. The skeleton of steel girders would be up in less than a month. He grabbed his hard hat, snapping his radio to his belt, and dashed out the trailer door. The closer he got to the pit, the more his stomach knotted with excitement. He started down the road cut into the side of the pit. He'd gone twenty feet when his radio crackled.

"Justin?" Belinda's voice cut out.

"Belinda? I can barely hear you, would you repeat, please?" Justin held his two-way radio close to his mouth. He covered his left ear and placed the radio near his right ear.

"There is someone who says her name is Diane holding on line two. Do you want to take the call?" Belinda's voice broke up over the speaker into his ear.

"Yes! Tell her to hold on. I'll be there in a minute," Justin answered. "Ed?"

"Yeah? What do you need, Justin?" the tinny voice of his foreman crackled over the radio.

"Tell the subcontractor I'll be down in about ten minutes, okay?" Justin said.

"No problem, Justin. He hasn't shown up yet, but I'll have him wait when he does," Ed answered.

"Thanks."

Justin sprinted back to the trailer. Breathless, he picked up his office phone.

"Thanks for waiting, Diane," he panted, "If your offer to stay is still open, I'd like to take you up on it."

"You sound like you've been running. The offer still stands, but we'll need to set some ground rules, which we can do tonight. I'm working late so call before you leave and we'll arrange for you to pick up the key," Diane answered.

"Sounds good. The detective in charge of my case informed me the investigation could take up to a week before I can go home. I'm being *allowed* to pack some of my clothes tonight but otherwise won't be able to get near the house for at least two days. Will that cause a problem?" Justin asked.

"No-o-o, but if it lasts longer than a week, I'm charging you rent."

Justin laughed, "I would expect it. Thank you, Diane. You don't have to do this, you know."

"I know. Call when you need the key. I have to go, Justin, client meeting. I'm sure you understand."

Nine

Justin strolled to the pit to wait for the subcontractor. *These guys usually work paycheck to paycheck. Missing an appointment that would put money in his pocket isn't an encouraging sign. I don't understand because he was highly recommended by the investor. When I talk with the broker on Monday, I'll have to ask about the guy again. Maybe there are two contractors in the area with the same name.* Justin slowed as he neared the lip of the pit. Each time he watched the equipment at work, he felt ten years old again. The roar of the earthmover as it rumbled from the bottom, belching smoke out the stack and groaning under tons of dirt sent shivers up his spine. He squinted at idle equipment. The echo of an engine powering up eased his anxiety. He had a great crew, and didn't want to end the week with a finger-shaking lecture about time and money. He strode the last couple feet toward the descending road when his body was slammed to the ground by a crushing wave of sound and flash that momentarily blinded him. He lay dazed on the hard surface.

Belinda appeared in the doorway of the trailer, her face twisted in horror. She started running to Justin when a second explosion pounded her to the ground. For what seemed an eternity, neither Belinda nor Justin moved. Belinda jumped up first, yelling Ed's name. Justin pushed to his feet and shook his head. He realized Belinda was running straight for the hole and the explosions. He raced to stop her.

"BELINDA! Run back to the trailer and call 911. We need help NOW."

The urgency in Justin's voice stopped her. In the distance, the sound of a siren coming toward the construction site indicated someone had already made the call. Justin sprinted to the lip of the pit with Belinda on his heels.

"Ed! Where the hell are you?" Belinda yelled. Lowering her voice, she sobbed, "If that SOB dies on me—I don't know what I'll do."

Justin grabbed her as she started down the road into the glowing inferno.

"If you get down there and there's another explosion, who's going to look after your kids, Belinda? Do you suppose Ed would die without a fight? I'll bet he's just gotten the wind knocked out of him. What do you think?"

Belinda's answer was lost in the rumble of the arriving fire truck and ambulance. The enveloping dust cloud started Justin and Belinda coughing. Slowing the truck, the driver of the fire truck leaned out his window.

"Hey, where do you need us?"

Pointing to the bottom of the large pit, Justin coughed out, "The explosions came from the work site at the bottom of the road. You'll find a tall, skinny guy in a hard hat who'll direct you to any injured workers."

Justin stepped back as the emergency vehicles thundered past him into the scene of destruction. A backhoe and dump truck jetted flames high into the sky painting the man made canyon in varying shades of red and yellow. Diesel fuel and dirt clouded the air choking workers scurrying away from the blazing equipment.

His radio crackled to life, "Justin? Justin, you there? We got three guys down with broken bones and a few concussions but nobody's dead. I think I might have broken my wrist when I was knocked to the ground, but everyone's accounted for and headed topside. Sorry about the backhoe and new dump truck," Ed was hollering over the roar of equipment fire.

"Thank God," Justin muttered, rolling his eyes skyward.

"The emergency equipment is on its way. Let those guys do their job, Ed. Sit down and let them work on you. I didn't hear the gas tanks go on the equipment. Did the explosions blow them completely?"

No sooner had Justin asked than the gas tanks of both vehicles exploded, sending everyone running for the nearest cover.

"Christ, Justin," Ed yelled, "Don't ask any more questions! I hope those were the last explosions we'll hear today. The firemen are dousing the equipment now, and three more trucks are on the way. The ambulance driver is calling for back up because they can only fit two semi-invalid bodies inside at a time. So, I'll wait for the next run. Justin?"

"Yes, Ed?"

"Is Belinda okay?"

Grabbing the radio, she replied, "You bet I am. Don't be getting any ideas about not helping around the house just because you broke your wrist, Bud."

Chuckling, Ed answered, "Wouldn't dream of it, sweetheart. And, yes, I'm okay. I'll see you at the hospital."

Belinda leaned into Justin's arms. She put up a good front, but anyone who knew Ed and Belinda knew she would be lost without the ornery construction worker she'd been married to for over ten years. Two ambulances rumbled through the dust cloud settling on the site. Flashing red and white lights pulsated through the orange flames shooting from the dump truck in the pit and black chimneys of oily smoke wound their way to join the clouds hovering overhead. Several emergency vehicles arrived and formed a convoy into the hole in the earth. A black and white police car carrying Corey Williams followed the procession.

"Come on. We need to get you into the trailer until the ambulance gets up here," Justin wrapped his arm around Belinda's waist and walked her to the trailer. She busied herself gathering up insurance forms to take to the hospital while he headed to his office. The door squeaked open. A metallic groan and the slight pitch of the modular office announced the arrival of Detective Williams.

"Belinda? Is Justin here?" he asked. Belinda pointed to Justin's office. Again, the squeak of the front door announced the arrival of a visitor.

A young man's soot smudged face poked through the open door. He reeked of smoke and diesel fuel. His paramedic shirt, identifying patch on the shoulder, bore black smoke and dirt streaks. "Excuse me, ma'am?

Are you Ed's wife?"

"Yes," Belinda said.

"Would you like to accompany him to the hospital?" he asked.

"Justin!" Belinda hollered toward the back of the trailer.

Justin poked his head through the door. "What?"

"I'm riding with Ed in the ambulance to the hospital. Can you handle things here?" she asked.

"Belinda? Get the hell out of here. Go!"

Belinda followed the paramedic out the door, slamming it shut as she left.

"Great intercom you got there, Justin," Corey grinned at Justin.

"Yeah, works real good. What brings you to my world?" Justin asked.

"How about several explosions that rocked all of Oakdale," he answered. "What happened, Justin?"

"Your guess is as good as mine. I was supposed to meet a subcontractor down there fifteen minutes ago to discuss plans for putting in the stanchions and pouring the concrete. Guy never showed. Now—maybe he's the one who's trying to kill me. What do you think?" Justin wisecracked to Corey.

"Don't be such an ass. The guy could be tied into this for all you know. How'd you decide on him? Is it someone you use all the time or is it someone new? How many times did you talk with him before today? There are a lot of questions that need answering. I'll need his name and business phone, Justin. We can't take anything for granted," Corey took out his green notebook and pen.

"Oh, get serious, Corey. This is Oakdale not LA or New York. People don't go around killing each other here. A lot of unconnected incidents have been happening near me; like my house, for instance. Someone probably went to the wrong block. Haven't you guys been watching a house two blocks over for drug activity? Well, it's probably connected to a bad drug deal. Some idiot got lost and tried to blow up the wrong house.

"As far as today, unfortunately, when you mix construction

workers and gasoline, you get accidents. I'm sure when the fire department's investigation is over, they'll find someone knocked over a gas can and one of the guys flipped a lit cigarette into it. I've told them to smoke away from the equipment dozens of times, but I can't be out there mothering them every minute. I'm not going to harp at them about the small stuff. These are just bizarre coincidences. Okay? I'll give you the guy's number and you can see for yourself. He probably went out last night, had too much to drink and blew off our meeting. Let's see," Justin looked through the papers on his desk, "it's not here so let me check Belinda's files."

He walked into the outer office and looked through her paperwork. He recalled seeing the subcontractor hand her a business card. He slid open her desk drawer and after a quick search, found it. Funny, the card's appearance bothered him. Justin rubbed his fingers over the face and noted it wrinkled as if it were paper, not card thickness. The printing appeared smudged. Hell, he was letting Corey get to him. There was nothing wrong with it or the subcontractor he'd hired to do the job. He probably had only one card left and Belinda made a copy of it on the copy machine so she could have something to which she could refer.

"Here," he handed the copy to Corey after writing the guy's name down for his files. "This is a copy of the guy's card I was supposed to have a meeting with today. If you can't get him, try this number," Justin wrote down the number of the investment broker whose client had recommended the subcontractor. "Said I could call day or night and someone would get hold of him."

Corey took the cards and scrutinized the numbers. The subcontractor's name struck a chord in the back of his memory, but it was common and he could have seen it anywhere. On the other hand, he recognized the name of the investment broker. Corey studied the name and tried to recall where and why it seemed familiar. Oh, well, he'd eventually remember.

"Look, Justin, I'm concerned you don't get yourself 'just hurt' to death. All right? If anything unusual happens, contact my office. You'll have to close the site for the fire inspector to do a thorough investigation.

Have you thought about a vacation?"

"Very funny. I can't afford a vacation. I need to be here in case Ashlee decides I can see my daughter. I want to be around to help my guys. While workman's compensation will pay for hospital bills, somebody has to help these guys with rent and food for their families. I intend to see they don't starve or get kicked out of their homes."

"Well, it was just a thought. We've received a bit of information I thought I'd share with you," Corey ventured.

"What?" Justin jumped to his feet.

"Don't get excited. It's a good-news bad-news situation. The good news is we know who owns the van Edna saw in front of your house. The bad news is who owns the van—the law offices of Manning and Manning."

"I don't believe it," Justin said.

"Now, don't go jumping to any conclusions. I told you this was a good-news bad-news situation. We've discovered through our investigation they'd reported the van stolen the previous night. So while we know who owns the van, we still don't know who was at your house trying to make 'people confetti' out of you," Corey grinned at his own joke.

"God, Corey. I still can't believe anyone would want me dead. If I'm alive and working, Ashlee or anyone I can think of who might want me eliminated will continue to get paid. If I die, a lot of people go broke," Justin said. He started snickering.

"What's so funny?" Corey asked.

"Can you imagine Ashlee working down at Sallianne's Coffee Shop?" Justin snickered again.

Corey stood for a moment, picturing Justin's ex-wife in a form-fitting, white dress and black-pocketed apron, popping gum and taking burger orders. He started chuckling, "Absolutely not."

"I need to get down to the site and talk with the fire chief. I hope when the fire marshal completes his report and states this was just an accident, you'll back off from this murder attempt theory. This has just been a bad week in Oakdale," Justin escorted Corey out of the trailer.

Standing on the bottom metal step, he turned and locked the trailer door. *If only I can convince myself this is just a coincidence, maybe I can get rid of the knot beginning to permanently reside in my stomach.*

Corey sat in the patrol car and wrote himself a note. *Contact fire chief in the next twenty-four hours.* He wanted to be the first to know if this was an accident or another attempt on Justin's life. He couldn't shake the bad feeling his gut was telling him that Justin was in a lot more trouble than he was willing to admit. All he could do now was wait for the lab results. It was going to be a long weekend.

Ten

Ashlee lit her cigarette as she picked up the ringing telephone.

"Yeah? Yes, it's me. Cut the dramatics. What happened? Really? Lots of fire? Did you get Justin? *What?* Listen, you idiot, I don't want him hurt...*I want him dead!* If he's hurt and can't work, you'll have to get a real job. You know, get your hands dirty? Get back here as soon as you can and don't draw attention to yourself. I'll have to think of something else you can't screw up."

Jabbing out the remains of her cigarette in the nearest ashtray, she slammed down the receiver. Paul was athletic, muscular, and until she paid him the final $2,500 she'd promised, would do just about anything she asked, but thinking and reasoning were not his strong points. She'd never understand, nor did she really want to know how he'd disconnected the gas line to the house. He'd mentioned his cellmate had been inside for armed robbery and something else she couldn't remember at the moment.

However Paul had done it, she didn't care. She needed Justin permanently out of the way before Monday. She'd received word through a connection in the law offices of Manning and Manning that Justin had changed his will. In fact, her informant had said the way the new will was worded, she wasn't even allowed to handle the money Briana, her daughter, would inherit. She was entitled to the money. She'd given birth to Briana because Justin said he'd always support them. She loved her daughter, really she did, but she'd have been just as happy planning a medical miscarriage and going to Hollywood. She was determined Justin would keep his word—one way or the other. As soon as she could get

Paul to eliminate Justin, she'd eliminate Paul. When she hadn't fallen for Paul's line as he'd expected, he'd moved on. The rumor mill at the gym had him showing great interest in one of the aerobics instructors. Ashlee grinned. They deserved each other. She needed to figure a way to "terminate with prejudice" her ex-husband within the next forty-eight hours before the records department at the courthouse opened and his new will could be filed.

Deep in thought, she jumped when the phone rang.

"What? What do you need now?" she barked angrily. "Hi, lover boy." Anger changed to childish sweetness at the sound of her married lover's voice. "Oh, salesmen. They've been calling all afternoon. I've been trying to read, and this darned phone has rung off the hook. How've you been? Really. That's too bad. Did you feel the earthquake we had? I didn't think we were in earthquake country. It wasn't? What was it then? An explosion? Where? The construction site?"

Ashlee sounded truly concerned.

"Gee, I sure hope nobody was hurt. There were? Well, I'll have to call and see if Justin is all right. Can't have my source of income on the injured list. Well, maybe I am a little selfish, but I like my lifestyle, and unless you want to support me... I didn't think so. Anyway, I need to make sure my meal ticket's okay. I do miss you. But you know how tricky things are with Paul right now. He's unemployed again, so getting out of the house is difficult. I believe he'll be heading off to the gym tonight. There is a bodybuilding contest he's preparing for which means four to six hours in the gym every day. He told me before he left to do his errands, he felt the need to push extra hard tonight, so I may have the whole night to myself. Briana has been staying in Winchester with her grandmother all this week and will be there until Tuesday which makes me a free woman. What say we meet around seven Saturday night? Can you get away? All right. I'll see you then. Bye, sugar."

Ashlee shuddered. She'd been having an affair with a married man for nearly twelve years and while the benefits were marvelous, the payment was ghastly. When he'd been a younger man, she'd been able to pretend she enjoyed being physical with him, but he'd not aged well. Each tryst became more difficult with the passing years. He had no idea how physically ill she became after they made love. Using her excellent acting ability, she'd make this just another role that would pay off before Monday afternoon.

A flicker of a smile grew on Ashlee's face. Maybe she'd be able to eliminate the married lover, too. *This can be such a freeing weekend. When I receive the inheritance, I'll stay around for a couple of months longer than I planned. I can try to sell the house—there's that realtor in Billington I've heard doesn't ask too many questions—and claim the memories are too much to bear. Once the house is sold, everything else can be auctioned off. Then on to the Virgin Islands or Puerto Rico or anywhere the amount of cold wet days can be counted on one hand. Briana will learn to adapt and my family, those I choose to stay in touch with, will understand my need to be away from all these painful memories. I am so-o-o good!* Ashlee flipped on the television and waited for Paul to return.

The program on the television had barely gotten underway when Paul barreled his way through the front door, scowling.

"I hate being your errand boy. Next time you want something done, do it yourself!"

He stomped up the staircase toward his bedroom.

"Paul?" Ashlee cooed toward his disappearing back.

He stopped on the stairs and turned to face her.

"You did a hell of a job. It didn't turn out exactly as I hoped, but you did some major damage and didn't get caught. I think I'll go at this from another angle so you can put in more time preparing for your contest."

She slinked up the steps and wrapped herself around the blonde muscled body. "Do you *really* have to go to the gym, right now? I mean, we could work on some aerobic exercises, if you know what I mean," slithering a hand down Paul's chest to his thigh, Ashlee moved her body suggestively.

His hand stopped the movement of her fingers toward his crotch. Paul brushed his lips quickly across her forehead, "I know exactly what you mean. I wish I had time to aerobicize with you, but I'm behind on my workout schedule. I need to get to the gym and get busy. Don't wait up for me; I'm not sure how long I'll be tonight."

He peeled Ashlee off his body. She stuck out her lower lip and pouted. As Paul left, Ashlee noted his overstuffed workout bag. *He must be planning an extended aerobic exercise session with his new friend. Fine.* She was working on the problem of separating her ex-husband from his—make that her—money. She would have to employ her married lover. In so doing, she might be able to kill two birds with one stone. Ashlee tingled at the thought.

Eleven

Diane unlocked the door to her small advertising agency located on Main Street next to The Bar and flipped on the lights. She shivered. *How could it get so cold in less than twelve hours?* Adjusting the thermostat, she gravitated toward the kitchenette to start the coffeemaker. She wanted to formalize her ideas from last night. She grabbed the cup marked "I'm the Boss, You're Not" and stood waiting for the concoction to finish brewing. When the last bit of water had gurgled through the basket into the glass carafe, she filled her cup with steaming black coffee and left the kitchenette. She pushed open the door and was, again, assaulted with a blast of cold air. *I need to contact my landlord, Liz, about the ancient heating system in this building.*

Sitting at her desk, Diane went over the events of the previous evening. Her friend, Mark, had surprised her when she told him about seeing Retro Man on her patio.

"Listen, Diane, I just can't make it over tonight, however, Justin Anderson is in need of a place to stay. His house is under siege by the police department, and he won't be able to stay there for at least the next day or two. I know you think he's hot despite what you say so think of it like this, you get to observe him away from the bar. How about it?"

"What's up Mark? Did you move in with Jennifer even after you asked my advice and I told you I thought it wasn't a good idea?" Diane asked.

"Uh, that's not it. Really, I just have another obligation I have to keep. What do you say about Justin staying?"

Diane let the silence stretch out for a minute.

"Sure, Mark. But if anything happens, I'll hunt you down. I have your word this guy is a bona fide gentleman?"

"You danced with him, what do you think?" Mark countered.

"I think he was a gentleman in front of an audience. However, I do have Princess and she's pretty good about protecting me," Diane said.

"I remember," Mark said.

Diane giggled. She could picture Mark rubbing his hand in the spot Princess had nipped him when she thought he was getting too close.

"All right. Give Justin directions, but tell him he's got thirty minutes or the door locks for the night without him inside."

Diane realized this would give her the chance to observe Justin up close. So far, she liked what she'd seen. What surprised her was the way he made her feel; heart pounding, head swimming, stuttering like a schoolgirl with a new crush. She felt no control of the situation when he was around.

Justin's vulnerability touched her soul and stoked embers in a fire she thought long dead. She hadn't felt this breathless about a man since, well, since Ron. Diane smiled sadly as she unlocked her desk and opened the bottom drawer. A magazine with a picture of her and Ron fleeing the paparazzi graced the cover. No one in Oakdale knew anything about her previous life. She'd not found anyone with whom she was willing to share the pain, not even her friend, Liz.

Twelve

Diane's escape began right after high school. She had fled her abusive home life by marrying the first guy who'd shown an interest in her. Her marriage turned out to be as bad as the life she'd left. Andrew Betts had been attentive and loving while they were dating, but after the wedding, everything changed. He'd graduated from truck driving school the week before their nuptials and passed the test for his license the week after they returned from their honeymoon. Within seven days of receiving his license in the mail, he was on the road six to eight weeks at a time.

Diane found herself stuck all day in a small, dreary apartment having married a husband whose expectations of a wife's duties were rooted in the nineteenth century. She was his property and, as such, not to have a job where she might be exposed to other men. If he called and she didn't answer on the second ring, Andrew accused her of infidelity. Diane hated that she had built this trap for herself.

Andrew's initial visit home from the road proved to be the litmus test for Diane. Gazing out the small window of the kitchenette, Diane's skin prickled and her scalp itched. Andrew should be home any minute. She flinched when the screen door banged shut.

"Hey doll face, I'm home," Andrew appeared in the doorway holding a bouquet of carnations, Diane's favorite flowers.

"Oh, Andy. They're beautiful," She accepted the bouquet and buried her nose in their fragrance.

"Just like you, darlin'." Andrew slipped his arms around Diane and began gently nipping her earlobe. His lips traveled down her neck to her shoulders. "What say you give me a proper welcome home?"

"Let me put these in water first, okay?" Diane asked.

"Sure. I'll be in the bedroom. Don't make me wait too long," Andrew's dimples creased his tanned cheeks.

Diane quickly located an empty mayonnaise jar and placed the flowers inside. Filling it halfway full of water, she placed the carnations on a makeshift bookcase in the diminutive front room.

She hesitated, took a deep breath and entered the bedroom to find Andrew lying naked and erect. He stroked himself and licked his lips. His boldness made her blush even though she wasn't a virgin when they wed. She quickly undressed and slipped onto the bed next to Andrew.

"Come here, baby, Daddy's missed you."

Diane slid into his open arms, expectant and breathless. She closed her eyes and pursed her lips, reaching up to accept the loving kiss she'd been waiting six weeks to feel on her mouth. Andrew grabbed her arm, his fingers crushing the soft flesh beneath them, and shoved her on her back. Rolling onto her small frame, his weight crushed the air from her lungs as he mounted her, planting his leg between her thighs and opening them until she winced in pain.

"Something wrong with you? I can make it hurt if that's what you want," he growled into her ear.

"No, I'm fine," she bit down, leaving the impression of her teeth on her bottom lip.

"Good."

He spread her legs further. She closed her eyes tightly against the intense pain shooting into her pelvis. *He's going to split me wide open and kill me.* Diane bit down on her lip, tasting the blood that trickled down her chin.

Andrew placed his rock hard erection against her, ignoring her dryness and jammed himself inside her. He moved in and out two or three times growling lowly and finally shouting "Yes!" at his moment of release. He lay on top of her, breathing heavily for a few moments then rolled to the side and casually placed his hands behind his head. He stared at the ceiling as he talked.

"That was great. I've been thinking about that for six weeks. Great to come home to some loving." He reached to the night stand for his cigarettes. Lighting one, he inhaled deeply.

Diane lay still. When he had entered her, he'd ripped a tear into her dry soft skin. She had blacked out from the pain, and as she had returned to consciousness, she found his enormous bulk on top of her. She struggled to get air into her lungs, resisting the urge to push him off. She sensed the blood oozing down the crease in her bottom to the bed. *I hope he gets up soon. If he sees blood, who knows how he'll react.* She wiped the blood from her chin, careful not to draw attention to herself as Andrew blew smoke rings to the ceiling.

"I'm going out with Donny and Baker. Since you're not old enough to go with us, you'll have to stay home. I don't know when we'll be back, so don't wait up," Andrew rolled off the bed and padded into the bathroom. Diane lay on the sheets, feeling the dampness of his passion turn cold and clammy. Tears pooled in her ears as reality hit her. She gingerly dressed, careful not to reopen the tears in her skin and slipped outside to light a cigarette.

I've got a bad feeling about this. She was leaning against the porch rail when Andrew slammed out of the front door.

"I'm out of here. You need to go inside. Don't want the neighbors thinking you're a lady of the evening," Andrew lightly kissed Diane's cheek.

"See you later, hon," Diane couldn't shake the feeling of dread spreading through her. She went inside, stood by the wall next to the window and through the sheer curtains watched the old Chevy turn the corner and rattle down the pothole-strewn road.

She went into the bathroom and showered away all traces of Andrew. His smell made her gag. She stood, allowing the water to sluice down her bruised arms and caress her swollen and bruised pelvic area. Stepping out and toweling dry, Diane wrapped herself in the warmth of her terrycloth robe and went into the living room to mindlessly watch television until one in the morning when she went into the bedroom and allowed sleep to overtake her. The sound of shattering glass woke Diane.

She squinted at the alarm clock. It was three-thirty. Andrew stumbled into the bedroom, dropping clothes as he homed in on the bed.

"Hey, doll fash," He dropped onto the bed and jerked her to his side turning her face to meet his. "Kish, me."

Diane wrenched her face free from his grip trying to keep from gagging. He reeked of stale beer and endless cigarettes. She detected the scent of perfume in his hair. "It's late and I'm tired. Let's make love in the morning when you've had some sleep, okay?" Diane's stomach churned and she felt his body tense the moment she had spoken.

Andrew slammed her flat. One lumbering hand fumbled down her body, squeezing her breasts, pinching her nipples until they hurt. Diane squeezed her eyes shut. *This wasn't going to stop until he was satisfied.* She clenched her hands into fists. *God, if I could just knock him out cold.* Andrew mistook Diane's whimper of pain for a moan of pleasure.

"Now, that feels good, don't it baby?" Andrew's lips moved from her ear down her chest. His tongue, swollen and clumsy raked over her breasts and moved to her stomach. He shoved his hands between her legs spreading them wide. Diane's eyes rolled upward as the stabbing pain signaled he had torn her once again. She sensed the blood start to flow.

"You're my wife and I'll have you when I want." He hauled his body on top and jammed inside her. "Well, thas bedder. At leass your wet an happy to see me."

She felt a stab of intense pain as he ripped her apart further. He pushed and grunted on top of her for five minutes. Finally, the movement stopped. She struggled to breathe under his lifeless, drunken weight. *What I wouldn't give for a gun right now.*

Hearing him breathe steadily and thinking he had finished, Diane wiggled herself from beneath him. She snatched up her robe and bit her bruised lip to keep from crying out loud with the pain each step produced as she started to tiptoe into the living room. A board creaked.

Andrew struggled from the bed, his eyes burning hatefully and raging at the top of his voice, "You'll go wen I s-say go and shtay when I s-s-say shtay. You're my property, dammit, I'll do with you as I pleash!" He grabbed a handful of her hair and yanked her back onto the bed. She heard a crunch as he threw the first punch. Pain exploded in her head. Thousands of white lights flashed in front of her eyes as the blackness washed over her.

She woke on the floor the next morning to his snoring and a massive headache. Moving, so as not to wake him, she crept to the bathroom to assess the damage. Both her eyes were blackened and she suspected he had broken her nose. Tears ran down her swollen cheeks over her split upper lip and her own teeth marks tattooed her bottom lip.

This was her parents' house all over. She had run from the jackal to the waiting jaws of the lion. She tiptoed to the dresser and retrieved jeans and a sweatshirt. A rapid change and she started toward the kitchen. She stopped. Andrew's crumpled jeans lay on the floor where he had dropped them in his drunken stupor. Her intuition nagged at her. He was hiding something. She grabbed his shirt, jeans, and wallet off the dresser and padded barefoot to the living room. A search of his pockets revealed several match books bearing women's names and phone numbers. In his wallet, she hit the jackpot—a love letter from someone who signed herself, Alicia Betts. The letter bubbled about their wedding three days earlier. She "lovingly" awaited his return. Diane copied the name and address of the sender onto a small piece of paper and slipped the letter back into Andrew's wallet. She packed a bag with the few items she owned and fled the apartment. She crawled into her old truck and drove straight to the small town in New Mexico. Once there, she looked up the new Mrs. Betts. A pregnant, young woman answered the door of a small apartment, closely resembling the one Diane had just escaped.

"Yes?" she said.

"Are you Alicia Betts?" Diane asked.

"Yes, I am," she beamed, "Who wants to know?"

"Diane Betts. The first Mrs. Andrew Betts," Diane said.

Alicia paled and began to lurch. Diane pushed through the door and led her to a tattered couch in the living area of the cramped studio apartment.

"Are you okay?" Diane asked.

"I-I guess so. Who are you, really, and why are you playing such a mean joke on me?" Alicia, tears rolling down her cheeks, asked.

Diane showed her the wallet sized marriage license that had been issued to her and Andrew from the Justice of the Peace when they married.

"As far as I'm concerned, you are more than welcome to Andrew Betts," Diane said, "I just wanted to warn you. I don't need these," she pointed to the black eyes, "and I don't need him, either. Please be careful. Is there anyone you can stay with for a while?"

"Not really, Lisa next door helps out while Andrew is on the road. My family is in Florida," Alicia snuffled.

"So Andrew decided this is where you would live," Diane said.

Alicia nodded.

"I'm going to talk with Lisa and ask her to stay with you," Diane walked next door. She knocked and an older blonde answered the door. Diane quickly briefed the next-door neighbor on the situation and made her promise to watch Alicia. Diane's first reaction had been fury when she'd learned of Alicia but realized Andrew had smooth talked her just like he had Diane. When she felt confident the situation was handled, she drove back to her hometown and filed for divorce. The day the divorce was granted, Diane stood with twenty-five others pledging life and limb to the service of the United States of America in the Navy.

Boot camp was hell. It was supposed to be hell. Diane had lived through worse at her parent's house and breezed through the four months in Florida. She was thrilled when she received her orders to Hawai'i. Her military years were filled with school, friends, work, and fun. When she was honorably discharged, she decided to relax in Waikiki for a month. Lying on the beach, she watched the commercial airliners fly in and out of the airport. Getting paid to fly appealed to Diane. She applied at the airline offices, and when she was accepted, packed her bags for Dallas, Texas and ground school.

The years Diane flew with the airlines were happy ones but the constant traveling began to wear on her, and she found a Caribbean Island where she settled. She didn't worry about working—she'd find work, she always did.

Thirteen

Diane was working in a pub on her island when he walked in one day by himself and sat at the end of the bar. Ron Smythe. Yeah, that Ron Smythe, of the English rock band fame. The moment she glanced down the bar, she knew who he was. *If he's in this place, he doesn't want to be known.* She took his order for a pint of ale, walked back to her regular customers, and continued talking local events. She kept an eye on him, and when he signaled for another pint, she filled his glass.

"Hi, I'm Diane. If you need anything, just raise a hand."

"Thanks. Name's Freddie, Freddie Smythe. Just visiting your lovely island on holiday."

He'd used the name on his birth certificate, Freddie Smythe. She talked a little with him until her other patrons signaled. While she was at the tap, she held up a glass and gave Ron a questioning look. When he nodded affirmatively, she poured him a fresh pint.

"You know, my name is Freddie Smythe but most everybody knows me as Ron Smythe," he admitted after the third pint.

"Really, I would never have known," Diane smirked.

"You're having one on me, aren't you?" His eyes twinkled as he grabbed at his heart.

"Mmmm. Yeah. I knew who you were the moment you sat at the end of the bar, but I figured if you were hanging out in here, you were probably hiding."

"Yeah. Me and the boys were practicing for the concert we're supposed to be doing tomorrow night, but two of the blokes decided to get into a bloody row. I figured it was time for me to find a pub and have a pint until they decide to make nice to each other. I'll give it a couple of hours and head back."

"I doubt if any of the folks around here will say anything; everyone is pretty mellow. Like me, they figure if you're in here you don't want to be recognized. Besides, if an outsider comes in and starts the pointing and stuttering, we'll tell them you're a look-alike hired to put off the press. Okay?"

"Great idea," Ron's grin lit up his face.

They chatted until she closed the pub and he headed back to the hotel with her number tucked inside his wallet.

Diane watched him leave. *That's the last I'll see of him. Too bad, he's a hunk with a sense of humor. Oh, well, such is life.*

One week later, he breezed through the pub door carrying two-dozen red and white long stemmed roses. Behind him, trailed the members of the band.

"You, Diane?" asked Alex, the lead singer.

"Yes."

"Good! He's done nothing but talk about you all week long. Been driving us bloody bonkers, keeping us awake and driving away the birds—chicks, to you Yanks. Suppose you'll go out on a proper date with him and let us get some rest? How about a couple pints, luv?"

Handing the roses to Diane, Ron reddened as he spoke, "He's right, you know. I've been driving everyone bonkers. I couldn't get you out of my mind. I'd like to take you out, properly. You know, dinner, wine, moonlight, and dancing?"

Five pairs of eyes waited for her answer. Diane shifted uncomfortably. When there had been just her and Ron, things had been easy and fun. Now, with the group hovering nearby, she felt intimidated. However, she had no intention of being one of those old ladies who sat around and talked about what they should've done.

She looked him in the eye and answered, "All right, but I can't go anywhere tonight." Presenting the bar with a wave of her hand, she said, "I am otherwise engaged."

Ron smiled, took a seat at the bar and said, "That's fine. I have all week." Turning to his band mates he said, "All right, you're free to leave."

"We'll stay for a while," Alex replied, "But my fingers have been itching for two days. I need to get to the casinos and win some money!"

For three hours, the band ran Diane ragged while they dropped money in the jukebox, shot pool and danced with the older female patrons. Once they became bored, they tipped Diane the amount of two month's salary and bought the bar drinks for the rest of the night. Diane felt sure Ron would also disappear. She'd observed while the rest of the band was trying to drink the keg dry, Ron had nursed his pints. He stayed when the boys headed off to the casinos and until closing time when he helped Diane clean up.

"I don't normally do this, but would you like to come back to my place for breakfast?" Diane locked the pub door and turned to face Ron.

"Yeah, that would be nice. I'm getting kind of hungry and breakfast sounds good," he said.

They strolled leisurely to Diane's apartment several blocks away. Sitting on the small balcony off Diane's living room overlooking the placid bay, the conversation slowed to a comfortable silence. Looking at each other, they sensed something very special was happening.

Ron leaned across the table and gently cradled Diane's face in his hands. Pulling closer to her, he tipped her soft chin upward. Diane's heart thundered wildly in her chest, ears roaring with the rush of blood as she sucked the warm scented air into her lungs. Every nerve ending waited for his touch on her skin. Her hair ached to be caressed, and she found she was holding her breath. His lips lowered to gently brush her nose then found their home on her soft, full mouth. His tongue slipped between her willing lips, entering her warmth. She shivered at his touch, and her tongue danced to greet his with urgency. Ron slowly pulled back, tracing the outline of her mouth with the tip of his warm tongue as Diane exhaled slowly. Her heart was still pounding out a calypso and the top of her skin tingled. Her head felt light and little white spots exploded in front of her eyes. She took a deep breath and settled back into her chair, willing her stomach to stop tap dancing. Ron lifted one side of his mouth in a lopsided grin. He leaned back in the patio chair and slid her hand into his. They watched the starry Caribbean sky turn pink and orange with the streaks of dawn—silently—together. No one would ever believe they didn't make love that night, but they'd not wanted to spoil the feeling they were sharing. As the Caribbean sun began to rise in the sky and cook the landscape, they crawled on top of Diane's bed and slept in each other's arms until just before noon. While Ron showered, Diane, humming happily, performed a feat she hadn't accomplished in three years; she cooked breakfast. The warmth she'd felt the previous night hadn't disappeared with the sun. Ron emerged from the bathroom hungry.

"What smells so good? I could eat a whole pig by myself," Ron said. He sat at the table and powered his way through the eggs, bacon and toast and washed it all down with a large cup of coffee.

"Tell me, Ron," Diane asked, "is it my marvelous cooking or haven't you eaten in several days?" She was sitting across from him nursing her cup of coffee and watching in wonder as the food disappeared from his plate.

Ron smiled, "You're a pretty fair cook and I was starving. American restaurant food just doesn't seem to fill me up but this—this is like my mum's cooking."

"You're having one on me now, aren't you?" Diane looked shocked. "I haven't cooked a meal in over three years. I was sure I'd ruined everything."

"Well, I can eat just about anything. Ask the guys in the band," Ron said.

"Great! Should I be insulted or flattered? Don't answer that. I'm going to take a shower, and when I get out, maybe we can plan to do something today."

She put her cup on the countertop and skipped down the hall into the bathroom. She couldn't help giggling uncontrollably. This man made her feel so happy and lighthearted she wanted to sing at the top of her lungs. She showered and emerged to find Ron had done dishes and straightened up the place. It didn't quite fit with the image she had of rock stars, but she wasn't complaining!

"What do you think you'd like to do today?" she asked. She stood at the railing on the balcony, gazing out at the azure water and white beach.

"I thought maybe we could wander through the marketplace. I want to see if I can find some gifts for my family back in England." Ron moved behind her and placed his hands on her waist. He buried his face in her coconut-scented hair. "Mmmm. You smell good enough to eat."

Diane leaned against him, fighting the urge to turn and lead him into the bedroom.

"I'll lead the way."

She turned and Ron wrapped her against his warm chest. His lips found her willing mouth as she melted in his arms, the fire beginning to rage inside her. Reluctantly, she broke the kiss.

"If we don't leave now, we'll not make it out of this apartment," she said.

"That's bad?" Ron grinned and led her to the front door.

They ambled through the marketplace and window-shopped in the tourist section of town. Around two, they lunched at a small sidewalk café and meandered along the beachfront to Diane's apartment when they had grown tired.

Diane took Ron's hand and led him up the stairs, opening the door and pulling him inside.

"Don't you lock the doors around here?" he asked.

"Not normally," She turned and flipped the deadbolt. "But maybe I'll make an exception."

Diane led Ron into the bedroom. She pulled the vanilla sheer curtains over the open windows and turned to face him. Pulling him close, she slid her arms around his neck.

He leaned to meet her lips with his own. The velvety softness of her mouth invited him inside to explore its warmth. Ron's hands explored Diane's body. Expertly, he slid the buttons through the buttonholes on her blouse and edged his hand under the material of her cotton shirt. His hand met satiny, smooth skin. He slid a hand under her full breast and rubbed his thumb over her nipple, feeling it harden with excitement.

Diane groaned with pleasure. Her skin tingled as he caressed her, kissing along the line of her neck. She was sure the thudding of her heart must be the only sound in the room. Her hands roamed over his lightly haired chest, drawing circles with her forefinger. She heard his guttural moan when she lightly drew her fingertips over his nipple. Her knees started to buckle when she felt the hot, moistness of Ron's mouth on her breast, drawing in short, jagged breaths as he ran his tongue over her nipple and sucked it into his mouth. Diane's head lolled back in bliss, her eyes closing to savor the sensations running through her body.

Ron slid his arms under her shoulders and knees as he momentarily released her breast from his mouth, lifting her to the bed and languidly peeling her shirt from her shoulders. He fingers traced lines down her body to her waist where he deftly undid her shorts.

"If you want, we can stop here," he suggested.

"Don't stop," she breathed huskily.

He gazed into her smoldering dark eyes. She lit a fire in his soul no other woman had been able to touch. He wanted her, yes, but he wanted her to hold his heart as well. His hands tugged on her shorts, gently lifting her buttocks and sliding the garment to the floor. Diane lay on the bed, brown and inviting. Ron's heart beat so hard against his chest he thought surely it would burst. A feeling of pure joy was spreading warmly through his whole body, flushing his skin. He wrestled his shirt over his head and hooked his thumbs into his belt loops, jettisoning his shorts. His member pulsated with his pounding heartbeat. Ron stepped to the bed and gazed at this woman. *You are unlike any woman I've encountered. I know I can have you, but I want more. You've captured my heart and I want to know I've captured you too.*

"Is something wrong?" Diane lifted up on one elbow.

"No, it's just…" Ron found himself unable to voice his feelings.

Diane reached out and ran her hand down his arm. *If I don't say anything to him, I'll hate myself for the rest of my life. I don't have anything to lose.*

"Ron?"

"Yes?"

"I'm afraid you'll just have to live with the fact you've stolen my heart. I've never been this happy, and even if it's only for these few days, I'm glad you came into my life."

Ron looked again at the inviting body on the bed. *Is she reading my mind?* His smile slowly spread over his face and his heart began its staccato rhythm. He slid his body across Diane's. She groaned as his skin lightly touched her. He kissed deeply, holding her against his body, feeling her heart beat in synch with his own. He kissed down to the warmth between her thighs and gently moving her legs apart, Ron introduced his agile, talented tongue to Diane's pulsating sensitive womanhood. She arched her back and rolled her eyes to the heavens. He lovingly stroked as she arched higher and higher, her hands grabbing at the sheets and moaning that she thought she was going to explode. He then slithered up to introduce himself into her. Slowly, he maneuvered the slick narrow passage. When he had buried himself in her, the sensation of oneness overwhelmed him. He allowed himself to react naturally as he stiffened and exploded. Ron enveloped Diane in his arms.

"That was amazing," she said.

"Yeah," He replied. They lay arm in arm for an hour breathing together and caressing each other. Ron rolled on his side and gazed at Diane.

"Again?"

"Yes."

Too soon the afternoon melted away. Sated and content, they showered and dressed.

"Can I use your phone?" Ron asked.

"Of course, unless it's long distance," Diane smiled.

He picked up the receiver and dialed. "Alex, this is Ron. Yeah, can you send the limo to Fifteen Conch Shell Avenue? About ten minutes? Okay. See you at the airport."

Diane rinsed dishes and hummed softly while Ron gathered his things. A knock on the door signaled the arrival of the limousine.

Ron gathered her into his arms, recording her coconut scented hair and velvety skin in his memory. He gazed into her beautiful brown eyes.

If only you knew how you hold my heart in your hands.

"I wish I didn't have to go back tonight," he sighed, "It would be wonderful to sit with you on the balcony and watch the sunset. But we're under contract to record another album starting next week. I promise I'll call you."

Ron's earnest face almost convinced Diane.

"Of course, you will." She kissed him, holding his lips against hers, inhaling his aroma and trying to imprint him on her heart. Reluctantly, she turned him toward the limo waiting at the curbside. She stood in the doorway, waving and smiling woodenly as the stretch Mercedes disappeared down the street. *I know you won't call but what the heck? This has been the best two days of my life so far.* When it was no longer visible, she trudged into her apartment.

Grabbing a dust rag and broom, Diane began cleaning her small apartment. *Last week this place was just fine. Why is it so lonely now?*

Fourteen

One hour later as Diane, once again, cleaned the kitchen counter, the doorbell weakly dinked. Not hearing the first effort, Diane jumped when it dinked again. Looking through the viewer, she saw roses, in every imaginable color.

"What the...?"

She opened the door. The rainbow separated and Ron's smiling face appeared.

"I couldn't stand it. I got back to the hotel and walked into the room Marty and I are sharing. There must've been half a dozen girls in various stages of undress and, for the first time in ten years, I didn't care. I missed your voice and that impish grin you get when you're about to do something devilish. Most of all, I missed you—everything about you. The way your hair smells after the shower, the glow of your suntanned skin and, mostly, the way you are unimpressed with my fame. Diane? Please come to England with me. I talked with the boys and they think they can hold off the recording session for about a week. What do you say?"

Diane staggered into her apartment. She wasn't sure if the overwhelming aroma of roses or the shock of Ron asking what she'd just been daydreaming about was making her dizzy. She floated out to the balcony and gazed at the azure ocean and sugar white beach. The afternoon trade wind began caressing her cheek. She really loved being here, but lately restlessness had set in. She knew in her heart Ron was the man of her dreams. No one else had made her feel so...breathless and happy. When she felt his arms wrap around her waist, she realized he was waiting for an answer.

"Well, I'd need time to settle things here and," she looked at Ron, "I can't say I wasn't thinking about it" she grinned.

"Good. I've really got no choice," he retrieved a suitcase sitting on the front porch; "the flight is leaving about now. Your business shouldn't take too long, and we'll get to spend another week together in paradise."

He pulled her tightly to him and hungrily kissed her.

"I'm not sure I can guarantee much but a tour of Her Majesty's kingdom, English pubs, and lots of me going to work, but I won't abandon you. If you feel the need to get back to the colonies or even back here, just ask and I'll arrange it through my solicitors."

Diane bristled. "I don't need you or any other person to take care of me. I've saved enough money to take care of myself. If it's going to be such a bother, maybe I should just stay."

Diane turned to stomp off to her room. Ron caught and entangled her in his arms.

"I have a hard time expressing myself. I feel more for you than I have for anyone in my life. You don't make me feel awkward or silly. I say anything I like and you take it for what it's worth. You're natural, easy and make me feel the same. If I had to explain it to someone, I'd say I love the feeling we have and I don't want to lose it. Please say you'll go to England with me."

Diane started laughing at the pitiful expression on Ron's face. He was a very good actor. She decided to go.

A week later, they were ready to leave for England. Diane had found a replacement for her job at the pub, and they tidied up the furnished apartment where she lived. As the taxi waited at the curb, Ron and Diane gazed from the balcony one last time at the emerald mountains kissing the expansive sun baked beaches greeting the turquoise sea. Hollowness surrounded Diane's heart as she set out on her new adventure.

Ron took her hand and lightly kissing her on the forehead murmured, "It's time to go, luv."

"I know," she whispered. She surveyed her Caribbean island. "God, I'll miss you."

Fifteen

Ron and Diane, Diane and Ron. It was always said in one breath. In the five years since she had moved from her Caribbean island to London, she'd become a part of Ron and his life. She no longer worked but toured with the band—they'd done three world tours in three years—and did a fair bit of sightseeing in England. She'd been able to locate distant relatives and gather some family history for herself and volunteered with charitable organizations to keep busy.

She and Ron had a flat in London and a country home east of the Welsh border. They had cars, servants, parties, publicity and everything money could buy, but Diane wanted more—marriage and children. She'd not been trying to avoid having children but hadn't gotten pregnant. Two of the other band members had settled down, and their wives had given them children. When she approached the subject with Ron, he changed it. After trying to talk to him casually for a week, *she made an appointment* and sat him down in the library of the country house.

"Ron? I want to get married," she announced.

"Why? Things are fine. Why would you want to ruin a perfectly good relationship by getting married?" he asked.

"Ron. Things wouldn't change from what they are now, but I want our relationship to be more committed, and I want to think about planning children," she answered.

"I'll think about it," he said, "I'm going up to the studio."

He kissed her lightly on the forehead and fled to his music studio.

Six months passed without further discussion. Diane ruminated about what she wanted and just being Ron's ole' lady was not fulfilling her desires. They took a holiday and talked about the problem without resolution.

When they returned to London on the following Monday, Diane had made what she knew would be a life changing decision. She set an appointment with Ron's solicitors and removed her name from all the joint property. Then she stopped at the airline offices and bought a one-way ticket to the United States. Afterward, she returned to the London flat, packed those things she'd brought from the Caribbean, and a gift guitar Ron had given her from the group for her last birthday.

Tuesday, she took a cab to the airport leaving London and Ron.

Sixteen

Dulles Airport was gray as the rain mixed with snow muting the landscape and piles of slush lining the roads escaping the hub. Diane hailed a cab.

"Twenty dollars if you drive me directly to a residence hotel in Arlington," she waved the bill at the driver as she climbed into the warm cab. She peered out the smudged windows at the lanes of traffic spilling from the airport. As the cab gathered speed, urban steel began to melt into suburban sprawl. Light posts and billboards transformed into lampposts and evergreens. The driver piloted the cab to the curb. He opened Diane's door, offering his hand as he guided her to the entry. He brought her bags inside the lobby and placed them in front of the front desk.

"Thank you," she handed him the twenty dollar bill.

"Please," he pulled his billfold from his back pocket, retrieving a business card and handed to her, "If you need a cab while you're here, call me."

"I will," she said.

He smiled and with a quick wave turned and left.

She checked in and settled into her temporary home. The hotel was comfortably set up for stays of two or three weeks. Once inside her room, Diane dropped her bags in the closet and fell backwards onto the bed. It felt good to lie still. She felt as though she'd been on the go for the last four days. She knew Ron suspected something, and she would've told him exactly what she was doing but he'd disappeared as soon as they'd returned to London.

Right now all I want is a steaming shower followed by a hot meal cooked by someone else then twelve or fourteen hours of uninterrupted sleep. She called room service and ordered then headed for the bathroom. *After I eat, sleep—hours of uninterrupted sleep.*

She was drying her thick, brown waist-length hair when she heard a knock at the door. Looking through the peephole, the room service waiter and his cart had arrived with her dinner. She ushered him in and tipped generously when he left. Sitting at the dining room table, she was eating a meal she'd been craving for the last two months—an American hamburger and French fries. The burger melted in her mouth. She dumped ketchup on her fries and was slowly savoring every mouthful. The television was airing a program on a picturesque small community being touted as the most livable town on the East Coast. Oakdale, population 17,500, was located about two and a half hours out of Washington, D.C. in the Blue Mountains of Virginia.

"The same family has run the general store for five generations," the narrator stated. "Gas station attendants still wear ties, pump gas, and wash the car windows for you. A local pub called The Bar is said to have been a stopping place for Paul Revere during his infamous ride. But then every bar and inn throughout the original thirteen colonies makes that same claim. Paul must have been a very thirsty man."

Diane set her burger down for a moment and watched with great interest. This was exactly the kind of place she needed to be right now, small and friendly. She wasn't sure if Ron would come looking for her. He had the resources—if he was interested. She knew she wouldn't continue their relationship without the guarantee of marriage. The last time she'd talked with Ron he was less than enthusiastic about the idea.

Diane realized she was staring blankly at the telly screen. *TV screen. I guess I'm going to have to relearn to speak American.* Nearly five years in England and two years on a British dominated island had affected her speech. Either way, she was still sitting and staring.

She picked up the phone. "Please don't disturb me until after one o'clock tomorrow."

"Yes ma'am."

Crawling into bed, she fell into a deep, oblivious sleep.

She awoke at 11:00 a.m. Room service provided breakfast and a local daily newspaper. Skimming the main sections to catch up on the news stateside, Diane formulated a plan for herself.

"First thing I need to do is rent a car and check out that little town they showed on the news last night. If it's as pretty and friendly as they portrayed, maybe I'll start over there," she said. She folded the paper and got ready to leave for the day.

She rented a non-descript four-door sedan at the agency across from the hotel and drove off to find Oakdale. The courtesy road map showed it to be a hundred miles southeast from Washington, D.C., about an hour and a half's driving time.

"I really need time to pull myself together. I gave that man five years of my life, and I don't think I was asking too much of him when I asked for a commitment. I love him with all my heart and gave up a lot to be with him," Diane's chest ached and tears welled in her eyes. Through an increasing mist, she spotted the turnoff to Oakdale.

"Thank goodness," she sighed. She couldn't afford to fall apart. Her focus had to be on the future. Ron was the past. It was time to move forward.

Seventeen

Oakdale was beautiful. An old-fashioned town square featured a band gazebo in the center surrounded by storefronts, which had once been the mercantile stores. Now the old buildings were the antique and tourist shops of local artisans. Diane fell in love during the ten minutes it took her to view all of downtown Oakdale. A mile outside of town on the state highway that used to serve as the main passageway from town to town, she discovered a strip mall with fast food restaurants and boutique shops. Bordering the mall stood a Wal-Mart with gas station. It sat awkwardly in the country setting.

Diane executed a U-turn and drove back to the center of Oakdale. She parked at the post office and went inside to check the bulletin board. A job opening at the place called The Bar was advertised along with an ad touting a studio apartment for rent. She jotted down the information and decided to walk. She would get a better feel for the community.

Strolling, she window-shopped and wandered through the general store.

"Afternoon, Miss," a perky young blonde smiled as Diane wandered past the cosmetics counter. "If there's anything I can help you with, please let me know. My name is Debbie," she smiled.

"Thank you," Diane replied. "I'm just looking."

"Well, have a nice day." The blonde hummed softly as she stocked the shelf behind the glass counter displaying cosmetics and women's costume jewelry. Diane meandered out the front entrance of the general store and down the main street. Walking past an insurance office next to

The Bar, she spied a handwritten notice in the window for a part time opening. She went inside and spoke with a young woman behind the first desk about the position and was directed to the only enclosed office. The woman behind the desk introduced herself as the office manager and asked Diane to have a seat. After answering several questions, she was offered the job. This was as good a start as any.

She ventured next door to The Bar where she stood for a moment adjusting her eyes to the dark interior. Once she could safely navigate the floor, she strolled to the counter.

"Is the manager here?" she directed her question toward the back of the figure behind the bar. A thin, red haired older woman, cigarette dangling from her brightly painted mouth, turned toward Diane.

"That'd be me, hon. What can I do for ya?" she placed a coaster in front of Diane.

"I noticed on the bulletin board at the post office you were advertising for a bartender. Is the job still open?"

"Sure is. This for you, hon?"

Diane nodded.

"Well, what kind of experience ya got?"

Diane gave her a quick rundown of her years behind the bar.

The redhead stood back and looked Diane up and down.

"You're kinda skinny and small but you'll do. I really need some time off. Name's Liz," She stuck a bony hand out at Diane who shook it.

"I'm Diane. Does this mean I got the job?"

Liz started to laugh, triggering a coughing fit. When she'd caught her breath a few minutes later, she answered, "Yeah, hon, you got the job. Just got a little paperwork the state requires me to fill out then we can figure out a work schedule for you."

"I'm working part time for the insurance agency in the mornings so any time after noon will be fine."

"Okay, let's start you on Mondays, Wednesdays, Friday and Saturday nights from four in the afternoon until closing. All right?" Liz asked.

"Sure. Listen, there was also mention of a studio apartment for rent. Do you know about that?" Diane asked.

Liz furrowed her brow, causing lines to form between her narrowed eyes. A smile spread across her face.

"Oh, yeah. Maybe you'd better look at it first. Harvey," Liz called to an older gentleman sitting quietly at the opposite end of the bar, "watch the place while I show Ms. Diane the studio, okay?"

Harvey nodded.

Liz led Diane through the kitchen and out the back door. They turned left to a set of stairs, climbed to the second floor, and entered a small porch. Liz unlocked the door to a narrow hallway that opened out to a large room. A fireplace took up one entire wall. Liz steered Diane around the corner to a cozy dining area and self-contained kitchen. Turning toward the large living area, she guided Diane through what appeared to be two wall panels.

Behind the walls was a dressing room; full-length mirror on the closet door, built in shoe racks and dresser and extra closets for storage. One wall panel appeared to be a door while the other was a single pull down Murphy bed. Paralleling the closet in the back was a full bathroom.

The period furniture was well maintained. Diane stood in the center of the room gazing around in awe.

Liz mistook amazement for horror. "I know it's kind of a disaster. Haven't had anyone living in it for maybe five years, but I make sure it gets cleaned once a week, every week. So if you're not interested, I understand," Liz nodded.

"Oh, no, that's not it," Diane protested, "I was just wondering how much rent you were asking."

"Well, since I own the building…"

Diane raised her eyes, her mouth dropping slightly.

"I guess I can let it go for, mmmm, two hundred and fifty a month. After all, I know what I'm paying you and it ain't that much!"

Diane sat in the nearest chair. "Are you sure? Two hundred and fifty a month? How long a lease do you want me to sign?"

Liz laughed, "Honey, this is Oakdale. We don't worry about that kinda stuff. I know where you're gonna work, and if it comes down to it,

I'll just hold your paycheck."

Diane pulled her wallet out and counted out a thousand dollars.

"This should take care of the first four months," she said.

"Here are the keys," Liz handed her two brass keys on a cheap silver ring. "You can move in and sleep here tonight if you want. Let me give you a word to the wise. Around here if you don't want to stick out like a sore thumb, make a point of attending the Christian Church services on Sunday, whether you believe or not. The first week people will be curious and ask questions, but after the third week nobody will bother and they'll accept you more readily into the community. Especially if you're gonna work for me. I got a reputation you'll learn about soon enough."

Liz grinned at Diane. They closed the apartment and returned to the bar downstairs. Liz made out a simple receipt for Diane's prepaid rent.

Diane drove to the Wal-Mart outside of town to stock her small home with the necessities of living. Once she'd locked the door to her apartment, Diane headed to the rental car to drive back to Arlington. There were a few things she needed to get, like a truck then she could begin to put the pieces of her life back together. The Chevrolet dealership on the outskirts of Arlington was her first stop. Diane got out of the rental car and started examining pickup trucks.

"Hey, little lady. How are you today? My name is Stan. Let me know if you need any help finding some transportation." The salesman's smile was as phony as his tie was loud.

"I'm looking for a reliable pickup truck with low miles and good tires," Diane said.

"A pickup? I think I have a vehicle that would fit you better. I have a great little Camaro with very few miles and new rubber all around. Owned by a little grandmother in Richmond who drove it to Sunday school and the library. It's red with black interior and you'd look really great driving her off the lot today." Stan grabbed Diane's elbow and steered her in the direction of the passenger cars. She planted her feet and pushed his hand off her elbow.

"I said…I'm looking for a pickup truck, not a sports car. I want a three quarter ton pickup with a three-hundred-fifty horsepower engine, four-speed transmission, which has low miles and good tires. Do you understand what I'm asking for?" Diane asked him through gritted teeth.

"Well, well. I was just letting you know about a great deal I thought would be best for you. I'll show you some trucks, if that's what you really want, but I think the Camaro would be much better suited to you," Stan's insincere smile attempted to hide growing irritation.

"That's it," Diane stomped away from the surprised salesman who shrugged his shoulders and walked up to another couple looking at a sedan. She sailed past startled salesmen, puffing cigarettes and glancing at their watches, into the office of the sales manager.

"I came to this dealership because I like the product you sell. I have ten thousand dollars to spend on a pickup truck and I can't get your salesman, Stan, to hear anything I have to say. I'm taking my ten thousand and going to your competitor. Maybe someone on their lot will listen and help me spend my money." Diane turned and breezed out of the office, leaving the manager sputtering. She was striding to her rental car when another man in an expensive suit came huffing up.

"Miss? Miss? Please reconsider," he panted.

Diane turned to face him, "Why? The treatment I've received so far hasn't convinced me to put any confidence in your dealership. How are you going to change that?"

"Listen, tell me what you need and I'll guarantee the price, the warranty and the truck for two years," he said.

"And who are you to make such guarantees?" she asked.

"I'm Mike Morris. I own this dealership and two others in the area. If we don't have what you want on this lot, I can get any vehicle to you within two days. Guaranteed," he said.

"Okay, Mike. I'm Diane Wallace and I'll repeat, one more time, exactly what I require in a truck. I want a three quarter ton, three-hundred-fifty or more horsepower engine, four-speed transmission, with low miles and good tires. Now, I also want a two-year warranty, someone to give me a lift from my hotel in the morning to pick up my truck after it has been detailed and filled with gas, and I don't want to pay more than eight thousand cash for the deal. Those are my terms."

"What color do you want?" Mike began to walk in the direction of the truck lot.

"I prefer black." Diane walked alongside him.

By the time she crawled into the rental car and continued on her way to the hotel, she had exactly what she wanted. She would pay for the truck and finish paperwork on her way back to Oakdale the next day.

Returning the car to the rental agency, Diane observed a commotion out front of the hotel.

Must be some foreign diplomat. She walked past the photographers huddled on the sidewalk and maneuvered through half the lobby when flashbulbs started popping like firecrackers on the Fourth of July. Diane realized they were aimed at her. She ran and caught an opened elevator, hiding her face while the doors closed.

Who the hell told these piranhas I was here? Why are they targeting me? She was furious they had found her. She hadn't wanted the press or Ron to know where she was. For the five years she and Ron had been a couple, the paparazzi had been relentless in tracking them down. *Why would they care about me now? I'm not the famous one.* Peeking cautiously out of the elevator when the doors opened on her floor, Diane sprinted to her room. She needed to find a way out of the hotel tomorrow without having to deal with these jackals.

She flipped on the TV to see if there was something that would give her a clue as to why the photographers were camped on the sidewalk and in the lobby below. The news anchor talked about local news then segued into entertainment news. Pictured on the screen was Ron with a young, visibly pregnant, blonde flashing a huge engagement ring. The correspondent reported the couple was to be married the following weekend at Ron's country home. Their baby was expected in three months.

Diane gawked at the screen. She'd actually been feeling guilty about escaping England and Ron. She sat on the edge of the bed, mesmerized, as the photographers pushed and crowded around the couple.

"Ron! Ron! Tompkins from the Mirror. What about your Yank girlfriend, Diane?" yelled a reporter.

Diane shut her eyes tight. Straining, she heard Ron's reply.

"I'm sorry things didn't work out for Diane and me but sometimes that's the way it is. Faith and I are looking forward to our wedding and the birth of our child," Ron beamed at the camera.

Diane bolted into the bathroom and threw up. *That slime had been humping this little groupie while putting me off about getting married. What a fool I've been!* Diane broke down and sobbed, clutching her aching chest. She started hiccupping. A trip into the bathroom to get a drink of water showed a tired, emotionally drained woman staring back at her from the reflection in the mirror.

"Never again!" she growled through clenched teeth.

She washed her face, got a drink of water and fell into a restless sleep filled with dreams of castrating Ron.

~ * ~

Buzzing. What is that obnoxious buzzing? Diane fought through the haze. She realized the phone was ringing.

"Hello," she mumbled. "Who the hell is this?"

"Hello, Miss Wallace? This is Mike Morris. I'm calling to remind you about our meeting in forty-five minutes to finish the transaction on your pickup truck."

"Damn. Mike? Call me from the lobby when you arrive at the hotel."

Diane pushed the disconnect button on the phone and buzzed the front desk. "This is Diane Wallace in twenty-one twenty-one. Are there photographers hanging out in the lobby or out front?"

"No, ma'am. They weren't here at eight am when I started my shift, and I haven't seen any in the lobby all morning."

"Thank you. Can you get my bill ready?"

She cleaned up and waited for Mike to call. When he'd rung her room, she picked up her bags and, mentally crossing her fingers, made her way to the lobby where she spotted him near the door. He loaded her bags in the trunk of his vehicle and was opening her door when a TV cameraman's light temporarily blinded her.

"How do you feel about Ron and his pregnant fiancé?" asked the on-camera reporter, shoving a microphone toward her face.

Diane pivoted slowly to face him. She lowered her eyes and curved the corners of her mouth provocatively at the cameraman and reporter, "I hope the two of them are very happy. They deserve each other."

Mike slid his hand under her elbow and assisted her inside his sedan. The blazing light on top of the camera followed Diane's every move. She waved as the door clicked shut.

"Mike? Please drive as quickly away from here as you can," she said.

"You're that English rock star, Ron Smythe's, girlfriend, aren't you?" he asked.

"*Ex*-girlfriend," she made sure the emphasis on the *ex* was heavy..

Silently, they drove to the dealership. She completed the transaction of buying her truck and headed to her new home.

Diane couldn't understand how the paparazzi had found her. She didn't think anyone was aware of her real name; everything had always been about Ron. She wanted to be as removed from Ron and that lifestyle as she could.

Eighteen

A year passed uneventfully; no paparazzi, no Ron. Diane worked at the insurance agency Monday through Thursday mornings. Her afternoons were spent finishing up her college degree at the state college thirty miles away. She'd completed three years while she was in the service. Now, her GI bill was helping secure her bachelor's degree in Marketing. Her goal was to own an advertising agency. Liz rearranged her bar tending schedule to Thursday through Saturday nights and Sundays, on Liz's advice, she went to church. The first couple of weeks at church there had been questions, but after a while people went their own way and didn't bother her.

Toward the end of Diane's first year, she watched the crowd at The Bar getting noticeably younger. She wasn't sure she wanted to continue working there if the atmosphere was veering to college frat house. She enjoyed her older regulars. Timothy Crawford, rumored to think he was a ladies man, began haunting The Bar to catch Diane's attention. His smooth talk and good looks worked to break down her self-imposed resistance to dating.

On a chilly Saturday night in November before the noisier dating crowd arrived, Timothy, occupying his usual seat at the bar, called Diane over.

"Diane?"

"Yes?" she said.

"I would love to take you to dinner and share a bottle of good wine and conversation. How does that sound to you?" he asked.

"Well..." Diane hesitated.

"I heard you've been burned before, but I thought we could have dinner and talk, nothing more. Tuesday night at six o'clock all right with you?" Timothy's face looked so hopeful Diane relented.

"All right. Dinner, nothing more. I'll meet you here at five-thirty," she smiled as he reached across the bar and gently squeezed her hand.

Tim arrived at The Bar Tuesday night carrying a single carnation. He ceremoniously handed it to Diane as he kissed her cheek.

"This single flower, like you, needs nothing to enhance its beauty. Shall we go?"

Diane melted. Timothy escorted her to dinner in Billington, thirty miles to the west. After dinner, they danced at the adjoining nightclub until early morning. He drove her to the steps below her apartment and parked. Leaning over, he sweetly kissed her cheek.

"I had a wonderful time. Please say you'll let me treat you again?" he asked.

"I'd love it. This has been a lovely evening. I've enjoyed myself for the first time in a long time. Thank you," Diane pulled him to her and kissed him softly on the lips. She quickly exited his sport car and skipped up the steps. She was lightheaded and happy. A feeling she had all but forgotten. Timothy fervently courted Diane. Every night Diane didn't work, she and Timothy had a date.

Liz, her boss and friend, warned her. "Diane, I've lived in this town all my life. I've seen too many Timothys not to know what's going on. What does he do for a living? Has he told you where he gets his money? Hon, look, I tell you this guy is diggin' for gold. Be careful. Don't let him sucker you."

Diane chose to ignore Liz's warning. When Timothy proposed marriage, Diane said yes. She prayed she would finally be happy. She wasn't madly in love with Timothy, but people in arranged marriages made them work, right?

After six years of giving the marriage every effort she could, Diane filed for divorce.

Timothy had never understood the concept of marriage. He

couldn't understand why she got upset when he continued to date. After all, that's how he'd met her. The money he'd flashed on their dates and the sports car he'd been driving had been his first wife's. When Diane made the fact clear to Timothy he could no longer have her or her money, he threatened no one would have her. Diane swore out a restraining order he ignored.

One more time, she swore to herself, "Never again!"

Nineteen

What brought that on? I haven't thought of Ron in years. Diane frowned. *Whew, Justin must be stirring up feelings I thought I'd hidden. Apparently, not well enough.* Diane ambled to the coffee maker to warm her tepid brew. She needed to focus for her presentation at today's meeting.

Walking back to her desk, a thundering boom startled her. Everything in the office rattled and shook. A second muffled boom and rocking of the building followed. Diane set her cup on the nearest file cabinet and dashed to the reception area. Amanda Winchester, her accountant and Nora Thornton, the secretary, stood ashen faced and shaking.

"What happened?" Diane asked.

The two women shook their heads.

"Don't know, Diane," Amanda managed to utter. Nora grabbed a chair and slid onto the seat.

Diane instructed the receptionist, "Julie, call the police and find out what's going on."

She turned to the two bewildered ladies. "When Julie gets the story from the police, I'll buzz and let you know what's happening. In the meantime, why don't we go back to our offices and try to get something done? It's getting near the end of the month, and I know there are at least two projects I'd like to see completed." Calmly returning to her office, Diane felt the panic rise in the back of her throat when she heard the sirens in the distance. She sat at her desk and shuffled papers from one side to the other jumping when her intercom buzzed.

"Yes?"

"Diane, the police said not to worry. Some of the equipment over at the new construction site blew up. Nobody was killed but a couple guys got hurt bad enough to go to the hospital."

"Thanks, Julie."

Her throat dried and stomach lurched when she realized the construction site must be where Justin was working. *What had Julie said? Nobody was killed just a couple guys went to the hospital? Should I try to contact Justin? If I did, what would I say?* The distinctive creaking of old hinges on Diane's windowed door found her looking up into Julie's tear stained face.

"Lord, Julie, you look awful. What's the matter?" she said.

"Belinda from the construction company called and said my Lenny was one of the guys who went to the hospital. Is it okay if I leave now?"

"Good heavens, yes," Diane rose from her chair and crossed to her young receptionist. Putting her arm around Julie, she instructed, "Take the rest of the day off. Please call and let me know how he's doing so I don't worry. Okay?"

Diane had been steering her out of her office to the front desk where they collected her things and walked to the front door. Julie thanked Diane and dashed to her car.

Diane called Amanda and Nora into the reception area.

"Julie's information from the police is the construction site just outside of town had some equipment explode. Nobody was killed but a couple of guys got hurt. Julie's husband Lenny was one of them. I know this will affect all of us so I'm closing the office. I don't see how we'd get any work done anyway. Have a good weekend. I'll see you on Monday."

Not needing further convincing, the two women quickly gathered their things and disappeared out the front door and left. Locking the door, Diane strolled back to her office. Sitting alone, panic began to tighten her chest. She needed to know Justin was all right, that he wasn't one of the men sent to the hospital. Searching the papers on her desk, she located the pink phone slip Julie had given her first thing this morning. Justin had left a message on the answering machine with his number asking her to return his call. She lifted the phone. Hesitating, she replaced the receiver in its cradle.

"I won't get involved again. I won't, I won't, I won't."

She sat staring at the phone. *This is ridiculous. He's staying at my house and rescued me from Retro Man last night. I'm just showing normal concern for another human being. Yeah, right.*

She picked up the phone and called before she lost her courage. The phone rang busy. It rang busy for the next forty minutes. When she finally got through, she was frantic. Her heart was beating black and blue marks on her ribs.

"Anderson Construction. Can I help you?"

"Justin?" Diane croaked. She cleared her throat, "This is Diane. What's going on?"

"Well, somebody doesn't like the way I'm digging this hole in the ground and is determined to shorten my career. The fire marshal won't confirm or deny anything, but they're saying it looks as though the equipment was intentionally blown up. I've got a couple of good-sized bruises and a few scrapes but nothing more. The job site is being closed down until they can make a full investigation. So now, I have some unexpected free time. How about dinner tonight? I could make a reservation at the Pinnacle Restaurant in Billington? Say about seven o'clock? I have paperwork I need to finish here and a statement to make at the police station, but I could pick you up around six-thirty?"

Diane skimmed over her schedule. She had a meeting at 3:00 this afternoon with the hotel people. After her meeting, she was finishing up a project for her friend Liz. She realized her shoulders were unknotting as the panic drained from her body. *Why not? I need to eat and by six-thirty I'll be ready to leave the office.*

"Sure. I'll meet you in front of the building. It's three ten Main Street. See you at six-thirty." Diane grinned as she hung up the phone. *You have to give him credit. He's persistent.*

Twenty

Diane decided to use the quiet offered by the empty office and continue working on her ad campaigns. *Justin and I must be working for the same investor. It doesn't seem likely there's more than one major hotel going up around here. The explosion at the construction site could put an end to my ad campaign as well as his project. Today's meeting should help fill in the blanks.*

Diane chuckled when she recalled the first time she met with the client's broker. It had been overly cloak-and-dagger with the client insisting the meeting take place after her few employees had gone home. He'd also insisted Diane work on his account without *any* help from her office staff. She still had no idea who was bankrolling the hotel.

Robert D'Angelo, the client's broker, was muscular and expensively dressed. He had an intelligence he camouflaged with a quick wit and blatant exploitation of his Italian heritage. Most of his jokes were based on tired stereotypes about The Mob. When Diane had shown distaste for his inferences, Robert apologized.

"I'm sorry, Miss Wallace. Most of the business connections I have in Washington, D.C. have a difficult time leaving their preconceived biases in the video store."

"Well, Mr. D'Angelo, you will find, I'm not most people. Let's keep our business to the issues at hand and we'll get along fine."

Robert had the complete trust of his client, as his introduction letter detailed, and kept Diane assured she was headed in the right direction with her presentation. She discerned he'd get a kick out of the latest turn in her campaign. If Robert liked the idea, the client would be an easy sell. She was laying out the storyboards when the phone rang.

"Diane Wallace."

"Hello, Diane, it's Robert D'Angelo."

Diane had been expecting his call. If the construction site was closed down, she suspected the project would be put on hold for a while.

"Hello, Robert. I was expecting to hear from you. Has the project been shelved?"

"No, no, no," Robert chuckled in his smooth baritone, "we're just going to wait until the fire marshal finishes his investigation before we move ahead. Although I'm not sure we'll be using the same construction company. We need to be able to depend on them to get the job done on time and under budget."

"Listen, Robert, I'm familiar with the local company you're using. I'd venture to say, in spite of the recent difficulties; they'll come through for you. Don't be so quick to rule them out. This is a small community, and if you step on toes now, there could be problems for your hotel later. Think about this. If the best move for you is to go with someone else, then you have to do what's best for you, but remember you're putting a hotel in a small town where most of the people are related one way or another. I'm sure you'll guide your investor to do the right thing."

"You have a very valid point. Let's set another time to get together, say the same time in two weeks? Will that work for you?" Robert said.

"That works fine with my schedule. I should have the presentation completed, and we can go over the details at that time. Goodbye, Robert," Diane said.

Diane's mind traveled to her date with Justin. She felt her body flush when she thought of spending time close to him. She licked her lips and grinned; she had to give the man his due. Most of the men with whom Diane had been involved would have used today's misfortune to whine and throw up their hands. Justin seemed undaunted. He was unlike anyone she'd known. He joked about what had happened and was bold enough to ask her for a date. *How could I say no?*

Robert's call had just put her presentation on hold and her mind kept wandering to her dinner date. *Oh-my-gosh. I have a date. What am I going to wear? I don't have a thing that's fit to wear to dinner. I'll need to stop at Recycle City—and shop. First, I'd better go home and let Princess outside. I can be ready to meet Justin here by 6:30. Yeah, that's what I need to do.*

Diane drove home to let her greyhound outside and changed into comfortable jeans and tennis shoes. Every time she thought of Justin her heart skipped a beat. His voice felt like velvet on her ears and she had to resist the urge to run her finger over the slight cleft in his chin every time he was near. She was beginning to get excited at having plans for the evening instead of trying to decide what *not* to watch on TV. She knelt down and explained to her beloved dog what was happening as though she understood then left to find a new outfit.

Tonight she'd be diplomatic and give Justin the benefit of the doubt. She wouldn't think of the age difference; she'd think of him as an equal. Besides, he smelled great and whoever had designed the original pair of jeans, had his body in mind when they were doing it. Smiling, Diane pulled into Oakdale Plaza. The stores would have no idea what hit them.

Twenty-one

Justin leaned back staring at the phone. He'd done it. Interlocking his hands behind his head, he kicked his feet up on the desk and started chuckling. Not sure if the forces of nature were against him, considering the problem this morning, he'd asked Diane out and she'd said yes. Actually, said yes! *Things are definitely looking up.* Turning the chair slightly, he kicked over a pile of papers that had spilled out of his In-box. Groaning, he swung his legs to the floor and cupped his chin in his hands. He had a mountain of paperwork to wade through before 6:30. *First, I need to call the Pinnacle and reserve the table by the window. It has a beautiful view of the Blue Mountains I hope Diane will appreciate.* He flipped through the Rolodex on his desk and found the number.

"Pinnacle Restaurant."

"Yes, I'd like to make reservations for two at seven o'clock and I want to request the table on the west side that overlooks the river."

"We can set that up for you. Name please?"

"Anderson, Justin Anderson."

Justin set the phone in its cradle and grinned. The stage was set; a beautiful intelligent woman, great food, and a fantastic view. Every time he thought of Diane his heart River Danced in his chest. *I want—no I have—to know more about a woman who sets my heart to beating like this every time I think of her.*

He gathered the paperwork from his desk and realized most of this stuff required quick reading and his initials. Filling his out-box as quickly as he could, Justin had nearly depleted the paperwork mountain when his personal cell phone rang. He swallowed anxiously. With the exception of his phone call from Diane, the calls he'd received in the last twenty-four hours had not been welcome news. Would Diane cancel their dinner plans? Maybe she'd had second thoughts? He could let the voice mail take a message but what was the point.

~ * ~

Ashlee jerked the ringing phone from the cradle.

"What is it now?"

"--Justin—new girlfriend—"

"What? I can't hear a word you're saying. Speak up or I'll hang up," Ashlee barked.

"If you want to see Justin and his new girlfriend, be at the Pinnacle Restaurant tonight around six thirty." The voice was audible but spoke barely above a whisper. Ashlee couldn't identify the caller but the information was valuable to her. *Now to act.*

"Yeah, thanks." She slammed the phone down. *I can't make it out there myself tonight, but I should have* someone *I can get to help me. Randy, yeah, Randy.*

~ * ~

"Hello?"

"Hey, Justin. It's Tom Manning. Glad I caught you. I wasn't sure you'd be at the site."

Justin's body tensed. He couldn't help but feel Tom had knowledge of what was happening. It was an irrational thought. After all, he and Tom had been best friends since grade school. But a nasty little voice in the back of his head kept telling him Tom knew something.

"Hello, Tom. How can I help you?"

Tom reacted to Justin's chilly answer.

"Whoa, Justin. You and I've been friends too long to play this *polite* game. I just found out about the company van being stolen. Quite honestly, I didn't even know we had a van for our office. That's stuff the office manager, Mrs. Darcy, handles. All I know is when I need something, I ask Mrs. Darcy and supplies show up the next day. You know if I got mad enough at you I'd just sue. I've got more dirt on you than anybody in the county."

Tom's response eased the tension both men were feeling.

"I did call for a reason. Remember I told you I might have something on Ashlee? Well, my investigator found some paperwork that could change your legal standing regarding Ashlee and Briana. It'll take about a week but as soon as I've got verification, I'll contact you. And, Justin, if I can help, let me know."

"Thanks, Tom. I hate to admit it but you're right. You have more dirt on me than anyone. Guess that's my fault for being your friend since we were six. If your information can get me more time with Briana—great; if it's going to hurt her, I don't want any part of it. Call me when you get the facts verified. Bye, Tom."

When the company phone rang, Justin shook his head.

It was as busy as a normal Friday. He sure missed Belinda right about now.

"Anderson Construction."

"Justin? This is Corey. Where the hell are you? I need you to make a statement today so we can get it transcribed while Ida's still on duty. Do you suppose you could move your butt down here in the next thirty minutes before I send out a police car to pick you up?"

Corey didn't wait for an answer. He hung up. Justin sat looking at the receiver in his hand. He'd get mad but with Corey it was a waste of time. He hung up the phone and started making neat piles of the paperwork still on his desk. He'd come in Monday. There were several permits with time deadlines he needed to guide through the county system. He was determined to finish this project.

With the site closed for investigation, Justin had not been cognizant of how quiet the area could be until a noise outside the trailer startled him. He held his breath and strained to listen. Rising from his chair with as much stealth as he could muster, he crept to the door of the construction trailer. There it was again. Trying to pinpoint what he heard, he realized the sound was gravel crunching under a foot. He flung the trailer door open. Running footsteps ignited his adrenaline. Justin leapt past the steps to the ground pumping his legs as fast as he could in the direction he thought the intruder had disappeared. Losing any chance of catching sight of someone at the chain link fence surrounding the property, Justin stopped to suck fresh air into his out of shape lungs. He heard a car roaring down the road.

"Damn!"

He walked back to the trailer and called Corey. Relating the occurrence, Justin said he was worried about Corey's truck. "I'm not sure if it was tampered with or not, but I'd feel much better if you came out and took a look yourself. I'll stay in the office until someone gets here. I've got plans tonight at six-thirty, which I'm not going to screw up. If someone's not here by six, I'm calling a taxi."

This time Justin hung up on Corey. He smiled. He'd love to be at the police station now. The vision of Corey puffing furiously to his squad car set him to chuckling. Justin looked at his watch. He made a mental bet with himself Corey would show up in the next fifteen minutes. Ten minutes after Justin hung up the phone, Corey stood in front of his desk.

"Hey, Corey. Nice to see you. What can I do for you?" Justin smirked.

"Cut the crap. Let's go look at my truck," Corey said.

The men walked to the red monster parked near the trailer. Corey examined the exterior with his hands noting every blemish on the vehicle in his green book. He opened and inspected the engine compartment after which he crawled underneath and checked each tire and tie rod then ran his hands over the brake lines. Finally, he climbed in the cab, to Justin's great amusement, and checked the interior. The inspection had taken one full hour. As far as either man could see, nothing had been done to the truck, but Corey was insistent the vehicle be taken to the police lab and scrutinized by the experts.

Justin locked the trailer and hauled himself up into the cab of the red truck to follow Corey's police cruiser to the lab. Corey explained to the duty sergeant why he wanted the truck analyzed and motioned for Justin to relinquish the keys to a uniformed officer.

They drove to the station where Justin gave his statement and pressured Corey about his own truck.

"About your truck…"Corey hesitated and cleared his throat.

"What about my truck?" Justin asked.

"We didn't find any more issues," Corey started.

"I guess that's good isn't it?" Justin interrupted.

"Yes, but…"

"But, what? Corey, when can I have my truck back?" Justin's irritation was emerging.

"You'll be able to get your truck Monday. We took care to meticulously inspect your truck, inside and out. I'm having the boys replace your brake lines, which you'll pay me for Monday, after you pick it up. Any other questions? Oh, yeah, the house. We'll probably need to have it available all weekend. We were able to lift a partial print from the glass on the gas meter. It matched one of the prints found near the truck brake lines. You really need to change your routine. It's too predictable."

Justin sat opposite Corey trying to absorb the information Corey had nonchalantly imparted to him. He glanced at his watch and recognized he had less than two hours before he had to pick up Diane. But pick her up in what?

"Corey? Let me use your phone?"

"Sure."

Justin called the rental agency and, after several interruptions, was able to line up a rental for the rest of the weekend.

"Would you drive me to the rental agency in Billington? I finally got a car."

"Sure. Let me check out with the desk sergeant and we'll go."

Justin reviewed his schedule during the past week. It was uneventfully normal. With this new job, his focus had been trying to stay within budget and on time. There were two to three dozen people at any one time on the job site. A new face wouldn't have been cause for alarm. Justin rubbed his temples. He couldn't have a headache tonight.

Corey poked his head in the office.
"Come on. Let's get you a car."

Twenty-two

Randall had been working at the Pinnacle Restaurant since high school. He'd started out as a dishwasher and currently was waiter/assistant manager. At thirty-three, he still lived at home with his parents. He was finishing college this term and would have his bachelor's degree in Business Administration. Then, he'd move to Washington, D.C. or Baltimore or New York or anywhere except Billington or Oakdale.

He didn't date much because the highest goal for local girls was to get married and have babies. He knew there was more to life. So, Randall lived a quiet life punctuated by periods of intense excitement when Ashlee entered the picture. They'd dated briefly in college before she got involved with Justin Anderson. Once he showed up, Ashlee had eyes for no one else. When she and Justin divorced, she'd immediately run to Randall. He'd been flattered for about a week until he realized she was using him to try and make Justin jealous which hadn't worked.

Every so often, she'd drop back into Randall's life for a couple weeks then leave. It'd happened tonight. Before Randall had walked out the front door of his parent's home, he'd received a phone call.

"This is Randall."

"Hi, Randy," Ashlee was the only person he allowed to call him Randy. "It's Ashlee. I need you to do a favor for me. I'll make it worth your time," She was using her little girl voice.

Randall sighed. He knew he was in trouble. "What do you need, Ashlee?" he asked.

"If you see Justin, would you find out who he's with and call me?"

It sounded innocent enough, but Randall knew with Ashlee nothing was innocent. There was always an ulterior motive.

"Sure. You've still got the same phone number?"

"Of course. Speaking of which, why haven't you called?"

Randall knew she wasn't serious but mumbled some excuse about work and classes. Ending the conversation and leaving for work, he wondered what Justin had done to provoke the wrath of his ex-wife this time. He almost felt sorry for the guy. It'd been several years since Ashlee and Justin were married, but she still tried to control his life. It made Randall very glad he was single.

Twenty-three

Diane's shopping had been successful. She discovered a royal purple, figure flattering sheath dress that emphasized her dark coloring. She bought shoes to match and a sexy lavender teddy, with a garter belt, and silk stockings to complete the outfit. Although she'd be the only one who knew she had matching undergarments, it was the way they made her feel that mattered. She'd nearly forgotten what *sexy* felt like. Dressing at the office, she worked for an hour to artfully apply her makeup. Her final task was to brush her short dark hair upward. One last look in the full-length mirror put a confident smile on her face. She looked great tonight. If Justin didn't notice, well, he must be dead.

She heard a knock on the front door of the office. The butterflies in her stomach began to dive bomb relentlessly. Peeking through the mini-blinds, past the potted plant, she verified the knock belonged to Justin and opened the door for him. *I hope I look as good as I feel.* The stunned look on his face bolstered her confidence.

"Diane. You look—incredible!" he said.

"Thank you. You look pretty good yourself. Are you ready to go? I'm starved. How about we take my car and come back to pick up yours later?" Diane asked.

"Great idea. I had to rent one until Monday."

Justin held the door as Diane turned out lights. She locked the office and they walked to her Corvette. He lovingly ran his fingers over the sinuous lines of the fender to the passenger door while Diane unlocked it for him.

"This body style has great lines. I'd love to be able to drive something like this," Justin lightly caressed the leather interior.

"Why don't you?" Diane asked.

"Well, I will when I'm sure my business is on stable footing. I want to be sure my daughter…"

"Oh, you mean the adorable one?"

Justin sat taller, a slight smile playing on his lips, "Yeah, that's the one. I just want to be sure she has everything she needs. Right now that's the most important thing to me."

Diane shot him a sideways glance. His eyes sparkled and face flushed as he talked about his little girl. *This gorgeous man is undermining my determination not to get involved with him. He obviously loves his daughter very much. Real love for his daughter and great buns. I think I'm losing this battle.*

"That's the best reason I know for not treating yourself," Diane turned the car into the restaurant driveway and straddled it over two spaces in the back of the lot.

"Typical Vette owner, I see," Justin winked at Diane.

"Got a problem with that?" She grinned and started to get out her side.

Justin sprinted to open her door. Reaching in, Diane allowed him to raise her out of the car. He drew her so close to his body his fragrance tickled her nose. He looked into her dark eyes, noting the slim straight nose leading to full sensual lips. As he gently wrapped her in his arms, she could feel the rushing blood heating her body in the cool evening air. She caught her breath when their lips brushed together feeling her resolve slipping away as she closed her eyes and dissolved into his embrace. He pulled back slightly, breaking the moment.

"Thank you for having dinner with me," he murmured softly in her ear.

His taut muscular body, along with his aftershave, made her head swim.

"You're welcome. I need to lock the car then maybe we should go in? It's freezing out here," Diane's teeth started to chatter. Being in Justin's arms was undermining any strength she had left to fight the sensual feelings washing over her. She needed emotions of steel to hold her ground against becoming entangled. She'd made a promise—*never again.* She locked the car and they strolled into the restaurant.

Justin's upbringing took over. He opened the restaurant door then verified their reservation, finally holding out her chair. She'd forgotten that some men had actually been taught manners. The table, in the rear of the restaurant, provided a view of a snow-covered mountain under an ink blue sky sprinkled with more stars than Diane could remember seeing. Tall evergreens intermingled with an occasional maple or ash splashed red and yellow in the green curtain, soothed by the river running next to the restaurant. The two sat quietly taking in the beauty.

The maître d' walked to their table and cleared his throat. "Please excuse this interruption, but it is necessary for me to see your identification."

Diane and Justin turned from gazing out the window.

Diane stared in disbelief, "You're joking, right?"

"No ma'am. I'm required to see the identification of all our clientele. State law."

Justin handed his driver's license to the man who quickly scrutinized and returned the license to him. Diane rummaged through her wallet and pulled out her driver's license, which she handed to the officious man. He carefully examined the picture, looking at Diane then down at the card he held in his hand. After five minutes of carefully analyzing the license, he returned the card to Diane.

"It really doesn't do you justice. You are much lovelier in person, ma'am." He waved his hand and a waiter materialized.

"Glenn will be your waiter tonight. Glenn, please provide this gentleman and lady their first drink on the house," he turned to Justin and Diane, "I am sorry for the inconvenience. Please enjoy the rest of your evening."

As quickly as he had appeared at their table, he disappeared. Justin and Diane looked at each other and started to giggle.

"That was strange," Justin said.

"Really," Diane agreed.

Glenn took their drink order and disappeared into the bar. When Diane's strawberry margarita and Justin's coke arrived, they ordered the house special, prime rib. Justin added a bottle of the house red wine.

"I was wondering how you came to live in such a small town as Oakdale. I know you're not from here because I've lived here all my life and I would've noticed you. You don't really have to answer that," Justin said.

"Oh, I don't mind. I'll just give you the high points right now, okay?" Diane answered.

"Sure."

She put her hand under her chin and gazed at the silhouette of the mountain through the picture window. "This reminds me of a little place up the Willamette River just outside of Salem, Oregon; a quiet restaurant tucked away in the mountains with a great view. My family lived there for about two years while my dad tried his hand at logging. Like a lot of other careers, it didn't go very well, and we moved on shortly after he was laid off."

"I moved out of my folks' house as soon as I could. Unfortunately, I jumped to a situation just as bad. When my first marriage didn't work, I bolted. I globe-trotted a bit and found myself tangled up with a band member of a rock group. When my relationship with Ron Smythe ended, I moved back to the United States from England.

"Oakdale was the feature on a TV show the first night I was back. I needed peace and quiet and the town fit the bill. I decided to check it out. The people are welcoming once they realize you're here to stay."

Justin nodded his agreement.

"I really can't complain about growing up here. My parents, brother, sister and I are what most people around here call old timers. My great, great grandfather emigrated from Sweden and settled this part of the country when it was just Native Americans. He became so fond of the local chief's daughter he asked for her hand in marriage. Passing the tests set for him by the chief, they wed and started our family line right here in this valley. He built the plantation north of town. All the buildings were used until my father inherited the property. Dad wasn't much of a farmer but a great businessman. He made his money selling off parcels of the family estate. Just the mansion, outbuildings and three acres were left for us. He used the money from the sales to help keep his construction company afloat and build the shopping center at the edge of town."

The main course was delivered to their table and Diane noticed Justin pour himself half a glass of wine that he barely touched. She would have thought more about it, but they began swapping childhood tales and laughing. They'd lost all track of time when the maître d' appeared and asked Justin if he would settle the dinner bill.

Looking around, Diane and Justin realized they were the only people left in the dining room. Apologizing and tipping generously, a giggling Diane and smiling Justin left the restaurant. Diane handed him the keys to her car.

"Here, I *know* I can't drive. You've gotten me drunk and now you need to drive me home." Weaving slightly, she leaned in to him.

Justin took the keys and, slipping her hand into his, escorted her to the vehicle. He unlocked the door before gently pulling her into his arms, brushing his lips against her cheek. She responded by wrapping her arms around his neck. Her soft lips found his willing mouth. Her tongue probed deeply and sent a surge of passion through him causing stirrings deep in his body. Before he could embarrass himself, Justin reluctantly peeled himself away from Diane.

"Wow," he whispered. He stepped back on shaky legs. He was doing the best acting job of his life. He wanted to sweep her into his arms and kiss her breathless, while his body made other urgent suggestions. He opened the car door and lowered Diane to the seat. She swung her shapely legs into the car, causing her dress to part slightly and reveal the tops of her stockings. He groaned as he felt his animal passion rising and quickly shut her door. Breathing deep with each step he took, he muttered. *I've got to get control of myself. I don't want to lose this lady to stupidity. All right, Justin, slow down!*

He stopped at the driver's door to gather his thoughts and locate his self-control. When he lowered himself into the car, he felt he'd regained a bit of his restraint. Diane leaned over and turned his face to, hers placing her lips on his and kissed him hungrily.

"Take me home, Justin."

She sank back into the leather seat with a contented sigh.

"At your service, ma'am."

Justin fought the urge to speed to her house then sweep her into his arms and make passionate love to her all night. He wanted her, every muscle in his body ached for her touch, but he didn't want a one-night stand, not with Diane. When she sobered up tomorrow, he wasn't sure she'd feel the same lust she did tonight.

They'd spent a relaxing, comfortable evening together enjoying a great meal and sharing. Justin sensed Diane would probably withdraw until she perceived he was trustworthy. He glanced at her peaceful face. If she only knew how incredibly gorgeous and sexy she was, he'd never have a chance.

He pulled the car into the driveway. She pointed the opener at the garage door. Nothing happened. Furrowing her brow, she concentrated intensely as she pushed the button and watched as, this time, the door opened. Justin parked the car inside the garage and helped Diane. The closeness of her body threatened to start the fire raging inside him again. He opened the house and bowing slightly motioned Diane to enter.

"That's funny," she said.

"What?" he asked.

"Princess usually comes tearing down the hall when I come home."

Diane began to search through the house.

"You told me you let her out earlier," he said.

Justin joined the search. When he called the greyhound's name, the clicking of toenails could be heard pounding down the wood hallway.

"That does it. I'm sure I've lost my dog now," Diane crossed her arms.

"You can just take her out, Mister," She grabbed the leash from the hook behind the door.

Smiling and bowing subserviently, he took the leash from her hand.

"I'm sorry, Miss Wallace, it seems I have a touch with females."

"Get out of here," Diane laughed as she watched man and dog head happily down the street. She was falling for him. *Darn it all!* He was a real person behind those muscles and adorable smile. She really liked him and the wine she'd been drinking was inflaming her hormones. She wanted to make love to him this minute but the little voice in the back of her head kept saying she'd regret it later. She hated that little voice. It was usually right. Wistfully, she made coffee and waited for the pair to reappear. When Justin brought Princess back, he was breathless and pink cheeked. Diane couldn't help but giggle. Princess must have broken into a run. Once she started to run, she hated to stop.

"How about a non-alcoholic nightcap?" she offered Justin coffee.

"Sure," he panted as he sat at the dining room table.

"It's been a long day for both of us. I don't know about you, but I have to go in and finish up some work tomorrow. Not my idea of a great Saturday, but it pays the bills," Diane filled Justin's cup with coffee.

"Yeah, I've got to start working on clean up for the site. I don't want the investor to have any reason to back out." Justin put cream in his coffee and stirred. *This is so comfortable.*

"I'll be getting up at the usual time. If you like, I can get you up, too, and we'll drive back to the office and pick up the rental car. Sound like a plan?" Diane asked.

"Great. And Diane?" Justin looked seriously over the top of his cup.

"Yeah?"

"Thank you for having dinner with me tonight."

"You're welcome. It's been a long time since I felt comfortable enough to open up to someone. I'll see you in the morning. Could you lock up?" Diane's shoulders had sagged and her eyes were halfway closed.

"Sure. Goodnight." Justin watched her hips sway slowly, sensually down the hallway. She was making life very hard. He grinned at his own pun.

Twenty-four

When Justin and Diane showed up at the restaurant, Randall felt goose bumps rise on his skin. The thought that Ashlee might be psychic was terrifying. He recognized Diane as having worked at The Bar in town but knew she didn't recognize him. He asked for their identification. The scowl she gave him would've curdled milk. Randall used this time to memorize her address. Handing back her driver's license, he repeated the address to himself all the way to the podium. He called an acquaintance he had at the police station. "Hey, Kurt," Randall said. "I need a favor. I'll owe you a dinner with drinks if you do this for me."

Kurt hesitated. He and Randall had known each other since kindergarten. Nowadays, though, Randall only called when he wanted something. "I don't know, Randy," Kurt said slowly.

Randall shuddered at the nickname. It sounded different when Ashlee cooed it.

"How much trouble can I get into?" Kurt questioned.

"You probably run this request a dozen times every day. I need to have you verify an address on a driver's license. That's all. Did I mention I'd spring for a complete dinner with cocktails and wine?" Randall flinched. This favor could cost him nearly $200.00.

"Well, okay. I'm kind of in the doghouse with my wife, Angela. She caught me with the new dispatcher ,and I nearly got kicked out. I need something that'll get me back in her good graces. What can I do for you?"

"I want to verify that the information on a Virginia driver's license

125

is correct. The name is Diane Wallace; that's D-I-A-N-E-W-A-L-L-A-C-E. The date of birth is September tenth, nineteen fifty-nine. Will you double check the address for me?" Randall asked.

"Yeah, hold on a minute," Kurt answered and put Randall on hold.

Randall stood and hummed along with the recorded music. A distinctive click and the ending of the prerecorded song announced Kurt's return.

"There are two addresses on file for that license. The first listed is seven fifteen Elm Street, that's a residence then there's an alternative address of three ten Main Street, which appears to be a business address. She also has a Corvette registered in her name. The registration says it's black and only a couple of years old. Is that what you need?" Kurt said.

"Yes, thank you. Dinner for you and a friend is on me. Just call the restaurant and ask for me, I'll arrange everything," Randall replied. He then placed a call to Ashlee.

"Ashlee? This is Randall—Randy. Justin is having dinner with an attractive older woman with short dark hair."

"What else?" Ashlee asked.

"She's sort of slender," Randall said.

"And?"

"And dark," Randall said.

"Randy, quit beating around the bush. Tell me about the woman or--" Ashlee started.

"No. No ors. She's a tiny, slender, dark-haired, dark-eyed, woman who dresses well and appears to have money. She looks out of place in here. She owns a newer black Corvette and lives at seven fifteen Elm and, apparently, has a business or owns property at three ten Main Street. Is that what you want?"

"Yes, Randy. Thank you. That's what I need. I owe you. I'll pay up later. All right?"

"Sure, Ashlee. No problem," Randall wrote it off. He knew Ashlee was all talk. He also knew if you crossed her she could be vicious. He didn't want to be on the receiving end of her venomous temper.

As the evening progressed, Randall watched Diane and Justin. He could see they'd completely lost track of time. He envied the man. He sent the staff home and notified the two at the table they were the last customers left in the restaurant. He rang up their dinner ticket and discreetly tailed them outside watching as they headed to the only vehicle left in the lot, the black Corvette. Hiding behind a porch pillar, he observed as Justin fought to maintain his distance from Diane.

"Idiot. If a woman as beautiful as that threw herself at me, I'd go for it," Randall shook his head in disgust, walking inside to close the restaurant. He still had to go home and study for a couple hours. This time next year, he planned on being vice president with a company in a city far away from here.

Twenty-five

Ashlee hung up the phone. Randall was a worm but a useful worm. She'd suspected Justin was seeing someone new. She always suspected and he always denied it, but this time she had proof. According to Randall's information, this lady was quite a bit older than Justin. He was scraping the bottom of the barrel. She'd call her connection at the Police Department and see how far they'd gotten in the investigation.

Kurt answered the phone on the second ring.

"Hello, Oakdale Police Department. This is Patrolman Lee. How may I help you?"

"Hello, Kurt, this is Ashlee," she purred.

Kurt fumbled the phone. He knew Ashlee's sultry voice. She'd nearly cost him his marriage. Thinking about her now made his palms sweat and his pants grow uncomfortably tight.

"What can I do for you, Ashlee?" he dreaded the reply.

"Well, sugar, don't get yourself in an uproar. I need information I'm sure you have and can give me without losing your wife or job. How is Justin Anderson getting around these days?"

Kurt sighed in relief. He could give her what she wanted and he wouldn't jeopardize his life.

"He's gotten a rental car from an agency in Billington. I got to get back to work. It's nice hearing from you, Ashlee. You take care. Goodbye."

Ashlee would have been offended if she'd really cared, but Kurt was someone she'd used before. He was a typical guy that had grown up in Oakdale. *Boring.* She trudged up to bed. Tomorrow, she'd locate Justin.

Randall had given her two addresses where he might be. She couldn't resist the urge to taunt him. Maybe a note or scratching up the rental car... Ashlee rubbed her hands in delight.

Early the next morning, she dressed in dark clothing. She decided she'd use the white van Thomas Sr. had lent to her then she'd abandon the vehicle at the mall. A quick call to the police would direct them to the parking place and once recovered, Thomas wouldn't have to worry about legal entanglements.

Ashlee locked up and hiked to the garages behind the old mansion. She hopped in the van and motored to town. Observing the speed limits, she did nothing to arouse attention. She cruised past The Bar on Main Street and noted a white four-door vehicle with a rental sticker on the bumper.

That's got to be Justin's, she reasoned. She slid the van into a parking slot behind the building. Pulling up her gloves and retrieving a plain piece of paper from the floor, she scribbled a short note and meandered around front toward the car parked at the curb. It was seven on a Saturday morning, not many people were on the street as Ashlee moved closer to the car and slipped the paper under the windshield wiper on the driver's side. The piece of rectangular paper resembled a parking ticket waving in the early morning breeze. Pausing briefly before she turned the corner of the building to walk back to the van, she glanced back and smiled. This was the best way to ruin his day.

She'd park in the Wal-Mart lot near Billington. There was a specialty coffee shop close by where she would call Paul and have him pick her up. That is, if he was answering his cell. If he was with his new girlfriend, she could be stuck. No matter. She'd be out of the way when the police found the van. She slid behind the wheel and guided it to the main highway, noting a police cruiser apparently tailing her. Accelerating slightly, the police sedan equaled her speed, turning on the siren and lights. She punched the gas pedal and the cruiser closed the distance between the vehicles. When she crossed the county line, she was speeding. She screeched around the first left she saw then took an immediate right, sliding the rig into a parking spot at the back of a rundown bar. She sat in the back of the parked van for fifteen minutes until she'd calculated the officer had probably gone on his way. Climbing into the driver's seat, she drove to the Wal-Mart at five miles under the posted limit. She abandoned the van in a spot behind the huge building then strolled to the coffee shop to use the public phone.

"Oakdale Police Department."

Ashlee recognized Kurt's voice. She lowered her voice to just above a whisper.

"The white van stolen from the Manning and Manning law firm is in the parking lot behind the Wal-Mart building."

"Who is this? Hello?"

Hanging up the phone, she peeled off her driving gloves and tucked them in her bag, reversed her jacket and removed the stocking cap she'd worn, fluffing her short hair. Tucking in her shirt, she blended with the Saturday morning shoppers rubbernecking at the scene as the State Police showed up followed closely by Oakdale Police. Placing a call to Paul's cell, she got his message machine. She left a short concise message.

"Come pick me up at the coffee shop next to Wal-Mart, *now*, or I'll personally provide you a one way ticket to jail." Ashlee knew she had a ride home. She'd been in the room when Paul declared he'd rather die than go back to jail. She ordered a Cafe Mocha Light and watched the growing excitement across the way.

Paul stormed into the coffee shop and dropped into the chair across from Ashlee.

"I got your message," he growled.

"Yes, and it got you away from your new girlfriend, didn't it?" Ashlee reveled in the look of shock on Paul's face. "Do you think I'm stupid? I told you when we first got together I had connections all over town. What makes you think I don't know somebody at the gym? Anyway, the van's been recovered and we're out of the picture now. All we can do is wait. By Monday, I'll have the money that's rightfully mine. After the money comes to me, you and your new girlfriend can do anything you want. Until that time, Paul, I own you, body and soul. Do I make myself clear?"

Ashlee's crossed arms and set jaw convinced Paul the best course of action was agreement. He clamped his mouth shut and trailed behind her when they left the coffee shop.

The drive back to Oakdale was silently grim.

Twenty-six

Justin woke disoriented. The room didn't look familiar. *Where am I?* The fresh smell of newly laundered sheets and light vanilla that seemed to fill the house reminded him, he was a guest at Diane's. Stirring himself from the warm bed, he padded to the bathroom. Showering and shaving would help wake his whole body. He knew the hour was early but remembered Diane telling him last night she was going in to work today. He swung open the door and peered into the hallway. The rest of the house was still dark. He'd make coffee and get the paper. As he headed down the hall, he sensed a presence behind him. Turning, he found the silver greyhound at his heels. When he stopped, she nudged him to keep moving.

"I take it we're going for a walk?" Justin looked down at Princess.

The response was a tail-wagging streak headed to the front door.

"Okay, okay. But today, we walk. No racing. I'm too old to run that fast," Justin stated as he grabbed the leash and snapped it on Princess's collar. He stopped and made coffee first. *By the time we get back, the coffee should be brewed. I'll be ready by then.*

A quick detour to dress for a walk and Justin grabbed the house key on his way out. The two early birds journeyed into the brisk morning air. Justin would be glad when spring arrived. He didn't mind the cold but he enjoyed warmer days. Fifteen minutes later, Princess had taken care of her early morning duties and Justin was awake and ready for coffee and breakfast. He didn't normally eat breakfast, but the pace the greyhound set had stoked his hunger. Maybe, if he was quiet, he could fix something and not wake Diane. Opening the door, Justin's nose was seduced with the aroma of fresh brewed coffee and cooking bacon.

"What smells so good?" he asked, closing his eyes and inhaling.

"Could be the eggs and bacon I'm making," Diane replied with a smile.

"I thought you said you didn't cook?" Justin grinned.

Diane turned from the stove and stuck her tongue out at him.

"Wash your hands and sit at the table or I'll throw this stuff down the garbage disposal." She had set the table using place mats and new dishes.

"Wow, this is almost as fancy as dinner at the Pinnacle. What's the occasion?" Justin's voice held a hint of sarcasm.

"Well, smart aleck, when I was a kid the only time my family ever got together to do anything was at meal time. My mother insisted we all sit down at the table. Hell, I was twenty-four or twenty-five before I knew you could eat anywhere else. I like the idea you have to stop everything you're doing to sit down and carry on a conversation while you have a meal. If you want, you can take your plate to the family room and watch TV." Diane watched for Justin's reaction. He surprised her. The sarcastic smirk left his face.

"The last time I saw my family all together we were at the dinner table," he said. "In fact, my brother and I were arguing about who was better looking and better at sports. My sister was at a sleepover with her best friend and I was staying home because I had a test the next day and wanted to study. If I'd known it'd be the last time we'd see each other, I might've let him win the argument. My mom, dad, and Junior, my brother, drove off to one of his basketball games. On the way home, a car crossed the centerline and hit my folks' car head on at sixty-five. The driver was drunk." His eyes began to fill. He clinched his jaw tight and swallowed hard.

Diane couldn't stand it. She moved to his chair and gently placed her hands on his shoulders. "Justin, I'm so sorry. I didn't intend to bring up painful memories."

She ran her hands through his hair, her eyes filling at the pain she had caused him. His shoulders shook and he sucked in deep breaths. He put his hands to his temples, in an attempt to hide his eyes, as Diane stood stroking his hair, watching the large tears roll down his tanned cheeks. His breathing slowed and the tears dried. He left the table, returning with a freshly washed face.

"I apologize. I've never felt comfortable enough with anyone to let go. Talking about my family like that triggered fourteen-year old feelings. I-I promise it won't happen again," Justin's cheeks flushed red and he looked away from Diane.

"Please, don't say that," Diane lightly placed her hand on his shoulder, "I feel honored you trust me and I'm comfortable with you, which is something I haven't experienced in...I can't remember when. I know you have my dog's heart. She's never warmed up to anybody like you. If talking about your family is upsetting, we won't, but let me at least be a sounding board."

Justin smiled slowly. He wanted Diane to be more than a sounding board in his life.

"Thank you. I'll definitely keep you in mind for the job. Meanwhile, breakfast must be ice cold by now."

"That's what microwave ovens are for—reheating." She picked up his plate and in less than two minutes Justin had hot food again.

Justin looked at her across the table. "Last night was very nice. It's been a long time since I enjoyed myself enough to lose track of the time. Do you remember the pained look on the waiter's face?"

Diane snickered. "I've never seen anyone try so hard to look pleasant when what he really wanted to do was tell us to get the hell out. But you know, you're right, dinner was wonderful. We really need to do it again."

When they had cleared the table and put the dishes in the dishwasher, Diane handed Justin a key.

"What's this?" he asked.

"An extra key so you can come and go as you please," Diane said.

"You sure you want to do this?" he asked. He was holding the key in his open palm.

"Yes. Oakdale is a small town, and if you steal anything, well, I'll find out where you live and hunt you down. I already know where you work," Diane said over her shoulder as she headed to her room.

Saturdays, even at work, were casual. *I think jeans and a sweater will do just fine since nobody else is going to be there but me.* She emerged in a fitted pair of jeans that accented her shapely hips. The sweater had graduated shades of royal blue and forest green. She'd quickly run her hands through her short dark hair giving it a slightly mussed look.

Justin didn't realize he was staring until Diane looked at him questioningly, "Something wrong?"

"Oh, no," he said, "I've never seen anybody make jeans look so—so good."

Diane's cheeks flushed, "Thank you. You ready to go?"

Diane chose to let Princess have the run of the house today. They locked the door behind them and crawled into the black Corvette. Nearing the office, Justin noticed a paper on the windshield of the rental car waving slightly in the morning breeze.

"Oh, no," he groaned, "Not the way I wanted to start my Saturday. A ticket."

Diane parked the Corvette behind the rental car and they both climbed out. Justin pulled the paper from under the wiper and uttered a swear word when he opened it.

"What?" Diane asked.

"Look at this," Justin handed the note to Diane.

There were three simple words printed on the paper and no signature.

BANG! YOU'RE DEAD.

Justin slumped against the car and put his head in his hands. Diane handed him her cell phone and he placed a call to the police department. He was shocked to hear Corey's voice on the other end.

"What are you doing in on a Saturday?" Justin asked.

"Working on your damn case," Corey growled, "What do you need now?"

"I've just found a threatening note on the rental car. I parked it here last night when I went to dinner. It's been sitting in the same spot overnight," Justin said.

"Don't go anywhere. I'll be there shortly. And Justin?"

"Yeah?"

"Don't piss off anybody else in the next fifteen or twenty minutes, all right?" Corey said.

"Bite me," Justin hung up the phone.

"There's probably no chance of catching whoever did this but maybe there will be some witnesses. Corey wants me to stay here until he shows up," he said.

Diane slid her arms around Justin's neck and pulled him to her. Placing a lingering kiss on his lips, she told him she needed to get into the office. If they needed her, just knock on the door and she'd let them in.

Justin was stunned. The last thing he'd expected was a voluntary kiss from her this morning. As she began to break away, he pulled her back and wrapped his arms around her waist. He lowered his mouth to hers and softly running his tongue around her full lips, entered when she opened her mint-flavored mouth to his. Justin felt himself being drawn inside. Reveling in the sensations running up his spine, he broke with Diane at the sound of giggling. Two teenage girls whispering behind their hands and staring at the couple walked past them. Justin and Diane lingered before parting.

"Damn work," Diane muttered.

"What you said," Justin answered as he handed back her phone.

Diane gave a quick wave of the hand and disappeared through the door marked Diane Wallace Advertising Agency.

Corey pulled up in his police sedan.

"Justin. Got the note?" Corey lumbered from his car.

"Hi, Corey. Here," Justin handed the slip of paper to the detective.

"This could be the work of some of the local kids, Justin. This doesn't mean anything."

"Yeah, but it sure comes at an opportune moment. Why this car? It's obviously a rental." Justin pointed to the rental sticker on the bumper.

"I mean, have you gotten any reports of this happening to anyone else?"

"You're probably right, Justin, but this paper is scrap paper from who knows where and the writing is in ball point pen which can be bought at the Wal-Mart Store. All this proves is somebody doesn't like you. I'll take this evidence and file it with everything else, but unless you can come up with something more concrete, we're back to the beginning. Someone is trying to stop you from breathing. All I can do is warn you to watch your back, since you won't let me put you into protective custody."

"You know how I feel, Corey, thanks but no thanks."

The men shook hands and parted company. Corey drove to the police station and Justin stopped in to say goodbye to Diane. He knocked on the door. Diane ushered him into the office, locking the door behind him. As she turned, Justin pulled her into his arms and hungrily kissed her. She found herself wishing for more. Justin's hands began to explore. Diane's breaths came quick and shallow as she allowed herself to experience sensations she'd long buried. He moved his hand under her sweater and cupped her lace-encased breast in his warm palm. His thumb gently rubbed back and forth across her nipple. Hardening, the rosy tip pushed through the sheer material against his finger. She pressed against him, jumping when the phone rang. Justin slipped his hand from beneath Diane's sweater and grinned as she blushed and rearranged her clothing.

"Not here, not now," she huskily told him.

The phone continued ringing.

"I came to thank you again and head off to work," he said as he adjusted his jeans.

They gravitated together for another kiss, begrudgingly saying goodbye. Diane leaned against the door. She wanted him so bad her entire body ached.

She wondered why the answering service hadn't picked up the phone. Realizing she was the last one to leave on Friday, she'd forgotten to forward them to the service. Well, she'd answer this one call then forward the annoying things.

"Hello?"

"If you want to see your next birthday, you'd better walk away from Justin Anderson."

The line went dead. Diane glared at the phone in her hand. *Who knows Justin and I are even friends let alone call* here *on a Saturday?*

First, Diane panicked. Then she got mad, *really* mad, that someone had the nerve to think they could threaten her. What she did and with whom was nobody's business but her own. She sent the phones to the answering service and attacked the stack of paperwork on her desk. She'd finish Liz's ad campaign today. Diane leaned back in her chair; maybe she'd talk with Liz since the woman had been her best friend from the first day Diane arrived in Oakdale. She might have some idea who was behind the threat she'd just received.

Diane's mind began to wander to the moments prior to the call recalling the sensations she'd experienced. She hadn't felt this aroused by a man's touch since Ron and primal urges demanded satisfaction. Jerking back to the moment, she realized the reason she'd shut down those feelings was how overpowering they could become; having them was akin to addiction. She needed to focus on her business. Justin was breathtaking, literally, but would probably disappear when things got tough like most of the men she'd known. She couldn't afford to lose her objectivity over a physical sensation. She knew she was a dreamer when it came to relationships. Just ask her friend, Mark. How many times had he picked up the pieces and put her back together? He'd made it very clear the last time she stopped into The Bar, he wouldn't do it again.

Diane sighed heavily. Maybe this time…

Twenty-seven

"Paul, drive down Main Street then head for home," Ashlee instructed.

"Why? That'll take another fifteen minutes. That light in the center of town is the longest in the whole damn county," Paul complained.

"Don't ask why, just do what I tell you," Ashlee said through gritted teeth.

Paul had lived with Ashlee long enough to know when she wanted you to do something you did it the way she wanted, no questions asked. He headed through town on Main Street. As they passed the city limit signs, Ashlee spotted the black Corvette pulling up behind the rental car. She ordered Paul to slow down.

"Why? I'm doing twenty-five now," he grumped.

Ashlee glared at him, "Just do it."

He slowed his Camaro.

The action provided Ashlee an opportunity to watch her ex-husband and his new girlfriend. She watched the embrace with interest. Funny, she didn't remember him being that passionate after she'd told him she was pregnant. Paul uttered a four-letter expletive. They had to stop for the only signal in town. The interminable light held the Camaro immobile for an eternity. Ashlee watched from the side view mirror as Diane handed Justin her cell phone. The car had begun to inch forward when a police cruiser pulled up behind the Corvette and Corey Williams got out. Ashlee slid down in the seat.

If Paul noticed, he didn't say anything. He was busy brooding.

When they reached the house, Paul drove up the circular driveway and parked in front of the columned entry instead of parking in the garage. Slamming his door, he stomped in the house, leaving Ashlee to crawl out of the car by herself. She stormed into the foyer, heading directly to his room. He was packing a gym bag.

"Until Monday, you are mine. I have enough on you right now to put you in jail until you die. You and your girlfriend can fly to the moon Tuesday morning but until that time, you'll behave as though we're still a couple. Do I make myself clear?"

Paul turned and glared at Ashlee. What he'd ever seen in her he couldn't find right this moment.

"I have to go to the gym and work out. I still have two weeks until the contest, and," Paul said defiantly, "I won't be home tonight. I'll be moving things out on *my* timetable. Before you get too demanding, just remember who's done time. I know how, do you? Since I don't particularly want to do time again, I'll keep my end of the bargain. You'd better plan on doing the same. I want my money in small, old, non-consecutive bills. When this is done, so are we. Permanently."

Paul turned his back on Ashlee and zipped his gym bag shut. He shoved past her as she stood in the doorway. She ground her teeth together. If she hadn't needed him, she'd throw his stuff on the front lawn. Looking up a number in the local phone book, Ashlee placed a quick call. As she set the receiver down, the phone rang. Ashlee grabbed a cigarette, lit it and answered on the third ring.

"Yeah."

"Hello, muffin."

Ashlee choked. Coughing, she pulled the phone from her ear until she caught her breath.

"Hi, babykins," she purred.

"Listen, muffin, I'm able to get away tonight. We still on for dinner? I have a big surprise for you."

Ashlee hoped he didn't mean the one he always thought was so terrific in the bedroom.

As if reading her mind, he answered, "Not the one in the bedroom.

Although, if there's time maybe we can plan for that too?" He sounded hopeful.

Ashlee cooed dutifully and agreed they were still on for dinner at the Pinnacle Restaurant. She coyly mentioned she needed a new dress since they were going to some place nice.

Thomas Manning, Sr. chuckled, "All right, sweetie. Go over to the boutique and get something sexy. I want you to look especially good tonight. I'll see you later."

Ashlee hung up the phone. After changing her clothes, she walked to the garage behind the mansion she'd battled Justin to occupy after their divorce. She smiled smugly as she opened the garage door ,revealing her 1955 Chevrolet Belair. Her mother had given her the car, and Thomas had paid to have it restored.

Lovingly, she drew her hand over the polished body. She'd love to drive the car but didn't want the attention the aqua blue and white car garnered. She got into a late model four-door Toyota she'd bought for Briana and herself and motored to Main Street. She wanted to see if Diane Wallace had any courage. After she'd made the threatening call, she'd wanted to be in the room to see how Diane had reacted. Slowing as she passed the ad agency, she was surprised to see the black Corvette parked in front of the office. Well, Diane was either very brave or incredibly stupid. Ashlee wasn't sure which was more to her advantage. Time would tell.

At the boutique, Ashlee chose the most expensive dress in the store. Thomas had said he wanted her to look sexy and money was no object. The dress was form fitting, strapless and turquoise blue. When she modeled it in the store, every eye was on her. She had to have this dress. For whatever reason Thomas wanted her to look stunning, this dress was the guarantee she would pass his expectations.

The clerk reverently bagged the lustrous garment in a cotton wrapper and walked behind Ashlee to her vehicle where she hung the dress on the garment hook in the backseat, gently laying the excess on the rear bench seat. Ashlee drove back to the mansion. She felt the tingle begin at the bottom of her stomach. It was a good sign. Her intuition was signaling her something exciting was about to happen. She'd call her mom's house and check in on Briana to be sure the pre-teen wasn't giving her grandmother a hard time. A nap was in order before preparations for the command performance tonight. She would have Thomas eating out of the palm of her hand. Then anything she wanted was hers.

Twenty-eight

Thomas Manning replaced his phone in the cradle. He reached into the cherry wood humidor and pulled a tightly wrapped brown cylinder beneath his nose inhaling deeply. The distinctive aroma tickled his senses as he picked up the nippers from the desktop and cut the tip of the cigar into the ashtray. Lighting the end and puffing, two or three times, Thomas inhaled the acrid smoke into his lungs. *Ahhh, there's nothing like the taste of a good Havana*, he thought as he leaned back in his leather chair. He allowed his mind to wander.

~ * ~

He'd always admired Ashlee, and when she began returning his affections, he was flattered. Before too long, Thomas realized what the younger woman loved was his money and power. His physical person was a necessary evil. In the course of time, he used Ashlee as much as she used him. Her youth made him feel young and virile, so he paid for everything she desired. The year she'd become pregnant and didn't contact him was the most miserable of his life. He'd relied on his wife for what little physical affection she grudgingly doled out to him.

Arlene Manning had been the town beauty when she'd graduated from college, as well as a daughter of one of the richest men around, but after having children, she'd quickly lost her figure. She held the old-fashioned belief the only reason people engaged in sex was to procreate. She announced she planned to quit making love to him after the last of the children was born and turned a blind eye to his escapades.

Ashlee had bewitched Thomas the moment he'd laid eyes on her. He decided to concentrate on her as his only lover. Her boundless sexual desires and energy left him little time to fool around with anyone else. Arlene, while pretending blindness to his affair, had expressed concern Ashlee would expect to inherit money designated for their children. Thomas assured her Ashlee wasn't expecting anything when he died. He'd invested a portion of Ashlee's earnings in high yield stocks that would provide a comfortable dividend as long as the fund was not withdrawn. Arlene spoke no further about *the Ashlee thing* and he ceased to expect her to perform wifely duties.

~ * ~

Six months earlier, Thomas had been looking for a memo on his son's desk when he stumbled on Justin Anderson's file. Curiosity pushed him to open and read the contents.

Tom's administrative assistant was an efficient woman who took meticulous notes she transcribed immediately after any meeting. Thomas had despised wading through her notes after board meetings because of their fastidiousness.

Noted in Justin's file was a change in his will. He was asking about changing the executrix from Ashlee, Briana's mother, to his sister Irene. He was also asking what he could do to make sure Ashlee wouldn't be allowed access to any of the money.

Thomas whistled. Moving stealthily to his office, he slid behind his desk and picked up his phone. He dialed the number from memory.

"Hello?" Ashlee's silky tones aroused Thomas. "Hi, sugar. I have some news we need to discuss. Can you meet me tonight?"

"Sure. How about eight o'clock at my place? Paul is competing in a bodybuilding contest out of town this weekend and I can call Lynn to come pick up Briana for a sleepover. I'll have the house to myself," she said.

"Okay, see you at eight," Thomas knew if Ashlee found out about the change in the will from anyone else but him, he could forget ever having sex again. He drove to her residence and after a bottle of Zinfandel wine while they sat snuggled together on the couch, he broke the news.

"Ashlee?" Thomas tightened his arms around her.

"Yes, honey?" Ashlee snuggled deeper into the embrace of her lover.

"I want to let you know about something I've discovered. Justin is changing his will. He's decided to name his sister, Irene, as executrix and trustee of the money he will leave Briana," Thomas waited for the inevitable fall out, but Ashlee surprised him. She didn't rant or rave. In fact, she was so quiet Thomas turned her to him to see if she was all right.

"Are you okay, hon?" His brow was furrowed in concern.

"I'm fine. Has this change been made, yet?" Ashlee asked.

"No. I'll let you know when it happens," Thomas wrapped his arms around Ashlee and held her close.

The rest of the evening was hushed. Thomas left the mansion feeling uneasy. Her silence was atypical. He would have felt much more at ease had she raved and paced, but Ashlee's calm spooked him. She could be a *very* dangerous woman.

~ * ~

Justin jumped when his cell rang, echoing off the construction office walls..

"Hello?"

"Hi, Daddy," the distinctive voice of his daughter spread a smile on Justin's face.

"Hi, sweetie. How are you doing? Where are you? Your mom's not going to yell at you for calling, is she?" Justin asked.

"Naw, she doesn't know. I'm at Gram's house in Winchester. But Mom called and told me today you have a new girlfriend and probably won't be coming to see me. Is that true, dad?"

Justin gritted his teeth. His ex-wife was playing games again, and this time she didn't seem to care the person she was hurting was their daughter. Briana's hurt oozed through her voice.

"No, sugar. There's been some problems at my house and a friend of a friend, who just happens to be a woman, is letting me stay in her extra room until my house is fixed on Monday."

"Well, Mom said you guys were doing really gross kissing stuff like she does with that old guy that comes to our house," Briana said.

Justin straightened in his chair, "What old guy, honey?"

"Oh, I don't know who he is, but he has a really fancy car and only comes over when Paul's gone and they think I'm asleep. I mean, Paul is gross enough, but this guy is like really old, ya know, almost dead like. Anyway, you told me to call you if I ever had any questions I wanted to ask you. So, I just wanted to ask. That's all," Briana said.

"Hon, if I ever meet someone I really, really like, I'll let you know. Just remember, you're the first girl in my life, okay?"

"Okay, Daddy. Well, Gram is telling me I've got to get off the phone. I love you, Daddy," Briana said.

"I love you, too," Justin replied. He slammed his fist on the desk. The sound ricocheted in the quiet trailer. *There* has *to be a way for me to get custody of Briana. Ashlee is destroying her a little bit at a time with all the lies she's feeding her. I'll find a way for her to come live with me—somehow.*

~ * ~

Ashlee had begun hinting broadly to Thomas about getting rid of Justin. She wanted him dead and out of the way. Thomas had written off her threat as an Ashlee temper tantrum until she informed him she would no longer perform sexual favors until he guaranteed Justin's demise.

He'd recently engaged an investment company to help him diversify some of his money. His investment broker, who was of Italian descent, might know someone who could help him make arrangements to hire a professional to eliminate Justin. Thomas badgered his broker until the man had told him he would try to coordinate something.

Two things had happened in the last week. He'd discovered

through his own investigations that Justin had signed the new will and his son, Tom, was filing the change in the courthouse on Monday. Secondly, his investment broker had called and set up a meeting tonight, Saturday, with the man that who would remove *the Justin problem* for him and Ashlee. Maybe now, he'd be back in Ashlee's good graces.

Thomas' surprise was for Ashlee to meet the hit man tonight. Her love of danger would turn her on and he would benefit. Chuckling, he rubbed his hands together in anticipation. He could hardly wait. He phoned Robert D'Angelo to confirm their scheduled meeting. When Robert assured him they were coming, he relaxed, sitting in his chair and puffing leisurely on his cigar.

"What is that awful stench in my house?" Arlene tromped into Thomas's study.

Sighing, he tamped out the cigar. It was going to be an interminable four hours until she left to visit her sister in Billington.

Twenty-nine

Robert D'Angelo had moved to the Oakdale area on the recommendation of his friend, Chad Sanders. They'd been in the same fraternity in college and when drafted into the National Football League on the same team were assigned as roommates their first year. They got along so well they requested to continue as roommates throughout their pro careers. Chad had studied Police Sciences in college, and Robert had majored in Investment Banking. When their careers in pro football ended within a year of each other, Chad convinced Robert to move to a community near Oakdale.

Robert's representation of Thomas Manning was his most prestigious opportunity since his retirement from football. If the deal went well, Robert would be on his way to succeeding outside the sports arena.

He'd spent most of his life trying to convince people everyone with an Italian last name wasn't involved in the Mafia. The fact being the Mafia was a wives' tale from the old country. It didn't exist in America. Usually, people would nod their heads to make him happy. His new client, Mr. Manning, was insistent he must be a member of the Mafia. While Robert would have preferred otherwise, he didn't say yes and he didn't say no. He had too much at stake in this deal. When Manning began grilling Robert about finding someone willing to arrange a hit for him, Robert placed a call to his friend Chad Sanders at the police department.

Chad had been hired at the Police Department two years from the day he'd returned home. When the phone on his desk rang that Saturday morning, he was pleasantly surprised to hear Robert's voice on the other end. Robert quickly outlined his concerns about the general conversation having taken place between himself and his client. He didn't divulge the client's name because he wasn't certain the man was serious. Chad asked Robert if he would retell his story while Chad's supervisor listened. Robert agreed.

"Thanks. I'm going to buzz Corey," Chad said as he put Robert on hold.

Robert thought he might be overworking his imagination and began to feel foolish. In a three-way phone conversation, Corey asked questions throughout Robert's reiteration of his story, silence hanging heavy at the end of the give and take interrogation.

"Chad? Are you still there?" Robert asked, "I know this sounds like some kind of college prank, but I'm worried for myself. Just tell me I've lost my mind and I'll go on my way."

"No, Robert, I'm afraid this is serious," Corey answered. "We've had a situation occur in the last few days which verifies your information. I'm sure you heard and probably felt the explosions on Friday? Well, that ties in with what you're telling me. I've got an idea how we can begin to resolve this problem, but you'll have to work with us. Have you got someone willing able to maintain silence while we work on a plan I'm developing?" Corey asked.

"I have a cousin, living in Falls Church, I can trust, who would probably get a kick out of helping," Robert said.

"All right. Tell your client you've found someone who'll carry out his request. The party wants a meeting as soon as possible. We'll mic you two as well as have officers discreetly parked nearby. We don't want to ruin our chance to put this guy away. I don't need someone in my town trying to eliminate the townsfolk. Keep in mind, you will be in the line of fire, so the decision is yours to make," Corey said.

Robert thought for a moment. "I'll call my cousin."

"Good. Meet us here in my office at three o'clock. Call first and I'll meet you at the employee entrance in the back. At that time, we'll wire you for the meeting. And Robert?"

"Yes?"

"Thank you for your help," Corey said.

"Don't thank me yet. Once you put this guy behind bars then thank me," Robert answered.

~ * ~

Diane turned the storyboard sideway then upside down and finally around to its original position. She was having a difficult time concentrating. She kept feeling Justin's hand on her breast and the electric sensation it shot through her body. *I'm not sure how long I want to hold out. I'm beginning to feel alive again. Darn his handsome hide. I wonder if he feels the same way?* She put the work down and leaned back in her chair. *Why should I stop this feeling? I'm old enough to know better and still young enough to want to feel alive and this man is definitely making me feel alive! Damn you, Justin Anderson. Life was easy until you showed up and complicated things.* Diane shook her head. *I need to get back to work.*

She moved the storyboard in front of her and shuttled Justin to the back of her mind—for the moment.

~ * ~

Robert hung up the phone and sucked in a deep breath. *Why did this happen to me? I've worked so hard to avoid the stereotypes and* still *people won't believe all Italians aren't Mafia.* He picked up the phone and called his cousin. Anthony answered on the second ring. Robert quickly explained his predicament. Anthony's laughter took him off guard.

"Sure, I'll do it. Wouldn't Grandma have a fit if she knew after all her efforts to make sure we got an education, spoke with no accent and looked American, we're going to be acting exactly the way she didn't want us to?"

"You're right. She'd take that huge butcher knife she used to cook with and personally dismember us. That's why you can't say anything to anyone until this guy has been locked away. I don't want *anything* to go wrong before he's in jail," Robert warned his cousin. "Meet me at Sallianne's Coffee shop on the north side of the town square in Oakdale at two forty-five today. We'll be fitted with miniature voice-activated microphones to record the meeting on tape. With luck, that will provide enough evidence to take this guy off the street. They'll use double wiring—one backup in case the other has problems."

At two thirty, Robert drove his car to the police station, parked a block away on a residential street and casually walked the distance to the coffee shop.

I hope I'm doing the right thing. I don't know what I'll do if I can't be a broker. If this is some kind of joke, I know Thomas Manning will guarantee I don't have a future around here or anywhere else. He strolled into the coffee shop past his cousin sitting at the counter.

"Robert?"

Robert turned and looked intently at the dark-haired young man who had spoken his name.

"Anthony? My God, I didn't recognize you. Although, I don't know why, you look just like our fathers." The last time Robert had seen Anthony he was skinny, awkward and on his way to college. Not too many years past puberty. The person in front of him was a solidly built confidant man.

"Yeah, isn't it awful?" Anthony grinned.

"I need to call the detective handling this and let him know we've arrived. Then we can slip out the door to the alley and go the back way to the police station. He'll let us in."

Robert had a brief conversation on his phone and shaking his cousin's hand, walked out the café door and across the street. Anthony put three bills on the counter for the coffee he drank and left the shop to follow.

They were met by Chad and Corey at the employee entrance and led inside. Robert and Anthony were each fitted with a voice-activated recorder in a shoulder holster, creating a suggestive bulge beneath their expensive Italian suits. The wire was gingerly taped to their woolly chests and the miniature microphone, which resembled a gold tie tack, was worn on their silk ties. The meeting had been set for six o'clock that evening at the Pinnacle Restaurant in Billington. Robert and Anthony agreed the moment the meeting was over they'd return to the police station and turn over the equipment. A police clerk would transcribe the recorded meeting and the pair would sign the typed statements. If all went well, Chad and Corey planned to serve a warrant on the client before the end of the weekend.

"Well, I guess we must be Tony and Bobby now, huh?" Robert joked.

"You gotta a problem with dat?" Anthony smirked.

Robert and Anthony drove to Robert's house to pass the time until their evening meeting.

Thirty

Thomas thought his wife would never leave. She must've guessed he had plans to see Ashlee tonight because she hovered around his study for the next three hours. Once she'd finally packed the last suitcase in the car and headed out the driveway, he dashed upstairs and quickly changed into the new suit he'd bought on his last trip to Washington, D.C. He'd been sensing a lagging interest on Ashlee's side of the relationship, so he'd spent a great deal of money on a tailored Armani suit.

He modeled the designer suit in the bedroom mirror. *I look good for a man my age.* He didn't always exercise like he should but walked at least two miles a day. Arlene had quit caring about her weight as her size eighteen body witnessed.

Thomas called and confirmed the reservation at the restaurant. He decided to drive the black Jaguar. Tonight, he was feeling powerful. He cruised to the restaurant and parked in the back portion of the lot. While he waited, he listened to his favorite collection of Sinatra songs on the CD player.

Fifteen minutes later, the Toyota pulled up next to his car.

Ashlee must be excited. She's never been this early. A warming sensation started in the pit of his stomach and began to spread to his crotch. He climbed out of the Jaguar and opened Ashlee's door. As she emerged from her vehicle, Thomas let out a lusty groan. "My God, you look delicious," he said.

"You like it?" Ashlee asked. She could tell by his uncomfortable stance she'd made the impression she wanted.

"Oh, yeah. I just hope the surprise pleases you—a lot," he said.

Ashlee reached out a manicured finger down the front of his new suit.

"Well, aren't you the picture of fashion. This is Armani, isn't it? Even in this light, I can tell you look scrumptious, good enough to eat. Guess I'll just have to do something about that after dinner, now won't I?" Ashlee said.

A champagne-colored Lexus drove slowly past the two standing next to the Jaguar and parked a few spaces away. Recognizing Robert's Lexus, Thomas tried to make out the figures in the car through the haze of dusky twilight. All he could see were two silhouettes. His bravado didn't extend to approaching the car with unknown factors involved.

Robert exited and approached the couple.

"Mr. Manning? This meeting was to be private," Robert growled.

"The young lady is a trusted confidante and won't cause any problems," he said.

"I'll need to talk to my partner. Stay here for a moment." Robert headed back to the car. He slid behind the wheel and looked at Anthony.

"We got a problem."

"What?"

"He's got a woman with him. If he has any sense at all, he won't say anything and we'll have wasted our time. He's one of the most influential lawyers in this county, Anthony. You can't afford to lock horns with this guy. If you want to practice law and this goes down bad, he'll have you disbarred before you can try one case. You still want to do this?" Robert looked at Anthony.

"Yeah, the fact he's a lawyer who thinks he's above the law and won't get caught makes me angry. Hell, Robert, I can always practice law on the West Coast. California sunshine sounds pretty good," Anthony smiled at his cousin.

"All right, let's do this."

Robert got out of the car and motioned for the couple to approach. He opened the rear car door for Ashlee as Anthony moved to the back, leaving the front seat available for Thomas to occupy.

"Mr. Manning, let me introduce—Tony. He's the best in his field. Tony, Mr. Manning and…?"

"Let's just say my friend," he replied.

Tony grunted. Somewhere he'd found a toothpick, which was sticking out of the left side of this mouth. Robert turned and rolled his eyes.

"Tony," Thomas began hesitantly, "I need to have a situation handled."

"Handled. Like what handled?" Anthony pulled the toothpick out of his mouth as he answered.

Thomas stammered, "Well, you know, rubbed out, taken care of, wearing cement shoes, whatever you guys say."

Robert glanced in the rear view mirror at Anthony. He didn't know whether to burst out laughing or punch his employer.

"Look, Mr. Manning. Ya jus' asked me ta do tree differ'nt tings to da same person. Ya gotta make up ya mind. What exactly do ya want done? And to who? Evryting costses differ'nt. Ya catch my drift?" Anthony looked directly in Thomas's face. His skin crawled at the deadness he encountered in the other man's eyes.

"Tony, there's a man named Justin Anderson who's the contractor on the hotel I'm having built just outside of town. He's ripping me off. I want him killed and his body disposed of before Monday morning. I want everyone to know they can't rip off Thomas Manning Sr. The basement parking garage of my hotel is in the process of being completed. There's a lot of soft dirt. When they get back to work Monday or Tuesday morning, they'll be pouring concrete into the space. No one would find a body for a very long time. Clear enough?" he asked.

"Yeah, I got dat," Anthony answered, "That'll cost ya twenty grand. Half now, and half when it's done. Ya try to rip me off and I'll trow in a second body for free. Clear?"

Anthony gave his best menacing look. The man nodded and put his hand in his inside pocket.

Anthony jumped and shoved his hand inside his own jacket.

Thomas pulled his hand from his pocket clutching a folded manila envelope. He placed his right hand on the back of the seat and held the envelope up with his left hand where Anthony could see.

"Easy, man. Just going for the money. Okay?"

Anthony grunted.

He handed the envelope to Robert, who quickly counted the money inside. He nodded to Anthony and shook Thomas's hand. The meeting was finished.

Thomas climbed out of the car and opened Ashlee's door, offering his hand and lifting her out of the vehicle. As they crunched through the gravel, he provided his arm for support through the restaurant parking lot to the front door. The maître d' confirmed their reservations and escorted the couple to the private dining area.

"So what do you think, sugar?" he asked Ashlee when they'd been seated at their table.

"Oh, Thomas. That's the best present anyone's ever given me!" Ashlee's eyes danced with delight. "I'm so hot I'm surprised the curtains aren't on fire. Do we really have to eat?"

He wanted to draw out the pleasure as long as he could. It wasn't often Ashlee was this enthused, and he was determined to make the pleasure last.

"Well, sugar, let's eat a little something to keep up our energy. It's going to be a long, hot night," Thomas said with a wink.

Thirty-one

Ashlee looked at him with renewed interest. He reminded her of the man she'd fallen in love with all those years ago. What he'd done tonight was dangerous and daring.

"Babykins?"

"Hmmm?"

"I'm not really hungry." Ashlee's lips were in a full pout.

"How about dinner to go?" Thomas asked. Ashlee moved herself so she was sitting next to him. She hadn't sat next to him in so long he'd forgotten the last time. She was stroking his leg and making guttural purring sounds.

She looked at him—really looked at him. He was still handsome. The chiseled chin had acquired a fatty layer and the athletic body had acquired the sit-at-a-desk look. The once sandy brown hair was now silver but the green eyes still sparkled. The difference was, now Thomas had more power and money. Traits Ashlee found irresistible. She burned with an unbridled lust she hadn't felt for him in years. She wanted to act on her desire immediately.

He picked up the private phone from the wall.

"Hello, Randall? Yes. Can you make those orders to go? If you get them here in less than ten minutes, there is an extra fifty bucks for you."

She smiled coyly as she ran her hand up the inside of his leg. He knew if he didn't grab this moment of passion, like Haley's comet, it wouldn't appear again anytime soon.

"Why don't you bring the food and meet me at the cabin? I want to

157

get a fire going and pick up a little. Okay?" Thomas leaned down to kiss Ashlee on the forehead. She wrapped her arms around him and as he straightened, he pulled her up with him. She pressed her voluptuous body against his and kissed him deeply.

"I don't know if I can wait," she whispered.

He groaned as he experienced stirrings. "Try."

"If I have to." She pulled herself away and slowly ran her tongue around her lips to wet them. She knew this drove him crazy.

"I'll see you there." He moved away quickly, saving his dignity.

Ashlee blew him a kiss as he walked out of the private dining room. Lighting a cigarette, she waited for the meal to be brought to her. She remembered the first time she saw Thomas Manning, Sr.

~ * ~

The year between her junior and senior year at college, her mother had the only law firm in town. At that time it was named Manning and Holt.

Ashlee worked four hours a day, five days a week. Her job was to do filing, light typing, and anything else the office manager needed. Ashlee hated working. She was required to dress and act professionally while her friends were playing tennis and swimming. Her mom told her she wouldn't get any new clothes for school if she didn't earn the money. So Ashlee worked and complained, until the first time she met Thomas.

She'd heard rumors he was good looking and athletic but hadn't seen him because during the summer, business income from the big business accounts was slower than from private clients. So, Thomas Sr. came in only occasionally to catch up on the day-to-day happenings with his office manager.

The day she finally met Thomas was a Wednesday. Ashlee had chosen to wear the ice blue suit her aunt had given her, which set off her ice blue eyes. She'd worn her waist length dark brown hair in a loose ponytail tied at the base of her neck. She was bent over the bottom file in Mr. Manning's private office re-filing old cases.

"Well, hello, there."

Ashlee quickly stood up and turned to encounter the ruggedly handsome face of her employer. His blonde streaked sandy brown hair and green eyes set off the tan he sported supporting the talk Ashlee had heard of his playing a lot of golf.

"Uh, uh, hi. I'm Ashlee Cline. I'm the new file clerk," Ashlee stuttered and felt her cheeks starting to color. She was usually confident. Why did this man cause her palms to sweat and brain to deactivate?

"Hi. I'm Thomas Manning, Sr. Nice to meet you Ashlee Cline. I heard we'd hired summer help. No one said how attractive you were, or I would've made it into the office much sooner." He smiled revealing perfect white teeth. His aftershave was heady and impressed Ashlee immediately. He smelled like a man should smell. Great!

"I'll be done here in a minute then I'll be out of your way, Mr. Manning." Ashlee held up one more file.

Thomas frowned slightly. He took the file from her hands and looked at the label.

"Actually, Miss Cline, this is the file I need. Thank you. And please, my name is Thomas. Mr. Manning is my father. I'm going to take this outside to the patio so I can smoke my cigar."

Thomas moved to a square cherry wood box on his desk and removed a cellophane wrapped cigar. He rolled it between his fingers then removed the wrapping and repeated the action. He drew the cigar under his perfect straight nose, inhaling the essence of the tobacco leaves. Ashlee tried to quiet the butterflies in her stomach. This man was so sexy. Sticking the cigar into his mouth, he continued.

"I own the company and, come to think of it, I own the building, but if I lit this thing inside, Pam would fly in here with her air freshener and try to choke us to death," he said. "It was nice to meet you, Miss Cline. I'm sure we'll be seeing more of each other." He disappeared out the door.

Ashlee let out a long sigh as she leaned against the file cabinet. The rumors had proven true. Thomas Manning was incredibly handsome and athletic looking. She imagined his body pressed against her.

Pam, the office manager, rushed into the office, shattering her daydreaming.

"Well, I can tell by the expression on your face you've met the boss. Let me warn you, Miss Cline, stay away from that man. He can be overly friendly. He has a wife and four kids, one of whom, I believe, is just about your age. If I find out you've been fooling around with Mr. Manning, I'll fire you. Do you understand?"

Pam had taken on a tone Ashlee recognized from her own mother. She acted like the acquiescent child and nodded agreement finishing up her work for the day. If Pam thought she was going to walk away from a man like Thomas Manning, Pam was crazy. Ashlee did not deal well with being told she could not do something. Maybe Pam had been involved with the boss, got dumped and what Ashlee was hearing was jealousy. Oh, well, she'd get over it.

Ashlee began getting up earlier and planning what she would wear each day. She thought he was coming into the office more now, but he'd mentioned business had picked up unusually early this year. Ashlee and Thomas wound up in his office alone a month after their first meeting.

"Hello, Ashlee, how are you today?"

"I'm fine, Mr. Mann…I'm sorry, Thomas. How are you?" Ashlee answered.

"I'm just great. It's almost your quitting time. How about having lunch with me?" he asked.

Ashlee blushed and lowered her gaze to the ground.

"Oh, I see. Pam's been talking to you, hasn't she? Well, in my own defense," he smiled at his joke, "there's nothing wrong with the boss taking a new employee to lunch to welcome them to the company, is there?"

Ashlee smiled slowly. She couldn't afford to lose this job, but she wanted to be near him away from the office.

"Well, all right. But I can't be seen with you. Pam said she'd fire me."

Thomas's face began to turn crimson.

"Ashlee, please wait for me outside. I have one small piece of business before we go to lunch. Thanks, hon."

Ashlee picked up her purse at the front desk. Pam was glaring at her.

"I told you if you pursued Mr. Manning, I'd fire you. Guess you don't really want this job, do you?" Pam opened her mouth to say something else when the intercom buzzed.

Answering affirmatively, she went into Thomas' office. Ashlee waited as he'd asked her to do. Moments later, Ashlee witnessed Pam emerge from Thomas's office dour faced. She snatched her purse from the desk and stomped out the back door. Thomas soon appeared, equally grim faced. He indicated for Ashlee to follow him. They headed to a red Mustang convertible. He opened the passenger door for Ashlee. Upon slipping into the driver's seat, he picked up the car phone, making reservations at a restaurant outside of town. They drove in silence for ten minutes before Thomas spoke.

"I'm sorry Pam felt she had the right to dictate your actions toward me.

"She does have the right to tell you how to act in our office setting, but not how you can or cannot act toward me. I reminded her of who signs her checks, and if she wishes to continue having a check, she'll mind her own business. I gave her the rest of the day off to think about it."

He slumped into his seat. "We sure don't set a good example for learning to work in the real world, do we?"

Ashlee started laughing. He looked puzzled by her reaction.

"What's so funny?"

"Mr. Man…Thomas, I grew up very quickly. I've been in the real world since I was thirteen and my father mistook me for his wife. When my mother found out, she kicked him out without thinking about where we were going to get money to eat. Her father had made a name for himself, not money. So, we went from being 'in the circle' to waiting on the circle. I didn't take this job for the experience but for the money. You do pay well."

Thomas shook his head. He'd never met such a young person with such an old soul. He'd wondered what had happened to Michael Cline but not enough to ask anyone. He viewed Ashlee through new eyes. He shifted in the driver's seat. She was raising his blood pressure just sitting next to him. He'd have to tread very carefully. He couldn't afford to lose his law practice to lust.

Thirty-two

Ashlee and Thomas were soon sharing meals once or twice a week. She'd get off at noon and walk two or three blocks in the direction of her home. At a designated corner, he would pick her up and they'd go to the Pinnacle for long lunches. During one of these noon breaks, they discovered a mutual love of tennis. Not long after, they began playing on Saturdays. Summer flew by and before either of them was ready, school had started. Ashlee was finishing her senior year. Thomas offered her the option of working after school and on Saturdays if she wanted. She accepted...anything to stay close to him.

One month after school began Ashlee's perfect world nearly ended. It was a Friday and Pam had the afternoon off. Ashlee was sitting at the front desk answering phones and typing when she heard a ruckus in the conference room. Going to investigate, she observed a pudgy, bleached blonde in designer clothes wagging her finger at Thomas.

"Is everything all right, Mr. Manning?" Ashlee asked.

"Everything is just fine, Ashlee, thank you," he replied stiffly.

"Well, Thomas, aren't you going to introduce me? I wondered what was keeping you at the office so much lately. Now, I can see. Molly didn't tell me her daughter was so beautiful. Maybe we need to see if we can help her get a job at the Piggly Wiggly. I'm sure a girl her age would prefer to be closer to friends her age instead of around stuffy old people like us," Thomas's wife said.

"Arlene, this is Ashlee. Ashlee, this is my wife, Arlene Manning, who is just leaving for Washington, D.C. to visit her oldest sister. Please have a safe trip, dear, and don't worry about the money. Spend as much as you like."

"Count on it, Thomas Manning. If you think you've heard the end of this, you're wrong. I won't lie and say it was a pleasure to meet you, Miss Cline. Be warned, I'll be watching you like a hawk." Arlene Manning clomped out of the office.

Ashlee, crossing her arms, asked Thomas, "What was that about?"

"I'm sorry, hon, but Arlene sees every female as being in competition for my affection. You have the misfortune of being extremely beautiful. I apologize for her," he sounded weary.

"You think I'm beautiful?" Ashlee asked.

"Of course," he answered.

This can't be all bad; just puts me one step closer to my goal.

Thomas's wife began dropping in often. Ashlee always treated her with respect. She discovered from her mother Arlene had come up with the idea to give Ashlee the job at the law firm. The elder Mrs. Cline, plain looking and pleasant, fostered the hope for Mrs. Manning that Ashlee would resemble her. When she'd seen how beautiful the young woman was, Arlene's confidence was shaken.

Ashlee launched a campaign to win Arlene's trust. Within two months, Mrs. Manning was coming in as often to talk with Ashlee as to check up on Thomas. Ashlee's Valentine's Day present to him was the announcement she was pregnant and he was responsible. He told her there was nothing he could do to help, but he'd pay for an abortion. She informed him she didn't believe in abortion, and if he didn't come up with a better solution, she'd go to Arlene and confide how he'd taken advantage of her. Thomas found himself in a difficult position. Ashlee made him feel alive after many years of sexless marital boredom, but he enjoyed the position and standing in the community he'd acquired because of his marriage to Arlene. He needed a compromise.

"I'll support you if you keep secret my identity as the baby's father," Thomas chewed his lower lip and paced the floor of his office.

"That works great for you but what's in it for me? I lose my figure and my social life. Why don't I just put this baby up for adoption?"

Ashlee watched her lover pace the length of his office floor.

"No! I may not want you to admit I'm the father, but if you have this baby, I want to see this child and have a say in its life." He stopped abruptly in front of Ashlee's chair. His eyes lit up and the corners of his mouth began to curve upward. He snapped his fingers.

"I have it. This Friday night, Arlene is giving a dinner party for Tom and his football buddies before their big game on Saturday. Tom's best friend, Justin Anderson, will be there. I know he'll find you attractive. All you need to do is work your charms on him, and after a short while, you can probably convince him he's the father of your baby. Knowing Justin, he'll marry you. You and I will continue our relationship in secret, and you'll be an accepted member of the Oakdale society. Justin's family did leave him money."

"Oh, so I'm supposed to meet this young man and seduce him. I'll then convince him the baby I'm carrying is his, and magically he'll marry me? Then you expect to continue our rendezvouses on a regular basis? You still haven't told me what's in it for me." Ashlee crossed her arms.

Thomas knelt in front of her chair. "You're my life. You helped me recall what it's like to breathe and dream again when you came into my world. What do you want?"

"Money, Thomas, money. Set up a bank account in Billington I can get into anytime I want. Make sure the balance has lots of zero's behind it. That will help guarantee my silence."

He rose to his feet, pulling Ashlee up and embraced her. "You got it, sugar." He kissed down the side of her soft, supple neck.

"I'll meet this young man, but if the account is not open by Monday afternoon with the bank book in my hot little hands, Arlene learns about our baby Monday night. Clear?" Ashlee moaned as he kissed the soft depression at the base of her throat. His hand snaked around the front of her waist and moved to cup her breast.

"Clear. That's what I love about you, darling. No crap." His mouth covered hers as his tongue probed her warmth, fingers working to unbutton her blouse. Slipping inside the crisp material, he moved her bra up and cupped her bare breast in his palm. Ashlee pushed into his hand, her breaths becoming jagged with her stirring passion. He moved his thumb back and forth across her nipple until it hardened. She moaned and pushed her hips to his. He continued to kiss a trail down her neck to her nipple, sucking the pinkish brown bud into his mouth, flicking the tip with his tongue.

"Not here," Ashlee moaned.

Thomas freed his mouth for a moment, "You want me to stop?"

He pulled on her nipple with his warm mouth, lowering her to the floor.

"Yes, I mean no," Ashlee arched her back, pushing her breast deeper into his hungry mouth. "Someone could come in and catch us."

He pulled his mouth from her breast with a slurping pop sound. "I know. Don't you love it? Tell me if you want me to stop."

Ashlee pulled his mouth to her breast and popped her tingling nipple back into its warmth.

"NO. I love the danger." She moaned in ecstasy as he sucked hard on her stiff nub.

He unbuttoned and unzipped her jeans, gently lifting her hips and removing her pants. He traced her earlobes with his tongue while she unbuttoned and freed him from his wool slacks and jockey shorts. Ashlee's hand moved up and down his hardened member. She cooed and purred as his hands fondled her body and she lovingly stroked him. Moving slowly, he worked his way to her parted legs. He positioned himself between them. His aching member would wait no more and he entered her slowly, one centimeter at a time. They moved together for an eternity and when his body demanded, they climaxed on his Persian carpet.

Thomas cradled Ashlee's tanned body in his arms as he stroked her velvety skin.

"Do we have a deal?" he asked.

"Sure, why not?" Ashlee said.

They dressed and Ashlee slipped out the door to the ladies' room. She returned to gather her purse on her way home.

"I just got off the phone with my wife. Arlene wasn't totally thrilled with you coming to dinner Friday, but when I suggested we introduce you to Justin, her attitude changed. You are officially invited to the house Friday evening at six-thirty." He had taken a cigar from his humidor and was rolling in between his fingers.

"I guess I'll pencil it in on my calendar. See you there, love," Ashlee leaned over his chair and kissed him. He slipped his hand into her blouse and caressed her nipple with his fingers.

"Can't. Have to go buy the perfect dress for Friday," Ashlee reached down and squeezed his member, causing him to groan with anticipation.

"Think about next time." She turned and disappeared out the door.

That woman-child will get me into trouble yet. He stood up and headed to the back door. He needed a smoke.

Friday evening, Ashlee arrived in a peach colored, organza dress that set off her tan and turned the head of every man at the party.

Thomas pulled Justin away from his football conversation with Tom, Jr.

"Listen, I have someone I want you to meet. I know you boys have a big game next week, but I think you can take time to meet a pretty lady, don't you?"

"Mr. Manning, we need to talk strategy. Tom is going to start as the quarterback on Saturday and I'm his receiver. We need to go over all the plays until we have them set. If we win, we'll have a chance at a bowl game," Justin explained.

"Justin, I know you're right, but if you don't take some time for yourself, you'll wind up a shriveled old man. Take a break. Ah, here we are," he said.

Standing next to the fireplace in the family room, stood the most beautiful woman Justin had ever seen. Her waist-length dark hair undulated sinuously to her tiny buttocks, and when she turned to look at him, the clarity of her ice-blue eyes and the faint aroma of roses hooked him. His heart began to pound wildly.

"Justin," Thomas Manning began. "I'd like to introduce Ashlee Cline. Ashlee, this young man is like my second son, Justin Anderson.

You both are seniors in college, I'm sure there are things you can talk about. Ashlee, Justin is on the football team with my Tom at Old Dominion. That should help you get started. Feel free to fill your glasses at the bar, kids. I need to circulate among my other guests." Thomas was quickly absorbed into the milling crowd.

The slender tiny brunette turned her full attention to Justin. "You play football for Old Dominion?" Her blue eyes held him.

"Uh, yeah. I'm not the quarterback, that's Tom, but I'm his receiver. We've been a team since high school. Mr. Manning said you go to college too. Where?" Justin tried to find a way to stand casually. He was beginning to perspire.

"Oh, I just go to State," Ashlee moved closer to him and looked into his eyes. "Did you go to Oakdale High?"

"Yeah. Did you? I don't remember you."

"Well, probably not. I was pretty unremarkable in high school. I didn't really blossom until the year after I graduated." Ashlee moved as close to Justin as she could. She had been observing Thomas watching her over Justin's shoulder. *I'll fix him.* "Listen, Justin, why don't we go up to the bar and get a soda?"

"Great idea," Justin was relieved to have an excuse to move away from the little firecracker. She made his heart palpitate and brought his member to attention. He was amazed she was alone.

To irritate Thomas, Ashlee played up to Justin all evening. By the end of the party, most of the guests were discussing the new couple. Thomas silently fumed and Arlene glowed with delight. Soon, Ashlee and Justin were dating exclusively. When Ashlee realized Thomas was trying to pull away, she concluded to keep him , she needed to be unattainable.

Two months after they first met, Ashlee asked Justin to come pick her up after work. She knew he didn't have classes on Tuesday and would be able to make it to Oakdale from the university.

Justin walked into the law offices around five p.m.

"Hi, Pam."

"Hi, Justin. Come to pick up Ashlee?"

"Yeah. Guess we've got big plans, so I'm told."

When Ashlee breezed through the reception office, she slid her arm through Justin's and directed him out to his car.

"What's this all about?" he asked.

"Let's go to the park by the river," Ashlee said.

Once they parked, Ashlee turned to Justin, "You know I've fallen in love with you?"

He pulled her to him and wrapped his arms around her.

"And I love you, too. But what was so important you needed me to come over from school?" His lips brushed against her forehead.

"I've just found out I'm pregnant, Justin. I know you're the father because you're the only man I've been with. I'll understand if you don't want to have anything to do with me," Ashlee turned her face to Justin. Her large eyes were brimming with tears, her lip quivered slightly.

"Ashlee, that's wonderful. It's a little sooner than I had planned, but it's absolutely fantastic. Marry me. I want us to be together so we can raise our baby as a family," Justin kissed the corners of Ashlee's eyes.

"Are you sure?" she asked.

"Of course. How soon can we get a license?"

Ashlee couldn't believe how easy Justin was to manipulate. She'd show Thomas. Now if he wanted to play, he'd have to play by her rules. Before the end of the school year, Ashlee Cline became Ashlee Anderson.

Thirty-three

Justin dialed Diane's office number and got a busy signal. He tried again and got a busy signal again. After the note he removed from the car's windshield, he wasn't comfortable with Diane working alone. He hadn't wanted to leave, but her insistence he continue to his job was firm. *Come on, come on, somebody answer!* On the third try he found himself talking to Verna.

"Wallace Advertising Agency. This is Verna. The offices are closed for the weekend, may I take a message?"

"Verna?"

"Sir?"

"Verna, it's Justin Anderson."

Oh, Justin, how are you?"

"I'm fine. Where's Diane?"

"She forgot to switch the phones over last night. I guess she's at the office 'cause she switched over to us about an hour ago. I can go over there, hon, if it's an emergency," Verna offered.

"No, that's okay. I'll talk to her later."

"Well, if you change your mind, you have our number. Bye." The line went dead.

Justin felt his frustration rise. He smacked the desk with his hand. He could jump in the car and go over there, but if nothing was wrong, Diane would think he was an idiot. He'd just wait; he'd have to. If this overwhelming feeling of dread didn't dissipate by lunchtime, he'd just go and check things out.

Justin leaned back in his chair and stared at the paperwork threatening to avalanche across his desk. He'd accepted the need to get busy but didn't feel the motivation. The incident in front of Diane's office this morning shook him more than he'd wanted her to know. The handwriting on the note was Ashlee's. He was puzzled why she would threaten him. She lived in his family's home by their own agreement, and he paid his child support willingly and on time. She was tyrannical about his contact with his daughter, allowing visits solely on her terms. *What more can Ashlee possibly want? Could she have found out about the changes in the will? Tom, his law clerk, and I are the only ones supposed to know what they are. Why is it, when I've just begun to feel comfortable and start caring for someone, Ashlee seems to find out and try to ruin it? This time, I won't give up my happiness without a fight.*

Justin sat assessing the morning's events. He'd found a new battery for his cell phone but still jumped when it rang. "Hello?"

"Hey, Justin. It's Ed. I'm going to the hospital to see the guys. You want to tag along?".

"Great. I've been sitting at this desk pushing this mountain of paperwork from one side to the other and not accomplishing a thing. I need a good excuse to escape. I'll meet you there in—half an hour? Thanks, Ed." Justin restacked the pile of papers and dumped them into his In-box. He'd finish them later. He locked the construction trailer office and drove to the hospital.

Ed waved from the covered front entry as Justin maneuvered the rental car into a parking space.

"Thanks for reminding me to visit the guys, Ed. If Belinda ever gets sick, I know who I can call to be my secretary."

"You're welcome, but don't bother calling me if Belinda gets sick. You know as well as I do she'll be in the office if she has only two days to live," Ed grinned at his friend.

"Yeah, you're right. If this company ever gets back on its feet, I'll have to do something about that. She's one of a kind," Justin said.

"Got that right," Ed said.

The two men entered Lee County Teaching Hospital, the largest medical facility within the surrounding fifty miles. Working in conjunction with the community college, the hospital helped provide a training ground for the Licensed Practical Nurse program at the college. Justin and Ed checked in at the reception desk.

"Excuse me?" Justin addressed the young brunette in a pink-striped jumper and white blouse.

She looked up from her magazine, "Yes?"

"Can you tell me the room numbers of the injured workers from Anderson Construction?" he asked.

"Sure, what are their names?" She pulled the computer keyboard toward her.

Justin recoiled. *I haven't even asked Ed which of the guys were injured.* His shoulders sagged as he blew out an exasperated breath. *How can I be so selfish? I've been thinking only about Diane and myself.*

Ed cleared his throat and leaned slightly over the counter. The young lady looked in his direction, her fingers poised over the keyboard. Ed looked skyward counting on his fingers as he recited, "There's Carl Bernard, Dean Huntington, Artie Young and who am I missing—oh yeah, the twins, Denny and Lenny Devlin."

He pulled a small notebook and a pen from his shirt pocket.

"Let's see here. It looks like they're all on the fourth floor. Mr. Bernard and Mr. Young are in room Four-twelve; Mr. Huntington is in room Four-fourteen and Denny and Lenny Devlin are in room four-sixteen. Go to the elevator over there," she pointed to gray doors marked ELEVATOR in bright orange facing the reception desk, "and go up to the fourth floor. When you get off the elevator, take a left. The rooms will be halfway down the hall," she said. She pushed the computer keyboard back to its resting position and opened her magazine to resume reading.

"Thank you," Ed replied as he took Justin's arm and herded him in the direction of the elevator.

"Would you stop frowning?" Ed spoke as they rode up to the fourth floor, "The last thing these guys need to see is the owner of the company frowning. They're probably worried enough as it is."

Ed and Justin spent a couple of hours visiting their injured crew. The ride down in the elevator found the two men sharing silence all the way out to the entrance.

Standing under the archway of the hospital, Ed lit a cigarette.

"Those things will kill you," Justin said.

"Yeah, I know. Belinda's been nagging me to quit for as long as I can remember. Just haven't gotten around to it. Hey, Justin, what's up with the hotel? Are we still working?"

"I don't know, Ed. I haven't heard anything, and I can't afford to continue without some sort of indication where this is heading. I hate to think anyone might be out of work, but unless I hear from the investor or his broker before Tuesday, I have to figure the project is a loss and close the site down," Justin said.

Ed groaned.

"I know. What other choice do I have? I don't have many friends who can invest fifty to a hundred million in a hotel. Do you?"

"No. You won't mind if I start looking for other work, will you?" Ed asked. The two men started walking toward Justin's rental car.

"Naw. Let the guys know I'll pay them through Friday and I'll make sure these guys," Justin nodded his head toward the hospital, "will be covered by the company's insurance if workman's compensation doesn't cover them. You guys got families to feed and I understand. I wish things could be different, but this is the real world. I'll talk to you later," Justin unlocked the car's door.

"Yeah, see you later," Ed said.

The men shook hands and Ed ambled toward his pickup truck.

Justin dropped into the seat and sat with his hands clutching the steering wheel. He was feeling restless and unsettled. Working was pointless. Unless the investor contacted him, the project was done. He didn't have the money to continue until a backer could be found. Justin pulled his cell phone out and called Diane's office number again.

"Wallace Advertising. The offices are currently closed. May I take a message?" Verna's voice answered.

"Verna? This is Justin Anderson. Diane still has the service on?"

"Yeah, she hasn't called us back and said she wanted to answer the phones herself. You want me to put you through, hon?" she asked.

"No, I'll get ahold of her later. Thanks."

He started the car, fighting the urge to speed to Diane's office. Parking out front, he sat and surveyed the street and surrounding buildings. Nothing had changed. The black Corvette was parked in the same spot. He hopped from the car and pounded on the office door. Minutes that stretched like hours of Justin's frantic pounding on the front door brought Diane peeking through the blinds covering the window next to the door.

"Justin? What are you doing here?" she asked.

"Why is your service taking your calls? I thought we agreed to answer our phones?" Justin asked.

Diane ushered him into the office. He turned and swept her into his arms, kissing her hungrily.

"Whoa!" she gasped for breathe pushing him away. "To answer your question, after you left I got an unsettling phone call. The phone rang and a woman's voice told me if I wanted to see my next birthday, I needed to stay away from you. I had too much work waiting for me to play games with an old girlfriend of yours, so I transferred the phones to the service and figured if she wanted to waste her time talking with Verna and Elsie, she was welcome."

Justin dropped into the nearest chair. His face had drained to an ashen gray tone.

"What?" Diane asked.

"I recognized the writing on the note this morning as my ex-wife's. She can be devious and underhanded, but I didn't think she'd resort to crank calls and stalking. I'm sorry you've been caught in the middle. I wouldn't put it past her to follow you home. I don't want you or Princess harmed in any way." Justin slumped into the chair.

"Listen here, Mister," Diane started hotly, "I can take care of myself. Your ex-wife has no clue what I can do. I won't be threatened in my own office in a town where I chose to live. I can start bringing Princess to work with me. Trust me; she thinks that's where she should be anyway."

Justin smiled at Diane's brave front. He knew what Ashlee was capable of doing.

"I care for you more than I thought I would," Diane blushed at the admission. "I want to pursue this friendship. So my dog and I will take a chance. We have no plans to abandon a new friend. All right?"

Justin got up from the chair and embraced Diane. "Yes, that's fine with me. What say we have a quiet evening in tonight? Maybe, pizza, wine and videos?" he asked.

"I thought you were working. What happened?" she asked.

Justin's smile evaporated and a furrow appeared on his handsome forehead. Diane grasped his hand in hers and led him through the desks to her office where she motioned for him to occupy one of the comfortable chairs in the corner grouping. She sat next to him in a matching chair.

"Okay, tell me what's happening."

Justin settled himself into the chair.

"I drove to the office and stared at the paperwork on my desk. I was sorting things into piles when Ed called. He suggested we go visit the guys in the hospital. You know what, Diane? I had completely forgotten about the guys. I met him and we spent a couple of hours visiting with them and their families. As we were riding down in the elevator, the realization hit me really hard. I'm responsible for the livelihoods of fifty families in this town. Unless I hear from the investor or his broker by Monday, my project's finished. I don't have enough money to finance a fifty million dollar hotel. All my guys will be out of work unless the union can locate them other jobs. I have no idea where I'm going to find more work for myself. The insurance will cover the damaged equipment, but that doesn't help my guys very much."

The longer Justin talked the further down in the chair he slumped. When he finished, he sat staring at the floor. Diane didn't know what to say that would help relieve his worry. The shrill ringing of her cell phone broke the silence of the moment.

"Hello? Oh, hi, Liz. I'm fine. Yes, I have the campaign ready to go. I think you're going to love what I've created. What? Sure. Give us five minutes. Okay? See you."

Diane turned to Justin, a smile playing on her lips.

"What are you up to, Ms. Wallace?" he asked.

"I may have a solution to this problem. But you need to trust me. Think you can?" she said.

"I can try," Justin replied. He'd straightened up in the chair, and his face had lost the intense look of concern he'd worn a few moments earlier. Diane got up and pulled him to his feet. She wrapped her arms around his neck.

"I've protected myself so long I've lost out on a lot of life. No more. I trust nothing in this relationship is going to be boring. You fit in so well it's a bit disconcerting. I trust you will be honest and up front. If you want out, you'll say so," Diane pushed up on her tiptoes and gently kissed Justin's lips.

He responded by pulling her off her feet. Diane's lips parted and accepted the warmth of his mouth on hers. They molded to each other, feeling the simultaneous pounding of their hearts, the scent of lust lingering in the air. Grudgingly, they peeled apart, breathless and raw with aching. Staring into each other's eyes, they started giggling.

"I made an appointment with Liz next door in about five minutes. I'd like you to accompany me," Diane said.

"Why?" Justin asked.

"Don't ask. Please, just trust."

After locking the office doors and setting the alarm, Diane slipped her hand into Justin's and they strolled to their appointment next door at The Bar.

"I hate how dark these little bars can be," Justin complained as he and Diane stood inside the door for a moment, their eyes adjusting to the murky interior.

"I know. I figured out a long time ago that bar owners keep bars shadowy so people will lose track of time. That way, they'll stay longer and spend more money. Still doesn't make it any easier to see when you first come in." Diane walked to the bar with Justin who took a seat. She hugged the slender bartender who had come out from behind. She and Liz sauntered to one of the tables in the back and sat down.

"Did I see you come in with that adorable Justin Anderson?" Liz peered in the direction of the bar. He had turned and offered a hesitant wave when the two ladies peered his direction.

Liz hollered at the man who had moved behind the counter. "Donnie? Anything he wants is on the house, got it?" The man nodded and Justin ordered a soda.

"It's about time you paid him some attention. He's been in here for the past month and a half driving Mark crazy trying to find out about you. I'll tell you what, if I were ten years younger, I'd make a play for him myself. The way his buns fit in those jeans—whooee, does a woman's heart good. Now, give, I need details. I'm too old for this foolishness, but I can live through you. Fess up."

Diane looked at her friend and started laughing. "You are incorrigible. Nothing is happening, really. We've been thrown together because of circumstances. Thursday night when I stopped in after work, some out of town jerk tried to hit on me and wouldn't take no for an answer. Justin stepped in and helped get rid of the guy. Unfortunately, the jerk followed me home. When I looked into my sliding glass doors and saw the jerk's face looking back at me, I called nine-one-one but changed my mind when he disappeared. I didn't want to stay by myself, so I called Mark. He casually remarked Justin had shown up needing a place to stay because the police were investigating some type of break in at his house and wouldn't let him stay there. That's all."

"Right. Diane, we've been friends since I rented you a studio apartment your first week back from England. I think I can say I know you better than anyone else, and what I see is obvious—you care for Justin—a lot. It shows in the way the two of you look at each other. Don't write him off yet. Give this a chance."

Diane watched the smirk spread over Liz's face. Arguing was pointless; Liz was right. She knew Diane better than anyone.

"Liz, I came here to tell you about the ad campaign I designed to bring more business to The Bar. Can we talk about that and not my personal life?"

"Of course, hon."

Liz's smug expression irritated Diane. Her assessment of Diane's feelings was spot on and she knew it.

"Good. Well, the jerk from Thursday night looked like he was still living in the seventies. His appearance started me thinking. The fashions and hairstyles are resurfacing from the late sixties and early seventies. Why not go with the flow and cash in on the trend? We can start on Thursday nights; call them Seventies Flashback nights as well as Ladies' Night. I'm sure there are plenty of people who can provide music from that era and you can run a contest for the best seventies outfit. We'll put up some posters around town advertising the idea and get the radio station, W-A-L-K, to run some promo ads with Seventies background music. I think you'll be able to bring in a really good mix of people. The younger crowd thinks they've discovered something new and the older crowd will enjoy the memories. What do you think?" Diane finished.

"This is a fantastic idea! It would be like old times in here—people, music, and money. When do we start?" Liz's eyes danced at the prospect of the cash registers singing.

"I have a proposal I'd like you to help with or maybe you can point me in the right direction," Diane said.

Liz raised her eyebrows. When Diane started a conversation with, "I have a proposal", the result usually cost her money.

"Shoot."

"Justin's construction company is building the new hotel at the edge of town."

Liz nodded in recognition.

"Since the explosion, he hasn't heard from the backer at all. He's concerned the investment company will pull out and leave him with cleanup bills and no job. The hotel would have provided over two hundred jobs when it was built. You know we can use the employment opportunities around here. Do you know anyone capable of interesting investors in something so large? I know this is a long shot, but I figured if anyone in town would have the knowledge, it'd be you. Can you—will you help?" Diane asked.

"Diane, you know I'll do anything I can. Let me work on it. I should be able to give you an answer Monday at noon. How about lunch? Course, you'll have to come here, but at least it's not far from work." Liz patted Diane's hand.

The two agreed to have lunch Monday at The Bar.

Justin wandered to the booth where they sat. "You look pleased with yourself," he said.

"Well, I've asked Liz to try and find investors for the hotel," Diane put her hand up as Justin started to protest, "She's just looking into it. She may or may not come up with something. You'd be surprised at how many skeletons she knows about. Besides, looking and asking is better than sitting on our hands waiting for the end to come."

Justin could only agree.

Thirty-four

Robert and Anthony sat in stunned silence inside the Lexus. They watched the unusual couple stroll into the restaurant.

"Now, what was the reason you decided not to work in Washington, D.C.? If I remember correctly, it was the high crime rate and lack of morals in the town." Anthony looked at his cousin, "And this is different, how?"

Robert scowled. "Shut up. Let's drive to the police station and get this stuff transcribed. I need a shower. I feel grimy."

"Me, too."

Anthony regarded Robert, "I want to know how he knew I'd ask for that much money and where the hell did he get it on such short notice?"

"I told you he's very influential. He's probably seen too many movies and picked a number from one of them. I know he keeps at least fifty to hundred thousand in a safe at his house. He still has the Depression mentality his parents instilled in him and likes to have cash on hand in case *the banks fail*. The first time I saw it in his safe, I nearly choked. Let's get the hell out of here." Robert started the engine and pulled out of the parking lot.

Little was said on the ride to the police station. Robert slid the car in front of The Bar and the two men walked the three blocks to the courthouse. Chad had given them instructions to enter through the back door again. Anthony pressed a red button and they were buzzed inside.

The men wondered what Justin Anderson had done to piss off

Thomas Manning. The man had enough power to tie up Anderson in litigation for years. So why murder?

"Well, how'd it go?" Chad asked.

"Man, you got some bad people in this town," Robert answered.

Chad helped each man remove his microphone and tape recorder. He called in the police transcriber to start work immediately on the tapes.

"You guys want a cup of coffee?" Chad asked.

"No thanks, my stomach is already churning," Robert said.

"No, my stomach is just as bad," Anthony said.

"Well, I'm going to get a refill. When I return, you can fill me in on details of the meeting." Chad disappeared out the doorway and returned with a cup of steaming brown liquid. The aroma filled the room.

"There was a lady with my guy," Robert shook his head in disbelief.

"Robert, give us the man's name. It's only a matter of maybe an hour before we have it anyway. I appreciate you think his request might be a mistake, but he paid you, didn't he?" Chad was trying to be patient with his friend.

"Yeah, old, untraceable bills. Ten thousand worth," Robert said.

Chad choked on the slug of coffee now stuck halfway down his throat.

"Ten thousand! I can only think of one or two people in this town who've got that kind of money on hand. We're not talking about Thomas Manning, are we?"

Robert nodded affirmatively.

"Damn. You said there was a woman with him?"

Corey, coffee mug in hand, wandered into the office catching the tail end of the conversation.

"A knockout brunette with great legs and ice-blue eyes?" Corey inserted.

"Yeah, how'd you know?" Robert asked.

"I thought so. It's Ashlee Anderson, Justin's ex-wife," Corey said.

"Wow. She didn't say a word. Just sat there and stared at Anthony while he and Thomas conducted business. She looked excited by everything that was going on—gave me the creeps. She's so much younger than him. What's the story?" Robert asked.

"I'm telling only what I suspect. Thomas Sr. gave Ashlee a summer job when she was in college and things got hot and heavy until his wife put her foot down. That's when he introduced Ashlee to Justin. Soon after the wedding, their daughter was born. When Justin wanted out, Ashlee pitched a fit using their daughter as collateral until he handed over his family's home to her. She has a source of untraceable income I'd love to find," Corey finished as the transcriber returned with the documents for signatures.

Robert and Anthony read over their statements and signed where indicated.

Corey and Chad sat down and mapped out their next move, calling Judge Barton with a summary of the last forty-eight hours events. The judge accused Corey of drinking. Corey assured his Honor he hadn't touched a drop of alcohol.

Offering to bring over the recordings of the meeting, Corey anticipated the judge would trust his instincts.

"We've enough evidence now to arrest one person for solicitation for murder," Corey stated.

"Damn, Corey. I know this man. I've had him in my courts for thirty years. I can't believe he'd be stupid enough to do something like this," Judge Barton protested.

"Well, Your Honor, if it's any consolation, I think it has to do with Ashlee Anderson. He's tried to hire someone to kill her ex-husband." Corey related the facts from the evidence at his disposal.

"I warned him years ago that little tramp would get him in trouble someday. I'm surprised Arlene puts up with it. Well, you'd better be right. If you're not, it's your ass not mine. Get the warrant drawn up and I'll sign it. But you'd better get over here in the next hour. I need my beauty sleep."

Corey hung up the phone and grinned at Chad.

"Yes. We have that son of a bitch," He shook Chad's hand. "The judge gave us one hour in which he'll sign the warrant. We'd better get moving."

Chad hooted then called the District Attorney's private number.

"We need you to prepare a warrant for the arrest of Thomas Manning Sr.—immediately, Solicitation for the Purpose of Murder. Yes, I'm sure. We don't have much time. Judge Barton said within the hour or we'll have to wait until Monday. Yep. Bye."

Chad and Corey stood grinning at each other. They clinked coffee cups in celebration.

"Now, if we could just link the sabotage of Justin's home and vehicle to him," Chad started.

"That'd be too easy. Besides, Thomas would never get his hands dirty. My guess is it's Ashlee's doing. But she's slick enough to get someone else to crawl around and do the *dirty* work. Hopefully, we'll know Monday morning. It'd be so nice to put her in a cell right next to his," Corey said.

Coming out of Corey's office, Chad and Robert walked toward the front door. They'd worked hard and now the pressure was off. An elaborate trap had been set, and some elusive game had been caught just like their pro football days together.

"Now if we can just tie Ashlee to this," Chad was saying to Robert as they passed by the front desk. Chad nodded to Officer Kurt Lee on duty at the front desk.

Kurt picked up his cell phone and called Ashlee. He wasn't fond of her, but she'd saved his butt a time or two. He owed her this one.

Thirty-five

Ashlee snubbed out her cigarette and picked up the take-out bag Randall had placed on her table. She strolled through the restaurant to the parking lot, tiptoeing gingerly over the gravel so she wouldn't scuff her designer heels. Sitting and warming the car, Ashlee reflected how things had changed in such a short time. She relived the meeting with the hit man. Thinking of Thomas in this new light, her body ached to be with him.

Her cell rang.

Thomas must wonder where I am. How sweet.

She was startled to hear the voice of Patrolman Kurt Lee.

"Ashlee. This is Kurt."

"Kurt? What can I do for you?"

"I owe you for saving my butt a couple of times. I figure the information I'm about to give you will make us even. The District Attorney is issuing a warrant for the arrest of Thomas Manning for solicitation of murder. I'd suggest you be far away or they'll take you in too. We're even, okay?" he asked.

"Kurt, we're more than even. Thank you."

Ashlee set her phone to vibrate. The last thing she needed right now was to talk with Thomas. He'd excited her earlier but not enough to risk her life. She'd have to solve her problem with Justin another day. Meanwhile, overnight bags for herself and Briana were in order.

If I can sell the house, I'll have enough money to move away from all the rain and snow. I'll have to forge a deed of sale from Justin to me, but at this point, I've got nothing to lose and everything to gain. I can demand cash up front and by the time they find out I don't own the place I'll be laying on some beach under a tropical sun.

She put the Toyota in gear and drove back to the mansion. She'd leave the Toyota with the house and take the old Chevrolet Belair. Still registered in her mom's name, if it got noticed, she'd be in the clear. Once she got to her mom's house, she'd leave the Chevy and borrow her mom's sedan. She had no idea where she was headed. She just needed to be anywhere tropical that wasn't here.

Reaching the house, she parked the compact in the circular front drive. She barged through the door and, phone in hand, dialed the number of a realtor in Billington she'd once dated.

"Archibald Nelson Realty. May I take a message?" a nasal voice answered.

"Verna? This is Ashlee Anderson. Is Archie gone for the night?" Ashlee asked.

"Yes, he is. He left early tonight. I can get a message to him and have him call you right away if it's important," Verna offered.

"No, just tell him it's about the mansion. I'll be leaving to go to my mother's house. He can leave a message there. In the meantime, he won't be able to contact me directly. I'll contact him. Thanks, Verna."

She dashed into her daughter's room and pulled the suitcases down from the shelf above her daughter's clothes. Ashlee rummaged through dressers and closets flinging things into the bags. Everything else could be thrown in with the house or sent to the second hand store. After packing the Chevy, Ashlee called her mom.

"Mom? Briana and I will be moving in with you for a short while until I can figure out what to do."

Molly knew her daughter well enough not to ask why. "I'll tell Briana."

"Thanks, Mom."

Ashlee dumped all of Paul's belongings into a cardboard box she set on the front seat of the Chevy. She walked the corridors of the house she'd taken from her ex-husband, turning off lights and closing doors. She put her key in the dead bolt and felt the metal click into place.

At the car, she turned to admire the colonial elegance one last time. She'd have to mourn her losses later. Keeping the Chevy just above the legal limit, Ashlee drove to the twenty-four hour gym residing inside the old Woolworth's building in the town square and located Paul. Upon her threatened instruction, he followed her to the car. She opened the passenger side door and threw his belongings at him.

"I know you already have somewhere else to live so this won't break your heart. Goodbye, Paul. It was fun for a while," Ashlee said. "Oh, yeah, your money? Go whistle for the rest of it."

She slithered into the driver's seat, slamming the vehicle into gear, and squealed from the spot in a cloud of burning rubber before Paul could react. She calculated by noon Monday, Paul would be sitting in a cell next to Thomas.

Slowing for the drive out of the town where so much of her life had happened, Ashlee was numb. She realized this would be her first step toward moving to sunny days and balmy nights. A smile pushed the edges of her lips up then a chuckle rose from the bottom of her stomach becoming a full-fledged laugh. She would escape this nightmare unscathed. Her only regret was not being able to see Thomas's face when they picked him up.

Thirty-six

Thomas couldn't figure why Ashlee was knocking at the cabin door. She was the only other person who had a key. Maybe her hands were full; she *was* carrying their dinner from the restaurant. He carefully placed his smoldering cigar in the stand-up ashtray next to the overstuffed chair and ottoman. He crossed the polished bare oak floor and opened the door.

The shocked expression on Thomas's face told Corey the police were not who he was expecting to see at his door.

"Thomas Manning Sr.?" Corey asked.

"Corey, you know who the hell, I am," he said. "How did you know I was here?"

'Sir, I need you to answer yes or no to the question I've just asked. Are you Thomas Manning, Sr.?" Corey persisted.

"Yes. I'm Thomas Manning, Sr.," he growled.

"It is my duty to inform you that you are being placed under arrest on a charge of solicitation of murder." Corey stepped inside the cabin and placed handcuffs on a dumbfounded Thomas, reciting Miranda rights to him as he snapped the cuffs shut.

"You have the right to remain silent. If you give up the right to remain silent, anything you say, can and will be used against you in a court of law. You have the right to an attorney and to have the attorney present during questioning. You have a right to stop answering at any time during questioning. If you cannot afford an attorney, the court will appoint one for you. Do you understand these rights as I have read them to you?"

"Corey, what in the hell..." he sputtered.

"Mr. Manning., we'll answer your questions at the station," Corey said. "And as to how I knew about your..." his eyes surveyed the room, "love nest? Earl, your caretaker, is my dad's brother—my uncle. He's extremely proud of the care he puts into Ashlee's mansion and this place. He's told me on several occasions how quiet it is out here. You know, he's right. It is quiet."

Thomas, his jaw twitching, glared at Corey.

"Allen? Please make sure all the doors are locked and all the lights and appliances have been turned off. I smelled smoke when we came through the door. I wouldn't want Mr. Manning to have his cabin burn down because we forgot to turn off a coffee pot," Corey directed his officer.

"Yes, sir," the officer stepped around Corey and a scowling Thomas Manning toward the back of the cabin.

"Bob? Call Specialty Towing and have Mr. Manning's Jaguar towed to the impound lot. Tell them to give it the prestige treatment. We want to be sure there isn't a scratch on the vehicle when it is picked up later," Corey said.

"Yes sir," the deputy retrieved his phone from the holder and called the towing company.

Corey placed his hand under Thomas's elbow and directed him down the steps to his squad car. "Watch your head," he said as he placed one hand on Manning's head and with the other, gently lowered him into the vehicle. Corey bit his lip hard to keep from smiling. This was a scenario he'd only dreamed about. He climbed in the front of the car.

"Nelda?" Corey spoke into the microphone.

"Yes, Detective?" a woman's voice crackled through the tinny sounding speaker.

"I'm bringing in a suspect. His paperwork is in the center of my desk. Will you bring the file to the sergeant at the front desk so we can process him as quickly as possible?" Corey said.

"You got it, Detective," was the response.

The ride to the station was oppressive. Even the radio remained quiet. Thomas fumed. *There are only three people who knew about the meeting tonight. Robert and his cousin have too much to lose to say anything. I'm sure the Mafia would have them eliminated if they said anything. The only other person is Ashlee, and her reaction in the restaurant doesn't correspond with her setting me up. This would give her the money she feels she deserves. Then again, why after more than an hour of my leaving the restaurant had she not shown up at the cabin?*

By the time the police cruiser, with its well-known occupant, reached the station, Thomas was ready to kill someone with his bare hands. It was only through many years of courtroom experience he maintained his icy exterior. He was put through the booking procedure—filling out numerous forms, emptying his pockets, taking mug shots and fingerprinting—before he was shown to the holding cell. Corey had offered him a chance to make his phone call, but he needed time to gather his senses.

He was in a very uncomfortable spot. Arlene was in Billington visiting her younger sister, and he knew she *wouldn't* bail him out. No, she'd divorce him, taking everything he'd worked for because this was done for Ashlee. After all these years, Thomas could rely on his lover leaving town and grabbing what she could on her way out. He hated being right. He was left with only one alternative. He'd have to call his son. He sat on the bunk in the cell, head in his hands. Life as he had known it had just come to an abrupt end.

Even if he escaped from this thing, with everything in the open he was screwed.

Thirty-seven

Corey almost felt sorry for the man slumped on the bunk in the cell—decades of success down the drain because he couldn't keep his pecker in his pants. *Almost.*

"Mr. Manning? You can make your one call now. Use the pay phone down the hall. Here's your money." Corey opened the cell door and handed Thomas a handful of change.

"Thank you, Detective Williams." He shuffled to the silver pay phone box located at the end of the cellblock and called Tom Jr.

Corey gleaned from Manning's end of the conversation that he was going to spend Saturday and Sunday in jail. Bail would not be set until the preliminary hearing Monday morning.

Mr. Manning was going to have a long, lonely weekend.

Thirty-eight

Tom sat on the edge of the bed in the darkened room, the phone still in his hand.

How could things have gotten so out of control? His father was a highly respected member of the Bar Association in this State and had practiced in this town for nearly thirty-five years. *What the hell had happened?*

Hope, Tom's wife, slowly rose from the bed and gently touched him on the shoulder.

"What's the matter, honey? Anything I can do to help?" she asked.

"No, sweetheart. An important client wound up in jail, and I need to go see him tonight. I'm sorry I woke you. I'm not sure how long this'll take, so don't worry and don't wait up for me. I'll be home for breakfast."

Leaning over, he kissed her on the cheek. "Sleep tight. Goodnight."

Tom pushed up from the bed and shuffled to the walk-in closet Hope had insisted on having built in their master bedroom. At the time, he thought she was being extravagant, but it had proven to be a godsend. He didn't get many late night calls from his small practice in Oakdale. Still, he was glad he didn't have to keep Hope awake. She and the children were the best things in his life. He looked lovingly at her in the shaft of light from the closet. Twins and seven years of marriage had done little to fade her beauty. He was one lucky man.

He walked inside the closet and changed into a business suit. It might be the middle of the night and he'd just risen from bed, but his father would expect no less. A lawyer *always* wore a suit. He finished dressing and quietly slipped downstairs to the kitchen. He wanted a drink but would have to settle for reheated coffee. He needed to find out how his father had gotten himself in such a jam. Tom grabbed his briefcase and left for the jail. It was going to be a long night.

Arriving at the station in less than ten minutes, he was ushered into an eight foot by eight foot institutionally drab conference room where a table and two chairs were provided for inmates and their lawyers. Ten minutes later Thomas, sporting bags under his eyes and rumpled clothing, was escorted inside. A guard stood outside the locked door.

They stared at each other in silence.

"I guess I owe you an explanation," Thomas started.

"It will help in preparing a defense, Dad," Tom replied.

"Let me talk without interruption until I'm finished. This isn't going to be easy. Maybe you'll understand, maybe you won't. My life, as I currently know it, is over, so you best know the truth from me instead of hearing gossip from the rest of town."

Thomas Sr. leaned back in the rigid chair and began with the summer Ashlee started working at the firm. An hour later, when he'd finished, Tom sat mute. He was overwhelmed by the questions crowding his mind. He cleared his throat and leaned on the table.

"So, you're telling me," he started slowly, "Briana's *not* my best friend's daughter and my goddaughter but my half-sister? You were willing to have my best friend murdered because his ex-wife wants the money he's leaving his daughter—stepdaughter—which is rightfully hers? And all these years she made you feel—*young*? That about the way it lays out?"

"You make it sound so crass," Thomas started to complain.

"Dad, it is crass. You've just thrown away thirty-five years of practicing law and will probably wind up doing time with some pretty *uncorporate* people. Even if the judge and jury show some leniency for you, Dad, count on doing some hard time. I'd better call one of my classmates from college. He's the best criminal lawyer in D.C. I'm not sure I can be objective."

Tom felt guilty contacting someone outside the family, but at the moment, he really didn't care too much for his father. All his life he'd respected who and what he thought this man represented. He'd just discovered his father was a very flawed human being. All he wanted was to get out of the room as soon as he could.

Thomas looked at his son. Tom's rigid body perched on the chair, hands folded neatly over his briefcase, relayed to him that his son was holding back intense emotions. *Just like I taught him to do.* "Please, call your classmate in Washington. I'll need an excellent lawyer. I'll see you, Son."

Thomas knocked on the door, and the guard escorted him back to his cell. He sat on the thin mattress and put his head in his hands, weeping for the first time since Tom Jr. was born.

~ * ~

Tom, his head held high, walked deliberately to his car. He remembered the envelope in his briefcase the investigator handed him this afternoon in the office. Flipping the inside light of his car on, he ran a finger under the sealed lip. There was a photocopy of a birth certificate for Briana, but the line for the biological father's name was blank. A picture, obviously taken with a telephoto lens and dated in the lower right corner, of his dad and Ashlee captured the couple in a steamy embrace. Tom placed these items back into the opened envelope. He noted in pen, *Corey Williams/Justin Anderson* on the front. Moving through the public vestibule to the front desk, he instructed the desk sergeant to ensure the envelope, which contained evidence relating to a case he was working, found its way to Detective Williams. *Maybe it will help, maybe it won't.* His head was reeling with unanswered questions.

Returning to his car, Tom unlocked the door and sat immobile, gazing through the windshield. It was too much. In less than two hours, his father had turned upside down the life Tom Jr. had always known. *How could my father have fallen under the spell of a woman like Ashlee? Why isn't she being locked up? I need to talk some sense into*

Dad—tomorrow. Tonight all I want to do is snuggle next to Hope and be thankful for what I have.

Tomorrow would begin his family's journey down a very dark path.

Thirty-nine

Diane and Justin ordered delivery pizza, a specialty from The Bar*'s* menu. Driving separately, they met at the convenience store cum video rental, two blocks from Diane's home. Deciding against red wine to accompany the pizza, they chose a blush rosé. The couple, giggling at the absurdity of trying to pick wine for pizza, placed the bottle on the counter along with two comedy videos.

"Can I please see your ID?" the clerk asked.

"You're joking, right?" Diane replied in astonishment.

"No, I need to see both your ID's," he said.

Diane and Justin placed their driver's licenses on the counter. The clerk picked up each card and checked it carefully, comparing the pictures to the two people standing in front of him.

"I'm sorry. You two were having so much fun I was sure one of you was underage," he said. "More people need to enjoy themselves like you." He smiled as he bagged the wine and winked at Diane.

They walked out the front door and burst into laughter.

"I'll see you back at my place." Diane crawled inside her Corvette. With a wave of her hand, she zipped out of the lot and disappeared up the street toward her house.

While Diane changed into comfortable jeans and a baggy sweater, Justin popped the pizza in the oven and took Princess for a quick walk. The two got back as Diane was setting up the VCR.

The first movie's advertisements proved funnier than the film itself. Comfortably ensconced on the couch, sipping wine and talking, they realized they had a great deal in common. Both their fathers had been authoritarians and their mothers had chosen to give up promising careers to raise children.

"Diane, why did you choose Oakdale instead of some other small town? I know you said you saw a television special on Oakdale, but there must be a small town featured on the D.C. stations every night," Justin said, wanting to hear the long version of her story. He knew who Ron was, hell, everyone knew who Ron was, but his only interest lay in her part in Ron's life. Feeling comfortable and warmed by the wine, Diane decided to share her past with Justin. She told him the details of how she'd given her life to Ron Smythe, the infamous musician, only to find him incapable of committing to their relationship. She had pangs of guilt about leaving until she'd witnessed him and his pregnant girlfriend on television the day she'd first visited Oakdale. Liz's friendliness, and the feeling she'd found a home, convinced her the small town was where she needed to heal. She'd worried about being discovered.

"But, I never heard from Ron again," Diane finished her story without bitterness. She tilted her wine glass up finishing the contents.

"The man's an idiot," was Justin's only comment.

Diane smiled sadly, "That's what I thought too. But he and Faith are still married and expecting baby number five. I guess I was too American for him."

"It's still his loss. If given the opportunity to have you in my life, I'd make sure you didn't want to leave," Justin said.

"Thanks. Sometimes, I seem completely clueless. You'd think I would've learned from Ron, but no, when Timothy came along, I was feeling very lonely and anxious to start a family, so I fell for his smooth line. There was only one problem—Timothy didn't let marriage get in the way of his dating. But that's a story for another evening. Why don't we see if this other movie is better than the first?"

Justin raised his glass to her and toasted, "To new friends. Thank you for all you've done for me."

Diane picked up her empty glass and gently touched the rim to Justin's glass.

"To new friends. I want to thank you for helping me to trust again," Diane added.

Justin took both glasses and placed them on the coffee table. He pulled Diane to him.

"I'm still being a gentleman, so if you want me to stop, you'd better say something right now," he murmured in her ear.

"Am I stopping you?" she whispered.

He wrapped his arms around her waist, his heart soaring as she melted into his embrace. His mouth moved toward hers, tongue dancing on her lips then slipping inside. Diane willingly accepted his urgent kiss. She pulled back, slightly feeling the softness of his lips against hers. She could feel her heart beginning to match the beat of Justin's. His earthy scent filled her with a desire she'd almost forgotten. He abandoned his efforts to control himself, sweeping Diane in his arms and heading down the hall.

"Guest room or yours?" he asked.

"Mine," she whispered.

Justin pushed open the door with a foot.

The pedestal oak bed sat against one wall, a mirrored headboard running the entire length. Justin gently settled Diane on the bed.

"What about Princess?" he asked.

"If you hadn't noticed, I put her in the laundry room about thirty minutes ago."

"Oh," he said with a sheepish grin.

Diane pulled him to her. She wanted this moment to last, but his sensual body was testing her resolve to go slow. The gentleness of his caresses took her breath away. Unbuttoning his shirt revealed his lightly haired chest. When she'd conquered the last button, her heart pounding with urgent need, she deftly removed the shirt and ran her hands over the silken skin under the sparse covering protecting his well-developed chest and firm stomach. She moaned with the sheer pleasure of touch. It was a delight to revel in each sensation as it washed over her body. She knew from the tautness of Justin's muscles and the sizable bulge pressing against her he could easily give in to his need and the evening would quickly end, but he seemed determined to prolong the slow pace.

His hands explored gently beneath her sweater and, to his delight, he discovered she had removed her bra. Warm velvety skin easily slid beneath his fingers. He cupped Diane's breast in his hand, covering the side of her neck in butterfly kisses. She wiggled as he neared her collarbone and moaned when he started pushing the sweater over her head. He caught his breath at the sight of her small pert breasts. When she started to say something, he kissed her into silence.

"They're magnificent."

He stroked each breast, his fingers teasing the nipple until it presented itself hard and ready for his mouth. Then he trailed his warm tongue across her collarbone and between the small mounds to her nipples, flicking the tips then sucking one of the perfect mounds in his warm, wet mouth.

Diane let go all resistance with the sensations coursing through her. She lightly dragged her nails down his chest toward his engorged cock, feeling his muscles tightened in anticipation. He tongued languid circles over her bare chest to her hungry mouth, cupping her breasts in his hands as he gently played his calloused thumbs over her hardening nipples. Diane snaked her slender fingers beneath his waistband, targeting the hardened, pulsating bulge.

When her fingers wrapped around his velvety shaft, the growl he emitted reverberated through the room. It was the most beautiful sound Diane had ever heard.

Justin slid his hand under her waistband easily, using his thumb to slip open the button, and maneuvering the zipper down. He tucked his forefingers into the sides of the jeans and coaxed the pants over her smooth hips. A slip of material, mostly lace, barely covered her mons. Unconsciously he licked his lips, his fingers caressing the material covering the spot he most desired at the moment. He worked two of his fingers under the tiny bit of satin, moving it to one side only to be greeted by a warm, wet curl of dark hair. The wandering fingers slipped into the opening between the wet curls to explore the deep damp tunnel.

Diane arched her body and let loose a guttural moan. "I want you in me, now."

"Soon." The magical fingers moved in and out of the slick opening.

Diane pushed against the pressure, sending her senses soaring. She was certain she would explode if he continued like this, and she really wanted to feel him inside her walls.

Suddenly, the fingers were gone and just when she thought she would feel his rock hard cock inside her, she jumped at the sensation of warm mouth on her tender, throbbing clit. She threw propriety to the wind, moaning loudly each time he ran his tongue over the sensitive spot. After he had made several passes, Diane lay panting, the bed covers crumpled within her fingers. Now she was sure he would mount her. When her clitoris was pulled into his mouth and he sucked hard, she couldn't control the resulting orgasm. She sluiced her fingers through Justin's hair and pushed her hips against his mouth. He continued to suck and lick her to a frenzy then...he stopped.

"What...what are you doing?" Diane didn't want to believe he would walk away. She lifted her head to watch him undulate out of his jeans; his hardened member pointing heavenward.

Slipping back on the bed, Justin straddled her, inching his way to her wet, aching pussy.

She rotated her hips to bring him closer. When he was at her knees, he lowered his cock to the inside of her leg. With each rotation of her hips he moved closer to her wetness. When the smooth head of his penis kissed the wet opening of her pussy lips, Diane grabbed his hips to impale herself on him.

The suddenness of her move showed in his eyes, but he quickly recovered and set the rhythm with his thrusts; sliding with measured care at first allowing every inch of sensation to travel up his cock. Too soon his need overtook his desire to make the feeling last and he quickened the pace.

"I want us to come together," Diane moaned in his ear.

Justin leaned toward her and slipped his tongue around the soft shell of her ear. It was the final act that sent the two of them over the edge. Bucking and groaning the pair arched against each other in climax.

As the tide of physical ecstasy receded, they nestled in the afterglow. Justin pulled the covers over their naked, sweaty bodies and Diane burrowed into the shelter of his arms. They slept intertwined.

In the morning, she slid noiselessly out of bed and dressed while Justin continued to sleep. She looked at the angelic face lying on the pillow next to hers. *God, he's gorgeous. I can't understand how anyone could treat him as cruelly as his ex-wife has done. I've never met any man so masculine and loving. Where has he been all my life?* She started giggling. *He was in junior high while I was graduating high school, that's where! It's going to take a while to get used to this old soul in such a young body.* Looking at herself in the hall mirror as she passed, she winked. *I'll get used to it.*

Forty

Diane headed into the kitchen, opened the refrigerator and peered at the contents. She retrieved eggs and bacon. A pan from the cupboard, a spatula from the drawer and she was ready to create breakfast. Justin padded up clad in a towel and wrapped his arms around her as she cooked. Smelling lightly of her bath soap, he bent and kissed her neck and shoulders.

"If you're not careful, you're going to ignite a fire that will have to be put out immediately," Diane told him.

"Oh, darn," he countered.

Diane turned and Justin tenderly kissed her. He pulled away to admire her.

"You are the most incredible woman I've ever met," His eyes searched Diane's face.

She was so surprised by his sudden seriousness that it left her reaching for a response. The ringing of his cell broke the magic of the moment.

"Damn," he muttered as he answered on the second ring.

"Yes. This is Justin Anderson. Hey, Verna, what's up? Something wrong at the site?"

Diane turned the omelet onto itself and flipped the bacon one more time. Grabbing a plate from the set Liz had given her as a housewarming gift, she put the omelet and bacon on it and took the meal in the dining room. She poured herself a cup of coffee and, folding her leg beneath her, sat opposite him at the table.

"Count on it. Thanks, again, Verna." He placed the phone on the table and stared at his plate.

"Is your food, okay?" Diane asked.

"I haven't tasted it yet but it smells delicious. Verna passed along some information she knew I'd want to hear." Justin wrinkled his forehead.

"It seems my ex-wife thinks she can get rid of the house where she and Briana have been living. She needs money in a hurry, and she's convinced some realtor in Billington to put it on the market for her. I know she can't do anything because my parents left it to me, but if she's trying to raise cash in a hurry, that means she'll be leaving town and taking my daughter away from me unless I can do something. With the site closed down and no word from the investor, I don't have any visible income to show the state I'd be a reliable parent. Damn!" Justin slammed his fist into his hand.

He pushed away from the table. Getting up, he kissed Diane on the forehead and trudged down the hallway to the guest bedroom.

Diane remained seated, turning her coffee cup in her hands as a plan began to form in her mind. She walked to the hall closet, standing for a moment with her hand on the knob. Opening the door, she retrieved a guitar case from the top shelf and carried the item to the dining room table. Reverently, she flipped the latches on the side. Cradled in the deep blue velvet interior, rested a blonde, six-stringed electric guitar. There were five famous signatures on the body. The largest one read "*To the only love of my life, Diane*" and was signed Freddie "Ron" Smythe. Reaching beneath the guitar, Diane retrieved a sheet of paper with several faded phone numbers on it. She got up from the table, coffee cup in one hand and sheet of paper in the other. She poured herself a fresh cup and pushed the paper around the countertop for a minute, hesitating. *Once I implement this plan, there is no turning back*. Breathing deeply to fortify her courage, she dialed the first number. The accented British male voice, one she recognized, answered and she wavered for a moment.

"Hello, Ron? This is Diane Wallace." She could feel butterflies multiplying in her stomach.

"Is this some kind of bleedin' joke?" was the reply.

"No, Ron, it's not. However, if after this many years you still can't talk to me, I can hang up," Diane challenged.

"I've got no problem talking with you." He shot back at her.

"I have a business proposition. Do you remember a blond Les Paul guitar you and the guys signed for a birthday present the last year I was in London?" Diane asked.

"Criminy. You still got that? Should be worth a pound or two by now," he said.

"I'm sure it is. I'm also sure the five signatures on the guitar itself are worth more than a pound or two. More like one or two million, don't you think? I'm offering the guitar to you first because I'm sure Faith wouldn't be pleased having the world reminded I was in the picture before her. I'm giving you the first shot at making me an offer." For a moment, Diane thought the line had gone dead.

"You're right, Faith doesn't like being reminded you were the first love of my life," Ron replied. "Would we get to see each other?"

"No, I think the best thing would be to conduct all our business through your solicitors. If you're still using the same ones, I think they'll remember me. That way, you won't get yourself into trouble, and you can have them put the guitar away until Faith can deal with the fact she wasn't the first or you find a buyer." Diane amazed herself, sounding professional and cool. The truth was she felt nauseous and ready to pass out.

"Well, I'll give you two hundred fifty thousand American for it," Ron offered.

"Ha!" Diane laughed. "Forget it, Ron. I'll take it to an auction house in New York where they won't insult me. The price of the last guitar you guys put up for auction made the papers. This one happens to be signed with your birth name, remember? It should bring in a good price, and I'll bet the tabloids on both sides of the Atlantic will have a field day with the dedication. Well, I can see we have nothing more to talk about, so I'll ring off before you get caught. Take care, ta," Diane started to hang up.

"Wait! Wait!"

"What?" She winked at Justin as he wandered through the kitchen. His eyes focused on the guitar in the blue velvet case sitting in the center of the table. He ran his fingers lovingly over the fine wood.

"All right, luv, you win. I'll give you a million and a half pounds. Call the solicitors in the morning and make the arrangements. And Diane? Leave a number where I can reach you."

"Ron, you gave up the right to contact me when you made the choice to fool around with Faith. When I receive the funds, I'll arrange for the guitar to be shipped special courier to anywhere you want it sent. Goodbye, Ron," Diane hung up this time. Smirking, she leaned against the door jam.

"You are caressing a three million dollar guitar."

Justin jerked his hand to his chest.

"How much?" His mouth dropped as his eyes widened.

"Three million American, approximately," Diane started to giggle, "When I left Ron, I made sure I kept the guitar. I knew someday I'd be able to sell it for a good deal of money. So, this morning, I came up with what I think is a fairly good plan.

"I have a proposition for you," Diane sat down.

Justin gazed into her brown eyes.

"Okay, what's your proposition? Am I going to like it?" he asked.

"I hope so. Would you be willing to become partners?" Diane asked.

Forty-one

Justin sat back in the chair. He was afraid if he said something he'd wake up and this fantastic dream would end. She was making him an offer he wouldn't have thought possible three days earlier.

"How and in what business?" he asked.

"With money in the hotel business," Diane said. "If you can give me more information about the mansion and my suspicions are confirmed, I think we might be able to get some assistance from a historical group to renovate the whole property. I loved American History, and my memory is telling me this part of the country was very important during the Civil War as a link in the Underground Railroad to the North. The information you shared with me about your great, great grandfather would make the possibility very likely. His taking a non-white wife would not have set well with the Confederate sympathizers and would have made his mixed children subject to the discrimination all colored peoples endured. I'll bet if we look over the property, we'll find secret doors and hiding spots all through the old buildings. This is going to be so exciting!" Diane said.

"I love the idea of getting back into the family house. But I want to see how much damage has been done before you commit yourself to helping me," Justin said.

Justin picked up his ringing cell phone off the dining room table.

"Justin? This is Ed. What are your plans for today?"

"Nothing yet, Ed. What are you and Belinda doing?" Justin replied.

"Well, we thought we'd go over to Pinnacle and have brunch. Maybe go for a drive, you know, anything but sit at home," Ed said.

Diane had refilled their coffee cups. She watched Justin as he spoke, his face transforming within the short span of his call. His eyes began to shine and the corners of his mouth turned into a genuine smile. She could see he was plotting something.

"Ed. How'd you and Belinda like to have me in your debt until the day I die?" Justin asked.

"Great! Just as long as I don't have to kill anybody, we've got a deal!" Ed answered.

"Wait! You don't even know what I'm asking," Justin protested.

"Like I said, as long as I don't have to kill anyone, I'll be more than happy to have you in my debt."

"Okay, meet us in front of The Bar in about two hours. I want you and Belinda to listen to a plan Diane has come up with regarding the mansion. It'll involve a little deception, but the end result will be well worth it. See you then,"

Justin called the number of the realtor in Billington.

"Hello, this is Archibald Nelson. How can I help you?" a male voice answered.

"Yes, this is Professor Lyle Winthrop from the Virginia Historical Society. You have a home listed in Oakdale I would like to have an opportunity to tour, the Anderson Estate? We believe it may have some significance in the history of the state."

"Yes, Professor. It's located on Rural Route Two. Box One Nineteen. Do you know where that is?" the realtor asked.

"My assistant is a young lady familiar with the area. I'm sure we'll have no trouble finding it. Shall we meet you there at, say, two-thirty this afternoon?"

"Fine, Professor. I'll see you then. Goodbye."

"Until that time, Mr. Nelson," Justin hung up and grinned at Diane.

"You game?" he asked.

"This sounds like fun. You bet!" Diane jumped up from the table.

"Race you. Last one in the shower gets an ice bath," she darted down the hallway.

Two hours later, the couple was sitting in Justin's rental in front of The Bar on Main Street. When Ed's van pulled up behind them, they got out.

"Oh my God!" Ed's cigarette dropped from of his mouth. He began brushing his clothes trying to put out any live sparks.

Justin was dressed in a suit and tie and wearing a set of horn rimmed glasses. Scrounging around Diane's house, she and Justin had found an old pipe of Timothy's that had never been used. His resemblance to an Ivy League professor was uncanny. Diane was outfitted in a short blond wig, skin-tight mini-skirt below a form fitting sweater and five-inch stiletto heels. She wore glasses and carried a notepad and pencil. When Ed and Belinda finally stopped laughing, the four climbed into the van and drove toward the mansion.

"When we get there, I'll let Diane distract the realtor while I get into the library. I believe there is a family diary that tells about my ancestors' daily lives up through the time my father graduated from high school. Maybe we can find a starting point to research," Justin said.

"What are you talking about?" Ed asked.

"Diane suggested Anderson Acres may have been part of the Underground Railroad during the Civil War," Justin answered.

"You know, your dad used to talk about something like that. I guess he almost drove your grandma crazy hiding in all the nooks and crannies. He said it was a kid's dream. He didn't build a fort because there were so many great hiding places in the out buildings on the property near the mansion," Ed said.

"I don't remember what brought up the subject, but at the last party before your folks—" Belinda stopped, looking out the window of the van for a moment, then continued, "—were killed, Justin, your mom was talking about how you three kids would play hide and seek. Inevitably, somebody would hide too well and a three-hour hunt would follow until the culprit was found in one of the out buildings. She said she was probably the only mother in the world glad to see puberty happen."

Diane and Justin sitting in the backseat of the van looked at each other and started to smile.

"We can document the history and have the state declare this a national treasure. We might be able to get their assistance restoring the mansion to its original condition. You can provide work for your crew. There might also be some tax benefits. This could turn out to be a win-win situation," Diane said.

"This might actually work. The only other issue is money. It's going to take a lot to restore the mansion back to its original form. I don't have that kind of money and don't know where to get it. The company is barely making it, and if the hotel investor drops out of the picture, I may have to declare bankruptcy." Justin leaned against the seat and closed his eyes.

Diane scooted next to him and laid her head on his shoulder. Lowly and quietly she answered, "Trust me, Justin."

"I'm curious to see what this guy has to say about selling something he doesn't have any legal right to sell. Let's see what kind of money Ashlee thinks she can get," he said.

When the mansion came into view, Diane gasped. A mirror re-creation of George Washington's home on the Potomac, the white clapboard house perched on a small knoll reached by the cobblestone circular driveway. Large white columns held up the two-story porch. She could see a garage behind the house capable of holding three to four vehicles. Someone had lovingly planted and pruned every living plant on the acreage to appear natural.

Turning to Justin, she whispered, "Is the inside as breathtaking as the outside?"

His affirmative nod fired her imagination. She'd toured the homes of President Washington and Jefferson as a kid. She was anxious to verify the similarities. The van came to a halt in front of the home at the top of the drive.

A middle-aged man dressed in a suit coat, tie and slacks set about opening Belinda's door and offered a hand as she stepped out. He then opened the sliding door to the back of the van. When Diane's stilettoed foot appeared followed by her slender shapely legs, he stammered and offered his hand. She coyly thanked him and winked as he followed her to the front door completely ignoring Justin struggling to get out.

"This is working better than I expected," Justin grumbled.

Ed and Belinda laughed and caught up with the agent. Belinda took one of his arms while Diane followed, furiously scribbling in her notepad. Ed splintered off toward the garages and back acreage. Belinda and Diane lead the realtor through the ground floor of the house. In the formal dining area, Diane held back and caught Belinda by the arm as the realtor moved through to the kitchen. She muttered to Belinda, "Distract him. I need to slip upstairs." Belinda swept into the kitchen, pulling the agent along with her and began asking a barrage of questions about the woodwork, flooring, was the electrical up to code? She easily distracted the man whose confidence convinced the women he thought he'd made a sale.

Diane adjusted her glasses and diligently made marks in the notebook. She peered back to make sure Belinda had moved the realtor out of sight. She removed her stiletto heels, and holding them in her hand, bounded up the stairs two at a time. Puffing slightly with the exertion, she stopped at the top and looked down the passageway to either side. There must have been a dozen doors. How was she going to find the room she wanted? She leaned against the wall and stared morosely at the floor. She realized she was staring at the answer. She couldn't boast of being the best housekeeper in the world, but her floors got vacuumed at least once a week. From the look of the dust against the stair railings and on the runner carpet, Ashlee hadn't vacuumed in six months.

Thank you. Diane thought. She followed the trail of dirty runner carpet to the first door. Upon opening it, she realized it was not the room she wanted. The scent left in the room was definitely male. She closed the door and moved to the next doorway on the path. *Yes.* This was what she was looking to find. Entering the pink and cream decorated room, Diane looked around for a bookshelf. *There it is in the corner.* Tiptoeing to the shelf, she did a quick inventory reaching between the Math for the Ages and Spelling B's textbooks pulling out a couple of letters. Drawers were half opened, the contents spilling to the floor, closet doors flung wide and hangers dangled empty. Diane glanced at a small pink clock on the cream toned dresser. She'd been here for five minutes. It was time to rescue Belinda from the realtor. She slipped out the door, down the steps and at the bottom of the staircase put on her shoes and turned into the living room. She stood in the center of the room and tapping the pencil against her chin, a small frown line marring her forehead.

"There you are, Miss. I was afraid we'd lost you." The realtor walked up to Diane and eyed her suspiciously.

"Are the moldings authentic eighteenth century? So much of this has been updated I'm not sure I can recommend the professor take on this project. We really need a home with very little modernization. It is so hard to reverse the process and so costly," Diane wrinkled her nose and said, "Whoever lived here—smoked. I'm not sure we'd ever be able to get rid of the smell. Well, dear," she looked at Belinda, "we need to find the professor. There is much to consider and I need to provide him with a full report." Diane slipped her arm through Belinda's, and the two women ambled to the front door leaving the realtor gaping at their departing backs. He quickly recovered his composure and followed the women out to the front veranda.

The realtor stammered an apology to Justin and Ed, having forgotten them in favor of the women. They told him not to worry; they'd walked the grounds and outbuildings.

"I believe it's time we talk money here," Justin said.

The moment he mentioned money, the realtor provided his undivided attention.

"She's asking one and a half million for the mansion, six outbuildings, and three acres."

"Is she really?" Justin asked.

"I beg your pardon?" the realtor looked confused.

"You said she. Is Justin Anderson a woman?"

"While I can't divulge my client's name, that's not it," the realtor said.

"Well, that's very curious because my assistant thoroughly

researched the property before the Society decided to look at it, and the county records list Justin Anderson as the owner," Justin said.

The man shifted from foot to foot and slowly turning red, looked at his watch and mumbled he had another showing in fifteen minutes at a home twenty miles away.

"I would suggest you let your client know she can't possibly sell what she doesn't own. And since I'm in a generous mood, I've decided not to have you prosecuted for perpetrating a fraud," Justin said.

The realtor was quickly striding to his car and muttering with each step. He sped down the driveway and away from the mansion.

The foursome reentered the van, and Diane immediately slipped her stiletto shoes onto the floor, moaning and rubbing her aching feet.

"I'll tell you what, *Professor* Anderson, this had better been worth my aching feet. What did you and Ed find out?" Diane asked.

"When he took off with the two of you, I knew I'd be able to take my time in the library. What I found were several family diaries that document sales and purchases of slaves in the mid to late eighteen hundreds. It shows daily inventories of crops, purchases of feed for the farm animals and a lot of everyday items. I don't see anything that would indicate this was a stopping place for the Underground Railroad." Justin read the neat round entries written in quill pen by his great, great grandfather from one of three slender books he'd slipped into his jacket while he'd been in the mansion library.

"I don't think your ancestor would have openly written his intention to ferry runaway slaves from the south to the north. He could have been tried for treason. I'll contact the community college in Billington and talk with Professor Jeffrey Cornwall. He's one of the foremost authorities on the Civil War and events surrounding that time period. I'm sure he'll be able to give us some insight on what to look for in your grandfather's writings and direct us to the right agency to approach for help preserving the mansion. Okay?" Diane asked.

"Yes. Thank you for coming up with the idea, Diane. I didn't know what I was going to do. I hope this will work," he fretted.

Diane slid closer to him. "It will, Justin, it will." He wrapped his arm around her shoulders and pulled her to him.

"Will you live here?" she asked.

"If I can find a way to get Briana back into my life, I'll grit my teeth and bear the memories. It is the only home she's ever known," he said.

Diane looked up and gently kissed his chin.

"All right, you two, enough of this mushy stuff. What say we go shopping?" Ed looked at the couple in the rear view mirror and raised his eyebrows in question.

"Sounds good to me," Justin turned to Diane, "How about you?"

"You don't have to ask me twice to go shopping. Lead the way," she said.

The two couples spent the afternoon wandering the quaint streets of downtown Billington. They meandered through specialty stores whose windows advertised authentic revolutionary war antiques and collapsed at a table in a small coffee shop when their feet would walk no more. They talked about plans they envisioned for the mansion and ate scones washed down by strong black coffee.

"Oh, dear," Belinda glanced at her watch, "we really need to get back. Jessica can only handle our kids for about six hours when they're awake. If we stay away any longer, I'll have to try and find a new babysitter, and I really don't want to do that, again. We've hired almost every girl of babysitting age in Oakdale to find one that's reliable and gets along with the kids. I've enjoyed this so much. We have to do it again."

The couples finished their coffee and ambled back to the parked van. Back in Oakdale, Ed and Belinda dropped Justin and Diane off near their car on Main Street.

Leaning out of the van, Ed wagged his finger and smiled as he yelled to Justin,

"Remember, you owe me for life!" as he and Belinda drove off.

Forty-two

Justin was silent as he and Diane drove to her house. They changed into jeans and sweaters and settled on the couch.

She took his hand in hers, "I've got something I've been holding on to all afternoon. While touring the house, I conspired with Belinda to sidetrack Archie Nelson. She steered him into the kitchen while I slipped out of my shoes and dashed upstairs. I found the room that must be your daughter's, unless your ex-wife is into boy bands," Diane's eyes twinkled wickedly.

Justin opened his mouth to say something sarcastic but reconsidered and snapped it shut. Diane continued, "Most of the things a young girl considers important were gone except for a few trinkets. I found these and felt they were important for you to have," Diane handed Justin a couple of envelopes. The printed name on the front was in his daughter's hand.

"Princess and I need a walk," Diane got up and, putting on her jacket, gathered up her greyhound and left Justin to read the letters from his daughter.

Diane and Princess walked ten blocks to the high school and twice around the track. Princess kept peering over her shoulder at Diane, her brown eyes questioning. Owner and dog were cold and damp when they came through the door. Diane unhooked Princess's leash and towel dried her feet. She smelled the fire and heard the crackle of wood in the fireplace. The house had been straightened and a carafe and two mugs were sitting on the coffee table. She spotted Justin sitting on the floor in front of the fire. From where she stood in the kitchen, she was unable to gage his mood. When she'd removed her jacket, she wandered into the living room where Justin stood and wrapped his arms around her. His kiss was warm and welcoming.

"I needed to read those letters. It clears up a lot of things that have been worrying me." He reached for her hand and led Diane to the couch. When she was seated, Justin poured them warm frothy cups of cocoa.

Diane's brain exploded with unanswered questions, but she reasoned he'd explain in his own time. Before he could, Justin's cell rang.

"Damn!" he muttered as he set down his cup. "This had better be good. Hey, Corey. Actually, yes. It is a bad time but I know you wouldn't call if you didn't have a good reason. What's up?"

Justin's was sitting on the edge of the couch, but after five minutes, he slid against the back, shoulders drooping, face wearing a shocked expression.

"No way. Are you sure? I… I don't know what to say. He stepped in to help when my family died. You're sure there's no mistake?" Justin kept shaking his head and muttering, "I don't believe it. I just don't believe it."

He hung up the phone then drained the contents of his mug.

For the first time since Justin had arrived, Diane felt like a stranger in her own house.

"Corey says by tomorrow afternoon they should have this case wrapped up. It seems someone *was* trying to kill me. I just don't understand why."

Diane's heart ached for Justin. His face mirrored confusion and hurt. She couldn't stand it, and put her arms around his shoulders and kissed his cheek softly.

"They're idiots. Knowing why will help but anyone who doesn't know how wonderful you are is just an idiot." She was angry someone would hurt this man she'd begun to know well enough to love.

"Well, I guess that's the hardest part. They've got someone in jail for solicitation of murder, and it's the last person I would've thought hated me that much," Justin hesitated for a moment before he continued. Diane watched him struggle for words.

"When my parents and brother were killed by the drunk driver, my best friend, Tom, and his family were there for me and my sister. They offered to let us move in if my grandma couldn't handle two teenagers." Justin smiled slightly, "They didn't know Grandma."

"Tom's dad made sure we had everything we needed. He came by Gram's house at least once a week to check on us and seemed truly disappointed when I gave up my college scholarship to marry Ashlee," Justin stopped and swallowed hard. "They've locked him up for solicitation of murder—my murder."

Justin whispered the last two words. He dropped his head into his hands and started quietly crying. Diane hugged him even tighter. She'd never known a man who allowed himself to be this vulnerable, and it tore her heart to shreds. He stopped, took several deep breaths and wiped his face dry. He moved to the fireplace mantel and staring into the fire, began to talk.

"Since I'm having a hard time believing this, Corey's going to show me proof tomorrow morning. He says there are other people involved and right now they have an arrest warrant for at least one more of them," Justin turned and looked at Diane. "I hope I didn't embarrass you, but I've never felt comfortable enough to cry in front of anyone before. It seems to help."

He smiled. "Briana's letters were enlightening. She told me how much she loved me and that her mama was living with one yucky guy while this gross old guy kept coming to visit when the yucky guy was gone. She said her mama kept telling her I was going to pay them enough money so they could move away from Oakdale, which she really didn't want to do, and live at the beach all the time. She didn't understand why I wanted her to move to the beach, but she wanted me to know that she loved me anyway," Justin said. "Where did you find those letters? If Ashlee had known about them, she would've destroyed them."

Diane grinned, "When I was a kid, my father was prone to reconnaissance sweeps of the house for contraband. To him, contraband was anything that didn't fit into a suitcase, and with all the moving we did, he made sure no one took more than he deemed necessary. Consequently, I learned to hide things. I kept a diary he never got hold of because I hid it on the bookshelf next to the biography of Patton he prized. Dad's the one who taught me; hide something in plain view. I just checked the bookshelf in your daughter's room and found the letters between two school books."

Justin chuckled, "You're right. Ashlee hated reading and Briana knew it. How funny."

Justin pulled Diane from the couch, wrapping her in his arms and lowering his lips to place feathery kisses all over her face. He kissed to her ear and whispered, "Why don't you get a quilt from the hall closet and we can see to it this fire doesn't go to waste? I'd hate to be accused of missing a romantic opportunity."

Forty-three

Tom woke bleary eyed and exhausted. He recalled the conversation he'd had with his father at the jail Saturday night. The more he replayed his father's comments, the angrier he became. *I'm not sure if I'm angry from lack of sleep or the stress Dad is putting on the family. I can't believe he is giving up everything for that—tramp, Ashlee. I won't let him forget his duty as a husband and father; after all, he's a lawyer and sworn to uphold the law. If he doesn't turn her over for her part in this, I don't think I'll ever call him Dad again. She shouldn't get off scot-free while he serves time in the penitentiary. No way! I'm going back today and we're going to talk to someone about a deal. That little bitch,* Tom slammed his fist into his hand, *has twisted the screw for the last time.*

Tom called the police station and arranged to meet with his father and Detective Williams.

"Breakfast, Tom!" Hope hollered up the stairs.

Tom wandered down and sat at the table opposite his wife, watching her spread butter on her toast.

"Have I told you lately how much I love you?" he asked.

"Yes, you have, Tom, but I'm sensing something is up. What's going on? You tossed and turned Saturday night when you finally got home and came to bed and all last night. What's happening?" Hope searched her husband's face for an answer.

"Dad was arrested last night on solicitation of murder charges," he said.

The clatter of the knife against the plate echoed through the dining room.

"He WHAT?" Hope was visibly shaking.

Tom reached across the table and grasped his wife's hand. "I know this is a shock, but I want you to hear it from me first. Dad has been secretly seeing Ashlee Anderson for years. Apparently since we were in our last year at college. Recently, when Justin did something to set her off, she decided she wanted him murdered. Dad is still smitten enough with Ashlee to make the arrangements to have him killed. Unfortunately for Dad, the police were aware of the plan, and they recorded a tape of him arranging with someone to kill Justin complete with down payment. Saturday night, he was being stoic and wouldn't say Ashlee was involved. Maybe a couple of nights in jail will change his mind about letting her get away with this. I've set a meeting today to talk with the detective and Dad. I'm hoping we can make a deal to lessen his sentence then I need to call Dirk Sinclair in D.C. to represent him, because I can barely stand to look at the man right now."

Hope's eyes rolled back in her head and she fainted.

He leapt from his chair to catch her. He picked up her small form and took her upstairs where he tenderly laid her on the bed. Stroking her hand, he waited until her lashes fluttered open.

"Are you all right, my love?"

"Oh, Tom. I'm so sorry. I just felt so overwhelmed. This is so unlike your father. What will your poor mother say? Oh, dear, I feel so bad for her. I'll be fine, sweetheart, just fine." Hope patted her husband's cheek.

"You sure, hon? I can call someone to come help you with the kids. I don't want to leave you if you're not well," he said.

"I'm fine. If I was able to deliver the twins naturally, I think I'll be able to handle this. It just took me by surprise. Go help your father." Hope sat up and kissed her husband's cheek.

He grudgingly left her and snatched a suit coat from the closet. *To hell with the tie, Dad will just have to deal with it.* Grabbing his briefcase on his way out the door, Tom drove to the police station.

He was escorted to an interrogation room and seated. Tom noted the mirror and surmised the proceedings would probably be taped. His father was brought in needing a shave and looking haggard.

"Dad," Tom nodded his head.

"Tom, what's this all about?" Thomas stopped abruptly when Tom held up his hand.

"We are being observed," Tom pointed to the mirror, "and everything we say is being taped so speak carefully. Do you understand?"

"I understand." Thomas sat back in the institutional chair and crossed his arms.

"I called for this meeting. In about thirty minutes, Detective Williams will join us, at my request, to arrange a deal to try to lessen the time you'll have to serve—if you tell him who else was involved," Tom stated.

"I'm not making any deals," Thomas placed his ankle over his knee and set his jaw.

"Dad! I know you didn't hate Justin enough to do this to him. If you sit here like some patriotic martyr, you'll lose everything, and I can guarantee that in two months the woman you think you're protecting will have another sugar daddy to support her. Think about this." Tom pushed up from the chair, slapped his hands on the table and leaned toward his father.

"Do you care so little for the rest of us that you would throw it all away for—her?" he spun and walked to the wall, rubbing his forehead with his hand. *God, I'm getting a headache.*

Thomas stared straight ahead.

He's as stubborn as a damn mule. I don't know what he thinks he's getting from letting her go free, but he's killing our family.

A knock on the door announced the arrival of Detective Williams. Corey walked in and nodded at Tom and his father as he pulled out a chair and sat down.

"I just want it noted for the record that I'm not sure what I can do about the time you'll have to serve. That's up to the District Attorney but I can advise him of your cooperation. Mr. Manning, I understand loyalty. It's a good thing but when you go to jail for someone who doesn't give a damn, well..." Corey shrugged his shoulders.

"We just picked up Ashlee's live-in lover, and he's spitting out information like a ticker tape. He says she was willing to sell you up the river in a heartbeat. The only person that matters to Ashlee is Ashlee. Her live-in is giving us answers to dates, times, places and anything else we've asked him. I don't see the point of you being heroic when all it will do is result in a longer sentence." Corey leaned toward Thomas and looked him in the eye. "I, personally, don't like you, Mr. Manning, but why should you do any more time than you have to? You know she won't wait for you to get out of jail. No money, no power, no Ashlee. Think about it."

Getting up, he knocked on the door and strode out of the room.

The silence in the room pressed on Tom. He looked at the defiant man sitting across from him. Slow realization crossed Thomas's face and his whole body seemed to sag in defeat.

"Tom?"

"Yes, Dad?"

"Get Corey and the DA back in here. Let's talk."

Tom nodded at the mirror.

The door opened and Corey entered the room followed by a suited man with a briefcase and a young uniformed female officer carrying a transcription machine.

Corey introduced everyone and after reciting Thomas his Miranda Rights again, Thomas began providing the facts about the arrangement he'd made to have Justin murdered and just how much Ashlee was involved. He acknowledged she was present for the exchange of money, and at no time, did she try to stop him. He indicated she was the party he was waiting for when the police had arrested him on Saturday night.

"Since she hasn't shown up at her place, I can only guess she is going to her mother's house in Winchester to pick up her daughter and leave the country." Thomas said.

"Thank you, Mr. Manning. You have a hearing at two o'clock. Tom? Knock when you want to leave. There's a uniformed officer outside the door." Corey reached over and shook hands with Tom. Father and son were left alone in the room.

"Thank you, Dad," Tom said.

"Don't thank me. I hate to admit it but Corey was right. Ashlee could care less about anybody but herself. I decided to leave my family with some dignity," he got up and knocked on the door. The guard entered and escorted him out of the room in handcuffs.

Tom stared at the handcuffed back of his father. *I'll never understand him.* He gathered his things and left.

~ * ~

Corey shut his door and whooped. Jabbing a fist in the air, he whooped again. He'd finally seen the arrogant Thomas Manning Sr. toppled from his self-erected pedestal. It didn't get much better. Now, he needed to get hold of the police department in Winchester and have them pick up Ashlee as soon as the District Attorney provided him a warrant.

Corey no sooner had the thought cross his mind when there was knock on the door. "Come in."

The District Attorney walked in and handed him a signed warrant for Ashlee Anderson's arrest. "I believe you've been waiting for this?"

"Thanks," Corey smiled.

A quick phone call and the wheels were set in motion. Ashlee should be in custody before noon.

Forty-four

Diane groaned as the alarm went off. What she needed was a long vacation where someone else paid the bills. She realized Princess was not on the bed again. Oh, yeah, Justin had decided to stay in the other bedroom last night because he'd wanted to work out things alone. It was nice to find a man who knew sex didn't solve all his problems. She pulled herself out of the warm bed and got ready for the day. With the office shutdown on Friday, there'd be mountains of work waiting for her. Diane smelled fresh brewed coffee when she opened the door. Justin was up this early? She headed to the kitchen and found him putzing around making breakfast.

"I knew you had a busy day so I made coffee and took care of Princess,. Hope that's okay?" he held the chair out for her.

"Okay? I'll have to hire a maid, housekeeper, and personal assistant when you leave. Why are you up so early?"

She sat down. The paper was folded neatly next to her plate.

"I need to clean up before I go see Corey at nine o'clock, and quite honestly, I was having problems sleeping; too many things going through my head. I still don't understand Mr. Manning's trying to hire someone to kill me. I'll clean up here," Justin indicated the kitchen, "and bring the keys by after I see Corey. Okay?"

Diane's response was put on hold as the phone rang.

"Hello? Yes, this is Diane Wallace. Geoffrey! How wonderful to hear from you. Oh no, it's only about seven in the morning. No, don't worry; I was on my way to work. Yeah, I have my own advertising

222

agency. I take it you're still representing Ron? Do you remember the birthday party we had the year I left? You know the one at the country house? Yeah that one. The boys gave me a guitar with their autographs, and Ron had written a message especially for me. If I'd known he was fooling around with Faith then I'd have hit him over the head with the bloody thing; however, I brought it with me when I came back to the Colonies. I'm in need of cash right now, and I recalled how the group had sold one of their guitars for a large sum of money. I gave Ron the first opportunity to purchase this one. However, if he's changed his mind, I'll just take this one-of-a-kind guitar to an auction house in New York."

Justin was fascinated. The longer Diane talked to the person on the other end of the phone, the more British she sounded. He wasn't sure if she knew how much of an accent she was picking up.

"Oh. He's still interested? How much did he tell you he was going to pay? Good, that was the agreed upon amount. I'll tell *you* where to send the money, but if anyone on that side of the Pond finds out where I'm living, I'll sue you, luv. You'll have to come work for *me*. Once the money is in my account, I'll ring you. You can give me instructions where to ship it. Did you ever marry that terrific bird, Beatrice? Wonderful! Two? Boy and girl. That's fab. Well, Geoffrey, I've got to ring off. Time to earn my keep. Ta!"

Diane turned to face a smirking Justin.

"What?"

"Do you know how British you sound?" he asked.

"Oh, poppycock!" Diane protested.

Justin laughed and put his arms around her.

"Didn't say I didn't like it. See you later?" he said.

"You'd better let me know what's going on. I've been to hell and back with you this weekend. I'd sort of like to hear the ending. Hopefully, it'll be happily ever after."

After he kissed her, he waved her off to work.

Diane drove to the office. She found a note on her door from Liz saying she wanted to talk with her as soon as she was able. After Diane made the first pot of coffee, she took the system off forward, jumping when her the phone rang before she'd replaced the receiver.

"Hello? Wallace Advertising," she answered.

"Hey, darlin'. How ya doin' this mornin'?"

"Great. What's up, Liz?" She was relieved to hear her friend's voice.

"You heard what happened to the investor of the hotel, didn't you?"

"No, what?"

"He was arrested for trying to murder somebody," Liz said.

"You mean Thomas Manning was the main investor in the hotel?" Diane slumped back in her chair.

"Yep. That means the project is currently on hold," Liz added, "But I've got calls in to some friends who owe me favors up on Capitol Hill. I think I can have the funding by tomorrow morning. In fact, darlin, I'll guarantee it. What's the name of that investment broker?"

Diane searched her card file. "Here it is. Robert D'Angelo, area code eight-zero-four, five-five-five, nine-seven-two-one. And Liz?"

"Yeah, hon?"

"Put me down for a million dollars."

"WHAT? Where'd you get a million bucks? Maybe I should raise your rent!"

"Let's just say I sold my hope chest," Diane said.

"All right, darlin', but one of these days we're gonna sit down with a coupla drinks you buy and you're gonna tell me this story. I'm gonna give that Robert guy a call and see if he'll help my investors arrange a deal to keep the hotel going up. There are too many people in this area who can use the work. Besides," Liz said, "I'll own two out of the three bars in town, and I like that idea. I'll keep you posted, hon."

The door opened and Julie came in.

"Hi, Diane. How are you?" she asked.

"I'm fine. How's that husband of yours?" Diane said.

"Oh, he's going to be just fine. He broke his ankle diving for cover, but outside of that he's okay. He'll drive me crazy before this is over. If he doesn't find something to do, I'll personally choke the life out of him." Julie stowed her purse in the bottom drawer of her desk.

Her secretary and bookkeeper walked in and hung up their coats. It was beginning to resemble a normal Monday.

Forty-five

Ashlee crawled out of bed and stretched. It was a beautiful day. She wanted to get hold of Archie Nelson and find out about a showing he'd told her he had on Sunday. Maybe she'd be heading for the Bahamas before the end of the week. The thought made her smile.

"Ashlee!"

She heard her mom yelling down the hall of the little bungalow house and wondered why she didn't just come down and knock on the door.

"Ashlee Elizabeth!"

"Yeah, mom, what?!"

"Ashlee, get out to the living room this instant."

Good Lord. You'd think I was Briana's age. By the way, where is my daughter?

"I'm coming."

She changed into her jeans and a sweatshirt, and after slipping her feet into some tennis shoes, strolled down the hallway to the living room. Before she could react, she was turned, cuffed and patted down by a female police officer.

"Ashlee Anderson?" an officer asked.

"Yeah, who wants to know?" she scowled at the female officer.

"You are under arrest for solicitation of murder of Justin Anderson. I'll read you your rights then you'll have the opportunity to call a lawyer." The officer pulled a card from her shirt pocket and read to Ashlee from the card.

"Do you understand these rights as I have read them to you?"

"Yeah. I'm using my right to remain silent. I have nothing to say to anyone until I speak to a lawyer. The city can appoint one for me," she snapped. She glared at her mother and Briana clutching each other in the corner of the room.

The officer led her out the door and placed her in a police cruiser.

Briana turned to her grandmother, "I love you, Nana, but can I go live with Daddy?"

Molly Cline kissed her grandchild on the head, "We'll see, baby, we'll see."

Forty-six

Justin washed the dishes and made sure Princess was in her room. He locked the house and drove downtown to the Police Station. He was forty-five minutes early for his appointment, so he went next door to Sallianne's Coffee Shop. Reading a paper someone had been kind enough to leave behind and drinking coffee killed time until his nine o'clock meeting with Corey. It was his hope they'd release his truck and let him go home. He glanced at his watch and realized he should probably get moving if he was going to make it on time.

He checked in with the desk sergeant who called Corey. The sergeant motioned Justin through the employee's door where, at the end of the hall, Justin saw the open door to Corey's office. He pointed to a chair and Justin sat while Corey finished a phone conversation.

"Great. Good work, Detective. Thanks for your assistance. If we can ever help you out, just call. We owe you." Corey settled the phone in the cradle for a moment and picked it up again. "Yeah, I've got a meeting for the next thirty minutes. Can you hold my calls and take messages? Thanks."

"I have good news," he leaned back in his chair.

"I can have my truck back and go home?" Justin asked hopefully.

"Well, yes. That and we've made a second arrest in the case."

"Another person?" he asked softly.

"Yeah. You ever meet Ashlee's latest live-in?"

"Yeah, she always made sure I knew who I was supporting. This one was Peter, Paco, Paolo, something like that," Justin replied.

"Actually, Paul. He's an ex-con with a smooth line. He likes *other* people's things. His fingerprints were the ones we found under the truck and at the house. He assumed you'd die in the gas explosion and got careless. We arrested him bright and early at the gym this morning. He'll sit in a cell right next to Mr. Manning."

"God, Corey. I don't understand what I did to either of these guys to make them want to kill me," Justin shook his head.

"Justin, you and I have been friends for a pretty long time, right?"

Justin nodded agreement.

"You need to hear this," Corey set up a tape recorder and turned it on. The clear voice of Thomas Manning asking to have Justin permanently eliminated reverberated through the office. A second unfamiliar voice asked if he was sure he wanted this done. Mr. Manning quickly said yes. The second party agreed to the murder and named a price. There was the sound of shuffling paper and Thomas Manning's voice declaring he had ten thousand dollars in cash in the envelope and would arrange to have the second ten thousand delivered as soon as the job was done.

When the tape ended, Corey continued. "I've known for a lot of years Mr. Manning and Ashlee had more than just a friendship going, but they were smart about keeping it out of the public eye. Tom Jr. came in last night and conferred with his father for about an hour and a half. When the meeting was over, Tom went out to his car and left this envelope with the desk sergeant."

Corey slid an envelope across to Justin. He lifted the flap and pulled out a photo and another sheet of paper from inside. The birth certificate didn't list the name of Briana's biological father. Ashlee had been working the situation to her advantage from the start. Briana might or might not be Justin's. In his heart, he knew Briana was and always would be his little girl. The photo, taken and digitally dated within the last two months, was of Thomas and Ashlee locked in a passionate kiss. He put the information back into the envelope and handed it to Corey.

"You keep it," he said.

"You sure?" Corey asked.

"Yeah," he said.

"When we pulled in Ashlee's latest, Paul, the officer in the patrol car said he kept muttering something about 'it was all her idea. Said it'd be over by Monday morning. If he hadn't changed his will everything would be just fine now.' You know what he was talking about?"

Justin's stomach lurched.

"I just signed legal papers after work Friday that I thought only Tom, his law clerk, and I knew about. I reassigned the executrix of my will from Ashlee to my sister and changed the wording so Briana won't inherit until she's twenty-five. I cut Ashlee out completely," he said. "I should've guessed she'd go to any lengths for money. Guess I caused you a lot of work, huh?"

"Hell, Justin. We've never had this much excitement in town," Corey said.

"Well, don't look to me to provide your entertainment. Have you arrested Ashlee? You haven't said anything about arresting her. Don't tell me she got away. And what about Briana? Where's my daughter? When can I get her? I do get to go home and get my truck back, right?" Justin asked.

"Whoa! This isn't twenty questions. Ashlee should be enjoying the hospitality of the department about," Corey looked at this watch, "now. We got a signed warrant just this morning and asked the Winchester Police to help us out. The phone call I was on when you came in was the detective in their offices letting me know the warrant has been executed. Ashlee will share the first rate accommodations of the Oakdale Police lockup the same as her lovers." Corey grinned. "Oh to be a fly on that wall. I'll ask Don to drive you to your truck and you can head home tonight. I tried to get the lab boys to clean up their mess, but I'm afraid they didn't do a very good job. Sorry." Corey stood and extended his hand toward Justin. "Thomas Manning, upon advice from his D.C. attorney, has decided not to *assist* us any further. I'll keep you posted. Go out front and I'll have Don meet you there."

Shaking hands, the two parted company.

230

Forty-seven

The patrolman followed Justin to the rental agency where they turned in the car then drove to the police lot where, for the first time in four days, Justin started his truck. The lab technicians had placed paper mats down after unsuccessfully trying to clean up the fingerprint dust.

Justin drove to Diane's office.

"Hi. You get your truck back?" Diane asked.

Justin nodded.

"Good. The hotel project was going to be abandoned because the investor is now sitting in jail; however, tomorrow you're going to have to go back to work. No more lying around."

Justin groaned. What didn't Thomas have his hand into?

Diane continued. "The project is being refinanced with new owners. Someone likes the idea of a luxury hotel in this out of the way area. You need to be on site tomorrow morning to meet the new owners. The investment broker will be the same, but the owners are new."

Justin sat for a moment digesting this new development. His cell phone rang.

"Hello? Ed, how are you? Yeah, I heard. Well, for once her charms didn't keep her out of trouble. My concern right now is getting Briana back. I know she's safe with her grandmother, but I want my daughter to live with me. Listen, we can knock all this around first thing in the morning at the site. Yeah, you heard right. Somebody's pulled this thing out of the fire, excuse the pun, and the hotel is a go. Great. It's your turn to bring donuts. See you tomorrow at seven sharp. Bye." Justin

231

watched her for a moment then asked, "You bought in to this consortium by selling your beautiful guitar, didn't you?"

Diane's smile spread slowly, "Every time I looked at that guitar I saw Ron's betrayal of me. His wife, Faith, hated that I was in his life before she was and went out of her way to downplay the fact. I knew one day he would pay big money to make this testimony of his love for me disappear. When I thought about selling, it only hurt until he named his price. Then, magically, the hurt vanished."

"That's blackmail!" Justin said.

"No, no, no. It's foreign investment in our community. We need the money the hotel will bring in with jobs and tourists. I'm helping infuse the community's economic index," Diane's eyes twinkled mischievously.

"You're incorrigible."

"Yes."

"By the way, if I haven't said this, thank you. Once again, since we officially met five days ago, you've come to my rescue. Isn't that supposed to be my job?" Justin teased.

"You tried that once and wound up with Ashlee, remember?" Diane answered.

"Oooo, ouch! Point to your team," Justin bowed slightly in Diane's direction.

"Well, I can't say I've done much better myself," Diane smiled. She moved from behind her desk and came around to face Justin sitting in the chair. He rose and took her in his arms. The attraction between them was strong. Diane asked him the question she'd wanted to ask all day.

"What's the story behind all this?"

Justin hesitated but plunged ahead. "Ashlee and Mr. Manning had been having an affair since we were in college. Something happened where they needed a patsy." Justin raised his hand, "And there I was. I was so involved in sports and school, I didn't see myself being hustled. Ashlee turned her big blue eyes on me and I fell hook, line and sinker. She must've gotten pregnant right away, because she was about three months along when we got married. Recently, I decided to change my will and have someone else besides Ashlee handle the money Briana will get when I die. I'm not sure about this part, but either Mr. Manning read my files or she had someone inside the law offices who tipped her that I was making the change. She decided if I died before the new will was filed, she'd still get to control Briana's inheritance. Now Ashlee is a smart woman in most things, but when it comes to money, her common sense shuts down and all she can see are dollar signs. She didn't think that even with my death, as long as it was signed and witnessed, the new will would be in effect. She sweet-talked Mr. Manning into paying to have me murdered before Monday—today."

Diane leaned against her desk for a moment. If she'd not been a part of the last five days, she would've thought Justin was lying to impress her. It wasn't the kind of thing that happened in Oakdale.

"Will your ex-wife be indicted?" she asked.

"They picked her up today in Winchester at her mother's house, but I'm really worried about my daughter who's staying with her grandmother. What's going to happen to her?" Justin's brow furrowed and his eyes clouded with concern.

"Are you worried about the grandmother? Is she like Ashlee? Is that what you're worried about?" Diane asked.

"Oh, no, Molly is nothing like her daughter. I don't mind Briana staying there because Molly is a wonderful, caring person—completely the opposite of Ashlee. I just don't want this to be a burden on her, and I'd like to have my daughter living with me," he said.

"Have you talked with Molly about this?"

"I wasn't sure how to approach it," Justin said.

"I think if she's as caring a person as you say, you need to tell her what you've just told me. I'll bet the two of you can work out what is best for Briana. A lot will depend on the Children's Protective Agency but you are her father, and that will play a big role in their decision. Right now, your daughter is safe in a loving situation. Don't worry so much." Diane gently placed her hand on his arm.

"You like kids, don't you?" Justin asked.

"I couldn't have them, didn't say I didn't like them. Of course, I like kids. Now stop worrying so much. It sounds as though the police have things under control, your daughter is safe and you still have a hotel to build. What more do you want?" Diane asked.

"You do know I've fallen in love with you, don't you?" His warm breath tickled her ear.

"I guessed it might be something like that. And," she hesitated, "I think I just might be falling in love with you too."

"What are we going to do?" Justin asked.

"I guess we'll just have to work on it." A smile formed at the corners of her mouth.

"What say we start now?" he said.

"Now's as good a time as any," Diane said.

Their lips touched as they held each other. They'd made it through this weekend. They'd make it through everything else—together.

About the Author
C. L. Kraemer
Fantasy, Sci Fi and Mystery writer

C. L. Kraemer has been a gypsy all her life. From her military child beginnings to her might-not-get-this-chance-again attitude after she left home, she's seen most of the continental United States as well as Hawaii and Alaska. She hopes to travel the world but is content to stay close to her family in the Northwest in Oregon—for the moment.

Three contemporary romance novels *Old Enough to Know Better; Sun in Sagittarius, Moon in Mazatlan,* and *If Only* are being rereleased by *Rogue Phoenix Press* as well as **Cats in the Cradle of Civilization**.

Healthy Homicide, the October 2008 launch book for a new publishing house, *Rogue Phoenix Press*, picks up the torch in the mystery world. In February 2010, she contributed to two Valentine's Anthologies at *RoguePhoenixPress*: *A Valentine's Anthology*, with a story titled, **Lending Library**, and **A Different Kind of Valentine** with a story titled, **The Prize**.

She has completed the base story for a Dragon Fantasy series, **Dragons Among Us**, which was released August 2010 by *Rogue Phoenix Press* and the first follow up in the series, **Dragons Among the Eagles**, released in 2011.

Meadows of Gold is another faerie story released by *RoguePhoenixPress'* in the March 2011's anthology, *A St. Patrick's Day Tale*. A third story featuring the Fae of the valley outside Eugene, Oregon, **Defying the Odds** was included in the **May Day Anthology** May

2013. This tale is entitled, ***Defying the Odds***. ***Boots and Blades*** will be included in a Christmas 2015 collection.

August 2011 saw the release of ***Shattered Tomorrows***, a Mystery/crime novel loosely based on the May 7, 1981 shooting at the Oregon Museum Tavern in Salem, Oregon where four lost their lives and twenty were wounded.

A motorcycle poker run is featured in her March 2013 release, ***Joker's Wild*** and the third in the dragon series, ***Dragons Among the Ice***, is yet to be released. For detailed information, visit her Web site for background on her books: www.clkraemer.com

Other books by Christie L. Kraemer
Available at Rogue Phoenix Press

Healthy Homicide

Two murders have occurred at the Barrel Springs Day Spa. Police hurry to find the method and reason before anyone else is murdered.

MANIC READER REVIEWS says: Healthy Homicide by C.L. Kraemer is an intriguing plot driven mystery. The plot is well written and pretty much carries the whole story...

Dragons Among Us

In a world full of anomalies such as the platypus and self reproducing Komodo dragon, is the human race willing to accept that dragons may be real?

Sapien Draconi-human-dragon shape shifters-all over the world face this dilemma every day. The question has become life and death as their species is plagued with unexpected and unwanted shifting in the most unlikely of places.

The Ancient Ones-full-blooded dragons-can offer advice, but few seem to put forward workable solutions to the problem.

The fate of the shape shifters hangs in the balance, and an answer must be found before the Homo Sapiens find, dissect, and hunt Sapien Draconi to extinction.

Dragons Among The Eagles

Aleda Sable faces the toughest decision of her life--to stay in dragon form, live as a two-legged or put one foot in the human world and one talon in the dragon world.

An urgent call from her newspaper editor sends Aleda to report on an accident whose driver appears to be a dragon. Authorities have the scene locked down and aren't allowing access to anyone. Television broadcasts flash pictures of scaly legs hanging from a crashed car. However, the bodies disappear into thin air. When the stations try follow-up reports, all they find are state highway workers busily tearing up the roads.

In determining the truth of the shifter disappearances, Aleda finds the truth of her own dilemma.

Shattered Tomorrows

Lucy Daniels has a secret--a deeply guarded secret.

Her life was going along just fine until she accompanied her best friend, Cassie, to her attorney's suite on top of the Equitable Building in downtown Salem, Oregon.

Once inside the lawyer's office, the world turned upside down and Lucy was forced to face a demon from her past. Thirty years ago, life had been different. Lucy had discovered Prince Charming and was headed to her happily ever after.

That's when the devil intervened and because of her brush with the devil, innocent people died.

Joker's Wild

Four brothers raised in the Northwest.

Two choose to stay and pursue life in Oregon. Two are seduced by the promise of Hollywood.

Life throws the Palmer brothers an ugly curve when two are killed in preventable accidents. Even more upsetting is the lack of justice in the trials of the perpetrators.

The remaining brothers will find justice using a shared passion of all the participants--motorcycle poker runs.

Cats in the Cradle of Civilization

Glenda Nagel, editor for Getty Museum's monthly magazine loves her home in the Juniper Hills and her cats. When an ivory and emerald statuette of the cat goddess Bastet makes its way to her home and sets her cats on edge, Glenda is panicked.

Who knows about his and why has the darkly handsome, new Director of Egyptian Antiquities become so determined to visit her high desert home? Doesn't Egypt have enough sand?

C. L. Kraemer
is also featured in these anthologies available at
Rogue Phoenix Press

A Different Kind of Valentine

A collection of four short stories:

Witness by k. J. Dahlen

When Colten finds an injured woman the police are looking for her, should he trust his own judgment about keeping her hidden from the law even if it means she might kill him?

The Prize by C. L. Kraemer

A computer geek learns valuable life lessons when he is given his dream car as well as a condo and the perfect job.

Crazy 'bout You by Clay Renick

Can a psychologist and a romance writer find true love in time for Valentines Day?

Time Changes by Nicolette Zamora

Laurie is just about ready to give up on love when she spies Rob Hender, her high school sweetheart's older brother.

A St. Patrick's Day Tale
by
Christine Young, C. L. Kraemer, Genene Valleau

Tumble through time…

…to Ireland in 1817, when tensions are high between Protestants and Catholics and fae people guide the fate of villagers. A lovely Catholic lass stumbles upon the weakly ritual fisticuffing between Irish lads. She falls into the lap of a handsome young Protestant. Family ties, grudges, and two conniving faeries threaten their budding love. But the faeries outsmart themselves when they hijack a time machine that has mysteriously appeared in their forest and are whisked to…

…Eugene, Oregon in the 20th century, amid a property feud between the local faeries and night elves. The conniving faeries from Olde Ireland try to stir up more mischief. However, a warrior gnome convinces the magic folk to control their own destiny, and forces the intruding faeries to take refuge in the time machine again, spinning their way toward…

…A modern day castle in western Oregon. An eccentric inventor is determined to reclaim his wayward time machine and save his beloved wife from her latest misadventure. If only they can travel safely past the black hole…

A Valentine's Anthology

The Lending Library-a fantasy by C. L. Kraemer

Faeries try to fit into the human world when the forest where they make their home is destroyed by a mysterious enemy.

Chasing Rainbows-a contemporary romance by Genene Valleau

An eccentric aunt, an inventive uncle, a mother who wears poodle skirts, and a brother who wears pearls provide a hilarious backdrop for the courtship of a young woman who yearns for a "normal" family.

The Gift-an historical romance by Christine Young

A man and a woman on opposite sides of the Civil War get a second chance at love after one final battle returns soldiers to their war-torn homes to rebuild their lives.